Elixirs and Elves

Astoria Wright

Faerie Apothecary Mysteries
Book 3

Elixirs and Elves

Copyright © 2018 by Astoria Wright

All rights reserved. No portion of this book may be reproduced or transmitted in any manner whatsoever without the express written permission of the publisher except for the use of brief quotations in a book review.

This is a work of fiction. All names, characters, businesses, places, events, locales, and incidents are the products of the author's imagination or used in a fictitious manner. Any resemblance to actual persons, living or dead, or actual events is purely coincidental.

Some content was inspired by centuries-old mythology, but the characters in this book are not meant to represent the actual Irish, Welsh, Scottish or any other deities, so please, no divine wrath be on me.

The main character's degree in pharmacy and the character herself are fictional. I am not in any way qualified to give medical advice and so, by extension, neither is she.

Published by Novelwright Press, LLC
http://www.novelwright.com

Cover Art by Viyiwi
https://www.fiverr.com/viyiwi

Edited by 529 Books
www.529books.com

NOVELWRIGHT
PRESS, LLC

Table of Contents

Chapter 1
    'Twas Hours Before 1

Chapter 2
    A Gift Horse 15

Chapter 3
    Present Danger 29

Chapter 4
    Christmas Spirits 35

Chapter 5
    Merry Matchmakers 43

Chapter 6
    A Christmas Courting 56

Chapter 7
    Frosty Fae 69

Chapter 8
    Worry in a Winter Wonderland 80

Chapter 9
    The Proof in the Pudding 91

Chapter 10
    Candy Cane Hearts 106

Chapter 11
   Old Acquaintances 119
Chapter 12
   Ghost of Christmas Past 130
Chapter 13
   All that Glitters 141
Chapter 14
   Carol of the Alarm Bells..................... 152
Chapter 15
   Redwood and Evergreen Lies 167
Chapter 16
   The Gift of Truth 173
Chapter 17
   The Magic of Christmas 178
Chapter 18
   All the Trimmings............................. 190
Chapter 19
   Truth in the Tinsel 198
Chapter 20
   Under the Mistletoe 210

Chapter 1

'Twas Hours Before

Not a faerie was stirring in the Seelie Tree Apothecary on that cold winter morning, not even a sprite. Carissa Shae unlocked the door, shook the snow off her mint-colored coat and hat, and hastened into the heated air. The owner of the natural pharmacy flicked on the lights and rushed past the blue shelves to the narrow hallway behind the back counter. She set her chartreuse purse and coat on the tall rack in the storeroom. Removing her light-green beanie revealed her unruly red hair and the pointed ears that marked her as a half-elf. Carissa straightened her fern-hued cardigan over her maroon-and-black plaid dress pants. Then, she went about readying last-minute orders at the counter.

'Twas the season for cases of flu and colds, which made her customers less than jolly. Carissa didn't mind. What did bother her was getting a late start. Her brown eyes scanned the shelves on the back wall behind the counter for ingredients. Miraculously, she filled the orders in record time—with the help of a little fae-magic. At 9:00 a.m., all was ready for a day that promised to be busy with customers and small-town gossip in equal measure.

The apothecary shop was open six days a week, except for holidays—both human and faerie ones. Naturally, it was open this Saturday, a week before Christmas. Carissa turned on the OPEN sign. It sparkled in the dusting of snow and light of the lazy winter sun. Her assistant, Maren Raines, walked in shivering.

Maren exaggerated with a "brrr!!" as she swished a hand through her light-brown hair and slammed the door so that the bell above hollered. She removed her crimson wool coat and fluffy, white scarf.

"It's freezing outside!"

A thin layer of snow on the ground hardly qualified as freezing, but Maren liked drama. Carissa didn't argue; the days were always more interesting with her best friend around.

"Good morning," Carissa said.

Her greeting fell on deaf ears as Maren continued on her rant, "Except for Christmas Day, I really don't see the point of snow."

To Carissa, that was like saying one didn't understand the greatest gift of the holiday season: fresh starts.

Snow was a transformation of all worlds. It was winter painting things over in white: a blank canvas to be filled with endless possibility. Watching the snowfall was like waiting for a story to begin.

Carissa, daydreaming while watching the flurry at the windows, snapped back into the moment to see Maren had passed her by. She followed her assistant only as far as the back counter, calling out as Maren disappeared into the storeroom.

"Can you get the herb baskets out of the fridge?" Carissa asked.

"Like they need refrigerating in this weather," Maren argued as she reappeared and made her way to the freezers.

Starting up the tablet that was their register, Carissa swiped away her assistant's ramblings with a change of topic.

"So, what happened at the marina yesterday?"

Maren came around the aisle with a basket full of witch hazel. "I don't even know how to describe it. It was breathtaking! You really should've been there."

Carissa would've been at the marina for the arrival of the King of the Sidhe and Elves if the Harbridges hadn't asked her to look in on Barnaby on her day off. The leprechaun, whose clothing shop co-existed with their haberdashery in the Otherworld, also shared space in their home in Cari's neighborhood, Crescent Circle. Good neighbors in Moss Hill looked out for each other, which is precisely what she did.

Yet, a half hour visit to a friend with the flu had turned into two hours of babysitting—complete with making soup and tea infused with an herbal tonic. While Carissa had used her apothecary skills and magic to speed up recovery, she still didn't know how to cure the flu entirely without at least some time and rest.

Maren set the basket into the stand on the side of the shop with a kerplunk and continued her description of the rare event from the previous day.

"King Finvarra's envoy arrived in three ships, and there were otters all around the boats—only, they weren't otters at all. They were some kind of fae because they transformed into something similar to the little nature faeries—minus the wings—and floated through the air right around the royal family. And do you know what the tiny fae traveled in?" Maren's excitement spilled into her wide-eyed expression.

Carissa worried that if she opened her mouth, a laugh might escape. The way Maren clasped her hands together, anticipating Cari's guess, was nothing short of childish wonder.

"What did the tiny faeries travel in?" Carissa asked.

"Bubbles! Like the kind you'd blow out of a bottle."

Cari laughed despite her best efforts. Maren's joy was infectious, and not in the terrible way that Barnaby's flu had threatened her the day prior.

"Sounds delightful," Carissa said.

Carissa would have asked questions, but Maren was a wealth of information and she generously shared whenever she had any.

"I couldn't see the king very clearly, but his whole family was glowing, and I don't mean it metaphorically. They were covered in gold cloth, and their crowns reflected light like something out of a dream."

Maren leaned over the counter with a starry-eyed stare. Carissa was two seconds away from waving a hand in front of Maren's face, but her trance seemed to break on its own.

"Do you wonder what the prince is like?" Maren asked.

Cari mimicked Maren's day-dreamy eyes on the opposite side of the counter, and teased, "Are you wondering what the prince is like?"

Dropping her hand, Maren straightened and frowned.

"It's a perfectly legitimate question."

Maren went back to the herbs arranging them like a bouquet as if they needed straightening out.

"The king and his family haven't been to Moss Hill in over 200 years. We don't know what they're like. We know nothing about them."

"Valid point."

"They could be rude and stuffy old bores."

"You do know you're talking about fae royalty? I wouldn't repeat that," Carissa warned.

She pulled out a locket from around her neck. One turn of the circle of herbs resting inside a larger ring allowed her to step into the Otherworld, the realm of faeries. It was about time to check for fae customers anyway. Unlocking the door, she turned her locket again and said a chant. Back in the human realm with her assistant, she could now see into both worlds at once. Maren corrected her statement as if she hadn't noticed Carissa's temporary disappearance.

"They could be kind and do a lot of good for the people of Vale."

"There's no one there," Carissa said.

Maren didn't acknowledge her.

Carissa walked to the stool that rested against the back wall, dragged it to the counter, and sat.

"You know," Maren kept on, "they could help Moss Hill by working with the mayor on his plans for restoration."

Cari put a hand to her chin. Maren was off in her own world again. She wasn't even looking at Carissa.

"That would be nice." Carissa had to agree.

Elixirs and Elves

"They could be wonderful."

Carissa leaned against the counter, crossing her arms and seeing how long Maren would continue.

Her assistant shrugged, saying, "The prince might want to get to know the humans."

"He was handsome, wasn't he?"

"Soo pretty." Maren swooned right into her seat.

"I hate to burst your bubble, but the prince is half-elf and half-sidhe. Even if he's been trained in diplomacy, he's not likely to take very well to humans."

"I know that." Maren sighed and shook her head. "I wasn't serious anyway. You know I'm going with Parker tonight."

Carissa tensed. Parker Greer, to whom Maren had given one chance months ago, had not seemed like promising boyfriend material. Maren had promptly returned from their date with a plethora of reasons why he wasn't right for her. Yet, he had invited her as a date to tonight's welcome party in Vale. As the son of the owners of the Failte Abhaile Hotel and a city hall councilmember, Parker had been invited with a plus one. Cari suspected Maren had been on more than a few dates with him already, but Maren wasn't spilling any secrets.

"Are you going with Cam?" Maren asked, suddenly popping up from the stool and deciding to begin the workday.

Carissa bit her lip.

Tilly Brier, Moss Hill's ace reporter and apparent wizardess of words, had worked her way into the event. Cameron Larke, Moss Hill's ambassador to Vale, and ever the gentleman, graciously agreed to bring Tilly as his plus one. A fumbled apology to Cari and an explanation that they were only going as friends did nothing to ease the hurtfulness of the situation. What did help was her continued denial that she felt anything more than friendship for Cam.

The boy she'd known since childhood had become a man bent on climbing the political ladder. While he did his best to make room for two on the ascent, they just weren't in step with one another. Maren picked up on her silence as she brooded about their relationship.

"You two aren't the only ones avoiding each other lately. Seems like Varick and Jane have taken a page from your book. Or, are you taking one from theirs?" Maren asked.

Cari began a high-pitched defense, then lowered her voice when a customer entered. A woman, possibly a tourist, responded to her "hello" and wandered through the store.

Carissa leaned over the counter and asked in a hushed tone, "What do you mean?"

"They've been avoiding each other for months, but they were on the platform together to greet Finvarra. The moment they did their bowing and greeting, they paused and stared at each other for a long while. Then they walked away without a word. Everyone was talking about it. I wasn't in the front row, but Hattie says that they were forlorn. Isn't that a sad word, *forlorn*? After that, there's no question there must've been something between them. Of course, they'd probably deny it, but you can't tell me anymore that it's just my imagination."

Carissa narrowed her eyes. "All I said was it's none of our business, and we shouldn't be spreading rumors about it."

It was a virtue in Carissa's mind to not spread gossip. To the people of Moss Hill, however, it was miserly to keep information to oneself. Maren made it no secret that she shared the latter opinion.

Maren waved a hand like she was swatting a fly. "I'm not spreading rumors, I'm talking to you. Goodness knows you won't say anything—you're much too sensible to speculate."

"Why do I feel like you're patronizing me?" Carissa asked.

Maren nodded. "Smart, too."

Cari broke into a wide smile and turned as the tourist placed a book, some newly added Moss Hill memorabilia, and an herbal tea mix labeled with the Seelie Tree Apothecary shop insignia on the counter. It had been Maren's idea to add the insignia and souvenirs to the store for tourists. She'd been right about it boosting their sales.

Elixirs and Elves

"I've never seen an old-fashioned pharmacy like this," the brunette American said with a friendly smile. "This whole town is so charming, how have I never heard of it before?"

Carissa and Maren both smiled. It was because Moss Hill was an island town with several faerie residents and a whole fae village not a few miles away in the Vale Mountain. They couldn't very well tell the tourist that an ancient godlike figure, a Tuatha de Danann, had kept them hidden just under the radar of the conscious awareness of the countries in the Atlantic Ocean around them. That was one secret all residents of Moss Hill did keep. Instead of explaining, Carissa replied, "I'm glad you're enjoying your visit."

"I am, very much," the woman said while paying and waiting for change. "Though my friends were less interested in the shops as in the show at the marina last night."

"You were at the marina?" Carissa's eyebrow popped up.

"I know it was a private show, but we could see some of it from the pub, just bits and pieces of the light show, but it was amazing."

It was magic, to be exact. Carissa and Maren exchanged nervous glances. This was why the Mossies had been reluctant to increase tourism to Moss Hill. The fae weren't always incognito around visitors. Months ago, a particular tourist had discovered far more of their secret dual nature as a town of both humans and faeries than they'd ever wanted an outsider to know.

At least this particular tourist had mistaken the fanfare of the King of Sidhe and Elves as something else entirely.

"Those light shows are amazing, aren't they?" Maren covered. She bundled the items together in a bag and handed them to the woman with a reciprocated "thank you."

Upon the tourist's exit, Carissa hastily said, "Why wouldn't the king come through the Otherworld?"

If her voice lowered in disapproval, it was because she recognized the significant risk they'd taken in showing human tourists their existence. If they'd stayed in the Otherworld, they would not have been visible to human eyes.

"Mayor Belkin and the Everlys ensured no ferry boats were due to arrive last night, and the marina was roped off to citizens only. Not every Mossie has your ability to see into the Otherworld," Maren said, "but since all of Moss Hill is under the king's domain, the mayor thought it was only right that all Mossies be able to see him."

The people of Moss Hill, Mossies, were some of the only humans on earth who knew of and interacted with their fae neighbors. It was understandable that the mayor would want to include them in an event like the welcoming of the King of Sidhe and Elves, leader of the two oldest races of faeries. She just hadn't expected that they would be so open with tourists around.

"Didn't Cameron tell you that was the plan?" Maren asked.

Carissa kept her head down, focusing on the inventory list on the tablet's catalog. Anything she said to that would be thrown right back at her. Cameron hadn't been telling her much these days, and Maren would only say it was her fault for being so distant with him. Part of her felt that Maren was right. She had been pushing him away, and the truth was even she didn't know why.

Hearing the sigh and seeing Maren's hand move to her hip out of the corner of her eye, Carissa decided to set the conversation back on track. "You'd think the king would know not to be so conspicuous."

"Now who's criticizing fae royalty?" Maren retorted, dropping her hand. She left the counter and walked through the store, presumably seeing what needed to be tidied, restocked, or re-shelved.

The bell from the Otherworld rang and Carissa, out of habit, reached for her locket to join the new arrivals in the realm of faeries. She stopped upon noticing the two forms appearing in front of her eyes in the human realm. Thank goodness the woman had left the shop or they'd be risking further exposure to faeries in the outside world. Had the fae of Moss Hill wholly thrown caution to the wind?

Elixirs and Elves

The two men shook the snow off of them, and one rubbed his hands together, breathing into them to warm himself up. The man behind him stood stoically at his considerable height and waited for the shorter one to compose himself. Cari didn't recognize the one in front, but the taller of the two was hard to miss.

"Varick, to what do we owe the pleasure?" Carissa had dropped the "sir" with which she was used to addressing the head of the sidhe guard. While she knew she was overstepping with the lack of formality in titles, she also knew that Varick had something of a respect for her. The familiarity of her greeting could continue so long as he allowed it.

Upon hearing Varick's name, Maren peeked her head out from behind the shelves. Curiosity brought her to the edge of the counter, where she watched the exchange of greetings.

It was not Varick, but the other man, a bit taller than a leprechaun's height, who spoke up. "That'd be me—that is: I would be the reason we're here."

The man in the Victorian tailcoat and red vest walked up to the counter with Varick at his heels.

"Toffee of Tir Na Nog, a visitor to Moss Hill and happy to be of service to the fine people here," said the adorable man with the hair and eyes the same color as his name. He bowed low, but his curly strands stayed perfectly in place.

Carissa nodded, returning Toffee's courtesy.

"Carissa Shae, apothecary," Cari said, "glad to be at your service this fine morning."

"Toffee?" Maren interrupted. She tilted her head to the side and smiled at him. "That's like Fudge, isn't it?"

Maren referred to the butler of the wealthy Everly family, prominent Mossies who owned what was arguably Moss Hill's most profitable company: *Everly Exports and Excursions.* Fudge had been their butler for many years, though Carissa had met him only recently. A dapper and somber sort of servant, Fudge was much like the man in front of him, with the pointed nose and sharp jaw of an elfkin, though the features were more severe on the older Fudge. The butler was also the taller of the two.

"Fudge?" The man appeared to recognize the name. "Is this where he's gone to? That's a relief. Why hadn't I thought to look here?" He scratched his head and mumbled as if he'd misplaced the elfkin like a lost toy soldier and was surprised to find him in the toy box.

"We have items to buy for tonight's dinner," Varick interrupted in his usual demanding voice. The sidhe guard crossed his arms, a sign of his impatience.

"Right you are," Toffee said.

He retrieved a minuscule scroll from his jacket pocket and flicked it open. The paper unrolled to reveal its ridiculous length.

"We'd better hop to it," Toffee said with a wink and a smile.

Maren helped him with his list, giving him her name and chatting with the elfkin as he followed her about the store. Carissa stood awkwardly with the guard.

"So," she tried her hand at small talk with a sidhe, "Toffee is from King Finvarra's delegation?"

Varick's eyes shifted in her direction. His blond hair in a top knot made his sidhe ears look even more pointed than any elf, and he appeared more like a guard than when he wore his hair down. His lean, muscled arms unfolded so that she wondered if he was trying to be intimidating or if he just naturally looked like he was flexing all the time. Eventually, a hand settled on the counter.

"He is the king's most trusted servant. I am to protect him as he gathers items for tonight's ceremony." He blustered at being relegated to the job of babysitter for the day.

Carissa wasn't sure what to say to that. As it turned out, Varick didn't expect a response. He slid a hand into a pocket underneath his black guard's jacket and retrieved a far smaller list.

"I'm in need of these three items," he said.

Elixirs and Elves

Carissa examined the paper. "These are an odd mix," she commented, only to be stunned by him gripping the corner of the note.

"I'd appreciate if you could get the items without comment," Varick said.

He looked behind him at the elfkin and Maren. Then, he let go. Carissa hesitated. Was Varick acting strangely? She couldn't tell. This was possibly the lengthiest conversation she'd had with him where he wasn't accusing her or her friends of a crime.

"No problem."

She flashed a quick smile that did nothing to cover her confusion. All three items were powerful sources of magic and herbal remedies, which meant they were all located on the shelves behind the counter. Turning around, Cari searched for the items requested. She picked out a vial, a liquid extract of Ginko Biloba.

The bell chimed at the front door. Cari and Varick both turned to see a stocky, unnaturally short woman with curly red hair, large blue eyes, and a full red-lipped smile.

"Good morning!" the woman called as she entered.

While Carissa's eyes twinkled at the woman's pleasant voice, Varick's hand hovered on the hilt of a sword at his hip. Carissa cleared her throat in a soft way so the woman wouldn't notice while Varick's attention went to her brow-raised warning. *Don't disturb my customers,* her look said.

He glared. Carissa was definitely overstepping what should be done around a sidhe guard, but Varick was one of the few with whom she could risk it. He took his hand off the weapon. He was on edge today, and it put her off.

She almost forgot to call out a "hello" back to the woman. Varick paced around the counter, keeping her and the front door in sight. Carissa's disapproval would not have been noticed even if he'd been looking. She knew he had to keep an eye on Toffee, but he didn't have to act so suspiciously of every stranger.

She took out two canisters to finish Varick's list. Her hand reached under the counter to snap two plastic bags out of the holder. She scooped a hearty amount of white willow bark from one of the canisters into one bag. Into the other, she pinched a tiny bit of mistletoe powder.

"I'll need more than that," Varick said.

She hadn't thought he'd been watching, so his sudden low grumble shook her hands. Some of the golden powder fell from the small wooden spoon. She set the utensil into the canister and ripped a paper towel from a roll at the edge of the counter.

"Mistletoe berry powder is extremely potent," she explained. "Too much can be harmful to a person's health, especially if used in magic. I'm sorry, but I can't give you more unless I know how it's going to be used."

His eyes bore into her like he was performing a mental lobotomy. She stood her ground, her chin lifted. She would not let his control tactics work on her.

Her pharmacy training had taught her that mistletoe could be harmful, especially the berries. But, her training as a half-elf, insufficient as it was, told her that mistletoe was the most potent magical herb one could find. That made it dangerous to give out freely in a town like Moss Hill—even if the recipient had the best intentions.

"It's for an elixir."

Cari nodded. That was simple enough.

"If you tell me what elixir you're trying to create, I'll be happy to make it for you."

"No," he said too quickly. "It's not something an elf can make."

Usually, he said "elf" as if jabbing at an open wound. Today, he was only matter-of-fact in his statement. It almost worried Cari.

Carissa put a pinch more of the mistletoe powder into the baggie. "That's the best I can do."

If it had been anyone other than Varick, she would not have given even the pinch. Since it was the most potent

Elixirs and Elves

magical herb for druids and fae, the regulation of mistletoe had been clearly established by the sidhe guard themselves, which Varick must've known.

The sidhe took out a fifty euro note, and Cari gave him his change. She had barely bagged his items when Varick grabbed the purchases and stepped away from the counter.

His sidestep revealed the short, jolly woman, basket in hand. She heaved the container onto the counter with a grunt and a thud.

"Goodness," the woman said, using her scarf to wipe her brow.

"Quite a lot you've got there." Carissa looked over the arrangement of herbs and supplements.

"I've just arrived in town," the bright-eyed woman expounded, "working for my old mistress and so happy to be here, too, and what should happen but I run into my old friend, Barnaby! He was trying to open his shop across the way. Do you know him?"

"Yes," Carissa's lips stretched across her face, amused. She'd been a little taken aback when the woman stopped her rapid speech to wait for her answer.

"Poor thing," she started up again. "He's sick as can be and trying to work. I sent him right home. Oh, I can see your eyebrows raising. You must know him then, surprised as you are that he'd listen to me. But I'm as stubborn as he is. What kind of a bean tighe would I be if I let him work when he's sick?"

Cari's eyebrows settled back down. A bean tighe—that made sense. She was a leprechaun just like Barnaby, but the title she'd given herself was a "little woman of the hearth." Leprechauns like her liked the name better, as they preferred to be known as caregivers and housekeepers.

"Well, I'm glad you'll be taking good care of him," Carissa said as she finished bagging the items, a good portion of which were remedies for Barnaby. It was overkill, even for the flu.

Astoria Wright

"You can be sure I will." She paid with crisp bills that appeared to be freshly minted.

Varick hovered around the area far too conspicuously with one eye on the leprechaun and one on the elfkin. It didn't seem to disturb.... What was her name? Carissa asked the woman that very question as she turned to leave.

"Why, it's Holly, my dear," the bean tighe said.

Cari smiled. It was a fitting name for the season and an excellent meeting to have made at the start of a long winter day.

Chapter 2

A Gift Horse

Hela and Fenigar's home was akin to a castle. The estate of the head elf's daughter and son-in-law made a fitting choice to host the welcome party for the royal family. Vale had no more stunning property, except perhaps Fairfield, the real castle, which resided at the border between Vale Mountain and Moss Hill. Carissa hadn't seen the house since it was first being built, which, admittedly, had given her a creepy feeling in its half-formed state. That, and it had been invaded by an unseelie faerie known as a leanansidhe.

Now, it was a sight of wooden splendor, twisted vines digging solidly into the earth and reaching up to form the elegant, arched doorway.

Carissa, wearing a silver gown that shimmered in the moonlight, knocked at the door. The faerie tailor, Barnaby, had outdone himself. The dress pulled together in an asymmetric neckline so that the cloth around her shoulders formed a knot at the left. A matching loop below wrapped around her waistline and draped to the floor so that she seemed to be flowing in strands of silk. Cari put a hand to the fabric, lifting the dress slightly to step over the doorway as the door opened.

A whoosh of air blew past her. It was fortunate her red hair had been pinned up in a loose braided bun, or it would've been in her eyes.

"Chaos, Hiya, and Cynth! Stop that and get back here," she whispered. "You too, all the rest of you."

The nature faeries she'd brought with her floated back in a cloud about the door. Their little wings fluttered, and their flower-made clothing wavered around their little bodies. A dozen teeny eyes stared innocently at the owner of their garden homes.

"I promised I would bring you on the condition that you would behave yourselves. The king will be offended if you're flying all about, causing a commotion. He might put you in the Fairfield dungeons."

She went a bit over the top, but from experience, she knew that it took more than a few warnings to keep the sprites in line. The faeries nodded. The three most worrisome of the bunch gave the most expressive acknowledgments. Chaos and Cynth crossed their hearts. Hiya saluted, and the group flittered away.

"The king's not as bad as all that." An elfkin dressed in the same tailcoat from this morning stepped out from behind the high door.

"Toffee," Carissa's dress swirled around her as she turned. "It's good to see you again."

"And you, Miss Shae." The elfkin bowed. "You have no coat?"

"Barnaby used enchanted fabric."

Enchanted fabrics had always been too expensive for Carissa before, but business had been good, and this was a special occasion. So, Carissa indulged just this once on this custom-made gown. She clasped the dress and bowed to the elfkin.

"Oh, don't bow to me, miss." The elfkin waved his arms to stop her. "I'm no one."

Carissa tilted her head. "No one is *no one*."

"There's a lovely thought." Toffee pushed the door shut, then he turned and stopped abruptly. "Looks like your nature faeries are not the only ones causing trouble."

Carissa turned and let out a gasp. Her eyes sparkled, reflecting the glow of dozens of bubbles floating above the heads of the guests in the massive hall. There was a glitter of

Elixirs and Elves

golden dinnerware on a long, thick wooden table to the right. The natural flooring circled outward in reddish ring grains, emanating from the center of the room as if they were standing on the base of a sliced tree stump. It was probably a redwood, as those were common here. To the left, a grand staircase led upward. The ceiling raised impossibly high with tiny dot lights streaming across it.

The bubbles reflected the light so that it glistened like stars above. Those not part of Finvarra's party, having never seen them before, stared in awe as the bubbles danced in a whirlwind. They made their way down toward the sprites.

Cari was surprised when, one by one, the bubbles burst to reveal tiny, human-like forms, wingless but able to glide down to the floor without injury. Maren had been right: they were like the nature faeries, except for their lack of wings. The sprites followed them in curiosity.

"What are they?" Carissa asked.

"Alvens," Toffee said. "They're a type of water faerie. They've got a nature like the waves—unpredictable."

The sounds of windchimes filled the hall.

"Excuse me," Toffee said. "That'll be the door."

It felt strange to Carissa, being here alone. She'd never had to mingle at a party by herself. It was lucky for her that the hostess of the event spotted her across the room.

"Cari!" The red-headed, beautiful elf-woman, Hela, seemed to glide over in her floral dress. It was a peach, light cloth with real snowdrop flowers along the collar. "Come and join us."

Instead of the usual hug, she clutched Carissa's hand and dragged her into the crowd.

Of course, the well-intentioned, meddlesome elf brought her face to face with Cameron Larke. He was engaged in discussion with Hela's husband, Fenigar, who bowed upon seeing Carissa. Cari returned a curtsy.

"It's good to see you, Fen," she said.

"And you, Cari. I was just inquiring about your arrival," the host replied.

"We expected you to arrive together," Hela explained.

"We're glad that you are here now," Fen said. Both elves completely missed the reddening faces of their two friends standing on either side of the married couple. Aside from not noticing awkwardness, Cari's long-time friend was not one to stick with a conversation for long. "Look, Carissa, there's Marnie!" Hela said.

"Dear, I think it's Maren," Fen corrected.

Carissa shook her head and stifled her laughter. Hela never had gotten her name right.

"Yes, of course, we'll say hello to her too."

Hela, who apparently hadn't understood, excused herself and her husband so they could make their way to the door.

Cameron ran an awkward hand through his chocolate brown hair. His dark eyes met Carissa's with the crinkle of a smile at their edges, just as the hint of one pulled gently at his lips. If it were possible for a person to turn the shade of a holly berry, that's what her face would be in another minute.

She smiled back with a simple, "Hi, Cam." Then she added, "Where's Tilly?"

The smile that he hadn't entirely given was gone. He answered by pointing across the room. There was Moss Hill's star reporter, speaking with the mayor. A frown tugged at Carissa's lips. Tilly, who only ever wore the casual attire of a writer or the tailored pantsuits of a reporter, killed in her red fitted dress that reflected the light perfectly around her curves. The twenty-nine-year-old's warm, flawless complexion was stunning, even in a room full of ageless sidhe and long-lived elves.

Cameron stepped closer to Carissa. "You know we're not *together* together. She asked to come with me because—"

"I know."

Carissa winced at the sharpness of her words. She hadn't meant to sound angry, annoyed, or in any way affected by the wedge between them in the form of the beautiful Miss Brier. No, that wasn't fair. She wasn't the only thing in their way,

Elixirs and Elves

but Carissa didn't want to think about the complexities of their relationship, or lack thereof, at the moment.

Luckily for her, Sal interrupted any further uncomfortable conversation. The tall, long-limbed elfkin strode over with an appetizer tray in hand. Carissa naturally smiled whenever she saw Sal. His black eyes, thin face, and pointed nose were not the most handsome in Vale, but there was a charm to his personality that made him easily one of Cari's favorite people in all the world.

"Hello, Sal." Carissa smiled warmly.

He grinned wider than Cari was capable of matching.

"Hello, Carissa. So good to see you, Cameron. Cheese?" Sal was trying to be formal for the occasion. It made him even more endearing.

Carissa's eyes glided over the appetizers. There was a large assortment of cheeses on gold toothpicks along with several other types of hors d'oeuvres. Cameron reached for a mini quiche but pulled back.

"There have to be fifty items on this tray, and they're all different," Cam remarked.

Sal shrugged. "Tof didn't want to leave out anyone's favorites. I filled him in on Master Rolin's tastes. He seemed pleased."

"Tof?" Cam asked.

"Toffee," Sal said, "King Finvarra's head servant."

"He's the elfkin who answered the door," Carissa clarified.

"Oh, yeah, I saw him with the king a second after he let us in. How does he move that fast?"

Sal and Carissa smiled. *If humans only knew what magic fae could do,* Cari thought. It was like the tray in front of them. As a human, Cameron was clearly puzzled by the placement of each type of hors d'oeuvre on the platter. He was hesitating, eying the food but not wanting to take someone else's favorite and make Sal have to refill it. But Cari and Sal knew better.

With an elfish smirk, Carissa said, "Take one and see."

Cameron lifted the mini quiche from the platter. The moment it left the tray another appeared in its place. Cam's jaw dropped like a child on Christmas who'd just been surprised with his favorite toy.

"Amazing," he said, biting into the appetizer.

Carissa took a moment to choose from the tray herself. She removed a tiny avocado and tomato wrap, the red and green seemed appropriate for the upcoming holiday.

"Mmm. It's delicious! Thank you, Sal," Cari said. Cameron dittoed the sentiment.

"Oh, not me. Tof deserves the credit," Sal said. "Exciting, this party, isn't it? And the alvens! Did you see them?"

Carissa chucked. "They're wonderful, yes."

"They are something special." Cameron glanced around, marveling when he spotted them around the unfinished Christmas tree along with the nature faeries.

"I never knew a party could be planned like this and in one day! I'm learning so much from Toffee in so short a time." Sal went on so that Carissa almost missed it when he abruptly changed the topic, "Oh, Cari, I forgot—your parents were looking for you."

Carissa's eyes widened, and she put a hand to her lips. It wasn't polite to leave her mouth wide open while she was eating.

"My parents are here?"

It was about time they were due to return from their latest expedition. Cari's father, the elf-historian found world travel to be the best means to inform his interpretation of history. It had often meant that her parents were away for long stretches of time. She was used to it from a very young age. This last expedition had been five months, and that wasn't even the longest one they'd taken.

"They came with the king." Sal's kind eyes softened and his brows tilted sympathetically.

"Thank you, Sal," she said as Cameron put a hand to his forehead.

Elixirs and Elves

"Great. Trouble ahead." Cameron ducked, looking away.

Carissa looked to see Maren and Parker approaching.

"Hi!" Maren said. She hugged Carissa, practically jumping with delight. "You look beautiful!"

"You too," Carissa said.

Maren's green dress with its white cotton trim was a tad on the garish side, but Cari wasn't going to say anything.

Parker nodded curtly at Cam. The tension between the two competitors layered over the air so thickly it clouded Cameron's judgment.

"Maren? You came with Parker?"

Carissa jabbed him lightly in his side.

"It's okay," Maren said, though her defensive tone said it was anything but. "Parker has been nothing but a gentleman, and he asked me here as a friend, which you would know if you came by the Seelie Tree every once in a while."

Cameron's eyes shifted in Cari's direction but fell short of meeting hers. Cari held back her thoughts on Cam keeping his distance. There was that nagging feeling twisting in her stomach that forced her to acknowledge that she was at least partly to blame, but she didn't want to think about it at the moment.

Parker chimed in, "You're not with the mayor, Cam? I would've thought you'd be right by his side. You're his plus one, aren't you?"

Cameron visibly seethed. Maren's face paled.

"Oh, don't look so mad. I'm only joking." Parker held his palms up. "I know it's the mayor's birthday, I'll play nice."

He put one of his hands out to Cam as if to offer a truce. Cam didn't take it. Maren looked between them, her face recoloring from pale to red. She pulled at her date's suit jacket.

"Look," Maren attempted a distraction, "the Everlys are here. Let's go say hello."

She nearly pushed Parker into the crowd, glancing back with a wince in Cam's direction as they left. Cameron's eyes focused like lasers, choosing the back of Parker's head as a target.

"Are you all right?" Carissa ventured.

"Two months ago, he wanted my job," Cam said. "Now he's trying for the mayor's."

Carissa put a hand on Cameron's shoulder. "The Mossies will see right through him."

Cameron stiffened. "Aren't they serving drinks? The spinach quiche had a little kick in it." He scanned the room until he found Toffee with a tray full of wine glasses.

Elderberry wine, Carissa guessed since that was the elves' specialty. Cameron took a step away. Then, he pivoted to look back at Cari.

"Do you want me to get you one?" It was not the way he usually asked her anything. The tone was flat. There was no feeling, no added look of care in his eyes.

Carissa put a hand up and tried to ignore the stinging at the back of her eyes. "No, I'm all right."

She watched him disappear into the assemblage of guests before turning to search for her parents. Not seeing the average-sized elf with dark hair that was her father, nor the blazing red-headed woman she called mother, Carissa walked toward the back of the room where she might get a better view of the guests. Women in dresses and men in suits talked near the fireplace and around the table, some danced in a space near the tree, and some watched the sprites chasing each other and playing hide and seek in the tree branches. The evergreen shook. Carissa hastened over to it with fire in her eyes.

"Hiya, stop it!" she whispered at the boy faerie jumping up and down on a branch. He was watching his sister, Cynth, who had snuck up on an alven and tagged him. The alven fell from the tree branch and promptly created a bubble around him to float. He and his transport were no bigger than what any child could have made and seemed just as unstable as it wavered in the air. Carissa worried that just breathing would cause it to burst.

Elixirs and Elves

The fae himself was a lot like the nature faeries, about the same size. Like them, he was a tiny human with an adolescent appearance, but without the beautiful butterfly-like wings. He was snow white with blue lips and hair like a polar bear's fur. The alvens all looked like this. Instead of the range of skin tones, hair colors and eyes of the nature faeries, they varied only in wintery hues of water and ice. The countenance of each was entrancing.

Inside his bubble, the little fae laughed and pointed at Hiya playfully, as if to say "fooled you!" Not paying attention to where he was floating, the alven bumped into a sprite on the branch behind him.

Chaos, the unfortunate faerie he'd hit, fell from the tree branch and onto her bottom on the ground before she could control herself enough to use her wings. She shook her fist up at the alven. Her little face twisted in anger and pain as tears welled in her eyes.

Carissa knelt and reached out a hand, "Oh, Chaos! Are you all right?"

Cari was both concerned and annoyed. Chaos could always sense her emotions. The nature faerie put out a stop-sign palm and looked away, eyes closed, refusing her help.

"You wouldn't have fallen if you weren't all playing so roughly," Carissa said to the whole group.

To her surprise, the sprites and alvens in the tree were laughing. Since sprites couldn't speak, and apparently neither could the little water faeries, it only sounded like the faint whispering of bells, a pleasant sound for so frustrating an action.

Carissa looked down to see Chaos, eyes still closed, moving her mouth as if mimicking Cari. The moment the nature faerie opened her eyes to receive her applause from the other sprites, she saw Carissa's unamused scowl and stopped her imitation. Putting her little hands behind her back, she tilted her head down and swayed back and forth as innocently as a guilty sprite could appear.

"You're lucky you only fell and the tree didn't topple right over on you. No more pushing or chasing each other around," Cari pointed at Chaos and then up at the rest of the sprites.

The alven sat in his bubble with wide, open eyes and nodded. Carissa wondered if anyone had ever reprimanded the mini water faeries before. When it came to her sprites getting hurt, she was not about to let any fae get away without a scolding. The sprites seemed to calm down. They would behave for a while at least.

The matter would have been over except that Parker's voice traveled over Cari's shoulder to the little faeries' ears.

"Doesn't faerie dust have magical properties? Who knows what magic those alvens have! I hope you've sealed the magic on that gift you brought or it'll be bad luck instead of good you're giving to the mayor."

The faeries stopped their play entirely and sunk into the tree branches. The base of the evergreen rattled. Cari reached a hand out to stabilize the tree.

"Foolish faeries," a surly voice mumbled.

In her periphery, Carissa could see Fudge rummaging through the gifts under the Christmas tree.

Chaos turned her pouting face away from Fudge and Parker. Carissa felt sorry for the little sprite.

"They didn't mean to cause a problem, and I'm sure they're very sorry," Carissa tried a delicate balance between sympathy and sternness.

"He's right, though," Fudge said. "Magical, mischievous misfits...."

Something had put him in a foul mood. Carissa looked up to see Parker's condescending I-told-you-so face turn back toward Maren and the crowd.

Fudge stormed away as quickly as he'd come, leaving Carissa alone with the sprites and the alvens. As hurt as they could get, the nature faeries recovered quickly. They had already resumed their play.

Carissa's attention fled from them to movement at the double doors that led to the back of the house. She rose and

Elixirs and Elves

followed her intuition around the tree to where she could spy the doors unseen.

She recognized Varick in a variant of his sidhe guard uniform. The dark boots, black pants, a sword at his waist, and buttoned jacket were the same, except for the jacket's length. It was a formal coat, draping nearly to the floor. Even in winter, Carissa had never seen him wear such garments. He opened a large door and slipped out of sight.

Carissa was curious, but even more intriguing was the woman in the gorgeous gold dress watching him from the other end of the room. Jane Everly was standing close enough to the door to have seen him leave but showed no sign of having seen Carissa. She was near enough to the window to peer through it to see where he'd gone.

Carissa's eyebrows knitted together, watching the young Miss Everly's head droop downward and her face elongating. Carissa left the sprites and walked over to her.

"Jane? Are you all right?" Carissa said.

Jane's blue eyes glistened. She seemed to be failing at a composed look. Her lips quivered before she could speak. Carissa put a hand on the young heiress's shoulder. Jane took a breath.

Now able to speak, she said, "I'm fine. It's just…" her eyes darted around the floor as she searched for the word, "stubbornness."

Carissa wasn't sure if Jane meant Varick's or her own. She had no idea what the whole mess between them was about. As much as Carissa cared about all Mossies, she had never mastered their knack for gossip. If Jane wanted to, she would share. It didn't feel right to pry. So, Carissa didn't say anything.

Jane seemed to regain her composure, patting Cari's hand to let go of her shoulder.

"I'm fine, really." Jane touched the tips of her fingers to her cheeks and changed the subject. "Aren't the decorations wonderful?"

Astoria Wright

Jane's eyes betrayed her smile as she looked at the hall. The room shone nearly as bright as Jane's golden gown. The antique candelabras danced in Jane's eyes, though that was all the warmth inside them.

"Yes, it's a beautiful party," Carissa agreed, trying to think of what else she could say to make Jane feel better.

"Jane, dear." Jane's mother, Arin Everly, in a solid red dress and poinsettia pin, swooped in to clasp her daughter's arm. She didn't acknowledge Carissa at all. "We are to be introduced to the king. Come."

Jane, the picture of propriety, said a polite, "Excuse me," like an automaton.

Carissa's heart broke for her. It wasn't just the nature faeries Carissa felt compelled to protect. When it came to her friends, no one could hurt them without expecting a scolding as well.

Carissa scooped up the hem of her dress and marched outdoors to give Varick a piece of her mind on behalf of Jane's heart. Her dress took on a sheen for a second then faded back to normal as if a force around it rippled from top to bottom. It was Barnaby's magic, working to keep the fabric from allowing the cold in.

The area where Varick was standing, a porch looking over a snow-covered garden, was somewhat icy at her feet. Cautiously, she stepped across the slippery surface to where Varick was leaning on the twisted, natural-wood railing. In his hands, he clutched some sort of vial. A red glow emanating from it seemed to mesmerize the sidhe guard captain. Her shadow on the bottle caused Varick to snap upright. His eyes flashed gold. His powers, tied to his emotions, were not usually worn so openly on his shoulders like this. Carissa put her hands up.

"It's just me," she said.

His eyes faded back to their usual green. She expected a reprimand. When he sulked back down instead, she decided it was safe to take a few steps closer. Varick took the vial of red liquid and placed it into an inner pocket of his coat.

Elixirs and Elves

"Is that the elixir you needed to prepare?" Cari asked.

Varick responded by lifting one hand off the railing and facing her. Even leaning, he was still several inches taller than her. It was a shame the height, broad shoulders, chiseled face, and long, blond hair was accompanied by his sense of sidhe superiority.

"Do you need something, Miss Shae?" he said flatly.

Carissa expected more condescension in his tone. She had prepared herself for a fight as she stormed out here to yell at him for whatever he was doing to upset Jane. But he wasn't trying to intimidate or belittle or even be rude to her right now. *He's sad*, she realized.

Carissa took a spot beside the railing, closer to him than she'd ever cared to get, and tried for sympathy. She took in a breath, hoping that by the time she exhaled she'd have something to say. The pause was a little longer than necessary, and she thought she saw an eye roll before she even said the first word.

"Varick, I know you're not used to confiding in an elf and certainly not a human." She had to watch her tone. She could easily slip into snippiness, which was not the emotion she was going for here.

Cari looked at his now downturned face. "I know you might not consider us friends, but I can see that you're hurting, and I know Jane is, too."

Part of Carissa was surprised that he hadn't interrupted her by now. She wouldn't have believed she'd be able to finish a sentence without an argument from him. She almost wished he would say something since she wasn't sure what to say next.

"I don't know what I can do to help or even what your argument with Jane is about, but maybe if you and Jane opened up to someone else, it might help you to see things in a new light."

She was sure he'd argue with her now, but, instead, his eyes darted around the garden as if thinking about what she was saying. His next words surprised her even more.

"You're right," Varick said. "Someone else. I need someone else to get Jane to see."

He was clearly speaking to himself, formulating some sort of plan. Of course, it was like him to think Jane needed to see and not that he needed a new perspective. Even without knowing the cause of their dispute, Carissa could see that his thinking was off.

"Not exactly what I meant," Carissa started, but his brows were still turned downward, and his face still overcast with a shadow. It moved Carissa to, against her better judgment, put a hand on his.

"I could speak to Jane if you want. What is it you two are fighting about?"

Varick's attention turned to Cari. His eyes wavered between green and gold. While usually, the emotion behind the gold meant anger, she knew from her own elf-light that fae powers were tied to all feelings. *He really is a mess.*

Eventually, his eyes settled back to green, and he straightened to his full, towering height. He removed his hand from the balcony, and therefore from Carissa's grasp. Still, his surliness did not return. His demeanor, surprisingly, was much like a gentleman's.

"Thank you," he said to Carissa. "Now, I understand what to do. Your offer will not be necessary." He bowed his head, just a dip of his chin, and walked past her into the party.

Carissa lingered a moment, puzzled. Her confusion left her staring out at the garden. Whatever enlightening thing she had said, she definitely hadn't understood it herself. And what exactly did Varick believe that he had to do now?

She bit her lip. She really hoped she hadn't just made things worse.

Chapter 3

Present Danger

Carissa's parents found her the moment she stepped back inside. She had left the porch almost directly after Varick and in time to see him bowing to the royal family before being excused. As the sidhe mingled back into the party, Carissa was left to face King Finvarra, his wife, Ona, and their son, Prince Zephyr of Tir-Na-Nog.

Carissa opened and shut her jaw shut like a snapping turtle, convinced that both the open-mouthed stare and the corrective action made an unattractive impression. Her dress, which she'd previously felt was among the most beautiful fabric she'd seen, paled in comparison to the queen's gorgeous gown. The sidhe woman glowed as radiantly as the diamonds gracing her neck. Her long, blonde hair cascaded over a dress that shined so brightly Carissa wondered at the color of it. Was it silver or gold? Or was it something else entirely?

King Finvarra, the elf, had a dark brow, light blue eyes, a strong jaw, and the elfish smile that Head Elf Rolin lacked. His robes and crown were fitted with jewels—too many to miss his status as royalty and too few to be considered gaudy.

Carissa barely had a second to notice the prince before her parents appeared on either side of her, effectively cutting off any route of escape. She hadn't seen them in months, and yet her first few seconds with them consisted of them ushering her toward the royals.

"Majesties," her father began, "allow us to present our daughter."

"Carissa Shae," her mother added. The way her mother gripped her arm, she wondered whether she had ulterior motives than just an introduction. Her mother looked at her with expectant eyebrows, and she nodded her head as if to tell her something.

It took Cari a second to realize that she was expected to bow. She curtsied as low and gracefully as she could manage. The queen approached, putting a hand on Cari's chin. She stood as Queen Ona raised her up with her hand. Her violet eyes, rare among sidhe, settled on Carissa. Like all sidhe's, they glowed with specks of gold as she smiled. Her smirk was not like her husband's simple smile. There was meaning behind it that needed decoding.

"Beautiful," the queen remarked.

"A charming girl," King Finvarra added, "and more than worthy."

Carissa hid her confusion by looking down at the floor. *Worthy of what?* The prince stepped forward.

"It's an honor to meet you."

He bowed to her. A blush appeared on Carissa's face as numerous sets of eyes began to fall on her.

Not only was he a prince, but he was more than handsome enough to warrant Maren's earlier squeal when she'd called him "so pretty" back at the apothecary shop. His eyes were blue, like his father's, but with a sunlit hue. It reminded Carissa of the ocean in the brightness of day. His hair was gold, his chin chiseled, his stature tall, his shoulders wide. Carissa's blush deepened as his bow ended and he looked at her again.

"We have heard of your bravery," the queen said, "and wish to reward you."

She waved beside her. Toffee appeared with a wooden box with gold clasps, which he opened to reveal an emerald necklace, earrings, and a bracelet. Just as the diamonds, the emeralds glistened with a shine unlike any jewelry Carissa had seen before.

Elixirs and Elves

Finding her voice, she thanked the queen and curtsied again. This pleased the royal family immensely, and the elves and sidhe broke into applause. Even her parents looked incredibly happy. Carissa wasn't sure why her simple action had warranted such joy or why it created such a knot in her stomach.

She was saved by the dinner bell, rung by Toffee. It took a few minutes for the guests to all gather around the large table. Toffee and Sal made sure that the guests were arranged correctly according to the place cards set out by the plates. Fudge, who had come as a guest, still offered his services to the other elfkin.

Carissa could hear Sal thanking him and allowing him to enter the kitchen, but Toffee had a different reaction. There was a moment while waiting for her seat where she could overhear the two in a heated exchange.

"I am pleased to be pleasant with everyone, even you in the past. But now? I daresay, I find it difficult to be kind." Toffee's voice could barely be heard over the clang of pots and the guests' conversations.

It was the politest argument she'd ever heard. Or, at least it was until Fudge said his part.

"You and all the elfkin with your silly smiley ways. You're all daft, the lot of you, and I'm proud I was never so ridiculous. You give away half of what you earn and you're always helping everyone like you are beneath them. Well, I'm not. "

Toffee retorted, "Look at you, spoken all high and mighty, but you serve others, too."

"I'm paid very well, thank you, and I will retire a rich man. I only came in here to help, and I'd have offered you this if you weren't so undeserving of it."

Carissa couldn't see what the "this" was that he was offering. Realizing that she was standing unnaturally close to the door, she smiled at people passing her and nonchalantly walked in to rejoin her parents.

Astoria Wright

Fudge opened the kitchen door with his back toward her and the other dinner guests and whispered nastily at Toffee, "I'm done with you, you and all elfkin."

Carissa hastened her step when the elfkin finally returned out of the kitchen. She followed her parents to the table, spying Fudge from the corner of her eye. The scowl on his face was so similar to his usual countenance, it was almost hard to tell that he was upset. Except he pulled at his necktie and balled his fists after helping Jane with her chair.

Carissa was placed beside her mother and across from Hela. The positions were honored ones, even though they were near the center of the table. The king and his family took places at the head of the banquet, the sidhe elders beside them, then the head elf and his family, Hela and Fenigar included, and then Cari's family. As the official historian and member of the Elven Council, he was esteemed by the king. Carissa was a little surprised that her parents had traveled together with the king's envoy but supposed that she shouldn't be.

They were loyal subjects to the crown and did much work for the council, gathering information about places around the globe. Cari had never really thought about the value of the work, only that it must've been essential to have kept them away from their only child for months at a time when she was little. It almost felt comforting that they were seated closer to the king than other council members. At least their work was valued.

Before sitting, the fae and humans turned to the king, waiting for him to be seated first. King Finvarra remained standing and began a speech. The guests quieted.

"I have been through the world and lived in a paradise of natural wonders in Tir-Na-Nog." His eyes scanned the table, resting on each individual as they passed. "Yet, I do not believe I have seen a more joyous sight than this—all of you. Fae and human together at one table as equals, as neighbors, and, as friends. The credit for this I must give to the people of Moss Hill. Rarely have I met humans capable of understanding our ways and living among us in peace."

Elixirs and Elves

Finvarra extended his right hand to beckon to his servant. Toffee scurried out with another box, this one seemed made of gold. The king waved for Toffee to take the box to the table where Mayor Belkin was standing.

"A gift for your day of birth, to show our gratitude." At the king's signal, Toffee opened the box.

The gold itself would have been enough. As it was, the sight of it alone lit Belkin's eyes. But there was a flickering glow when the box opened. The elfkin brought out a vial, much like the one Carissa had seen earlier in Varick's hands. The red liquid blazed as Toffee poured it into a glass.

"An elixir of long life," King Finvarra explained.

Toffee scrambled to fill the glasses around the table with the elderberry wine. Sal did the same. The difference was that Sal gratefully accepted Fudge's help in pouring the wine. He readied Jane's glass beside him and the Everly's nearby and even Carissa's and her family's.

When the drinks were all poured, Finvarra raised his glass. As was customary among elves, the elfkins stood aside from the guests and filled glasses for themselves. A toast, in fae lore, was not complete unless all present took part in it.

"To the leader of Moss Hill, good health and many years of happiness. And to the people of Moss Hill, a bright future."

Everyone raised glasses. Carissa almost took a sip. She brought her goblet near her lips, but Mayor Belkin did not let the moment pass without adding to the speech.

"Moss Hill thanks you, Your Majesty, and wishes you well in return."

Again, the guests raised their goblets. This time, no one was able to drink. A clang of glass striking the floor ended the toast then and there. The thud of a body falling was followed by the sound of every hand setting their cups down on the table. Gasps erupted through the crowd.

Most of the table seemed frozen in fear. Parker lunged to get a glimpse of what had happened. His sudden movement spilled his own glass in the process. Fudge dashed around the table. He was the first to get to the source of the sound. Carissa and a few others followed, braving their fears to help the victim on the floor. It was the elfkin: Toffee. Fudge held his fingers to Toffee's wrist.

"He's dead," Fudge said in wonder.

The sprites and the alvens wailed. The red liquid from Toffee's goblet was still spilling from the glass near his hand. The glow of it was unmistakable.

He had drunk the elixir…it had not granted him a long life.

Chapter 4

Christmas Spirits

The sprites and alvens would not settle down to sleep that night, especially Hiya and Cynth. This meant that the other faeries would not sleep either. In Cari's parents' home, the mini fae spread about the living room, some on the sofa, a handful on the rug by the fireplace, a few under the lamplight on the end table by the sofa, and the rest on the natural foliage decorating the walls. In fae homes, natural branches acted as shelves, with a touch of greenery strewn around them. Since the nature faeries were magically linked with flowers, their wings represented their respective flowers' petals. Being roughly the size of the blossoms as well, it appeared as though the entire room was filled with flowers. The alvens had no wings and were somehow able to blend so well with their surroundings that they had become transparent—except for when they moved.

None of the little fae had taken a spot on the windowsill. They were too frightened of the outside world. In fact, when Carissa re-entered the room after clearing the tiny thimbles of hot chocolate her mother had given them, they insisted that she draw the shade. In this case, the curtains were actually vines, and the sprites watched them sway until they became still. After much persuasion, they were considerably calmer than their earlier wailing at the abrupt end of the dinner party.

Varick had attempted to heal the elfkin, but it had been too late. He'd pronounced Toffee dead right then and there. The shock of witnessing Toffee's passing had sent the sprites into such a state that Carissa missed the sidhe guards' preliminary investigation. The nature faeries had immediately taken to sobbing or the chiming sound that was their version of crying. Though the music they made was beautiful in a melancholy sort of way, Cari could not stand to see them like that for long.

She had ushered them together and trotted them away from the area, then took them to her parents' home on the other side of Vale. The alvens came too, with permission of the royal family.

The alvens were easier to pacify than the sprites. In fact, some of them had tended to the nature faeries, hugging them while they cried or patting their backs in support. One particular alven, the one who'd knocked Chaos from the Christmas tree earlier, tried to comfort Chaos the moment they'd arrived at the cottage. His bubble had floated to where she had placed herself on the couch, and he smiled at her, but Chaos had dodged every attempt of his to hold her hand or pat her back. Eventually, the alven had scratched his head, slumped his shoulders, and sulked away in his bubble. He had joined the group on the branch-shelves on the wall.

Carissa's mother had coddled all the little fae as only a mother could. She'd made hot chocolate and asked Cari to find scraps of cloth from her sewing cupboard to use as blankets. Cake, hot chocolate, and the makeshift blankets had calmed them somewhat. Carissa would have left the room for the faeries to sleep in peace, but two little sprites refused to let her go.

Hiya and Cynth still required Cari's personal attention. Carissa took a seat on the large sofa. All the tiny faeries around the room looked on as Hiya sobbed and Cynth's whole face dripped with tears. Chaos sat between Hiya and Cynth, patting Hiya's back while Cynth wept into her shoulder. Carissa's lips pulled to one side, though her face hadn't quite decided whether she was smiling at Chaos's tenderness toward the two faeries whom she used to fight with or frowning in light of the night's events.

Elixirs and Elves

"Hush, now." Cari said, sounding more like her grandmother than she'd intended, "It's all right." She spoke softly to all the faeries, "You're all okay. I'm sorry you saw what you saw, but it's over now. You're perfectly safe here."

A sprite to her right stood up under the lamp. The faerie, Blue, who had wings like a bluebell flower and blue skin and hair that sparkled under the lamplight, began to gesture as if to drink, and then fell down, re-enacting what had happened to Toffee. He stood back up and put his hands up as if asking a question. Carissa knew what he was inquiring.

"No, Blue, he didn't make it," she said, which only upset all the little faeries again. "Oh, please don't be afraid. The sidhe will find out what happened and they'll catch the person responsible, I promise."

Chaos patted both Hiya and Cynth on their backs and then left them to fly to Carissa. She put two hands on Cari's shoulder and pushed. Carissa looked down with a puzzled brow.

"What? Are you sending me away?" Cari asked.

Chaos nodded. Then, she gestured toward the other nature faeries and straightened, pointing at herself.

"You want to talk to them yourself?" Cari asked.

Chaos nodded proudly. Carissa wasn't sure what Chaos could do or say that she and her parents hadn't already told the sprites that night, but she was tired and nothing they'd tried yet had worked as well as she'd hoped. She stood up.

"All right, good luck," she said. "Good night, all of you."

She silently stepped out of the room. In the hallway, she stopped and peered curiously around the corner to see what Chaos would do. The tiny nature faerie put both of her arms out like an orchestra conductor, but palms facing down as if to soften the music. Then she flew to each area of the room where the faeries lay and put a hand over each of them, sprinkling faerie dust on everyone.

It was magically calming and, as such, was sure to work. Carissa wasn't sure it was the most ethical, though, to use

37

magic on them like that. Had Chaos used magic on *her* like that before? That was a disturbing thought.

"Carissa?" a quizzical voice whispered in her ear.

Carissa jumped and turned to see Alden, the specter in full Grim Reaper form. The skeletal face shocked her, and she gasped. She clasped a hand to her mouth, hoping the faeries hadn't heard her. Regaining her senses, Carissa pushed the ankou farther into the hall.

"Alden!" she whisper-yelled. "I almost screamed."

"Sorry." Alden changed back to his human form. He once again appeared as the friend to whom she was more accustomed. His black eyes were the last to transform, their ocean-blue calmed her frazzled nerves.

Carissa signaled for him to follow her and walked past him into her father's study. The room was a forest of books. The walls were a mix of stacked stone veneer with pockets of redwood shelves set in rows. They were filled with ancient manuscripts, yet no dust collected in any corner. The furniture was eclectic. Toward the back of the room, a slip of the redwood curved upward, made of the same material as the floor yet serving the purpose of a desk. A chair behind it was perfectly contoured for comfort. It was seamlessly carved as if it had grown from a tree ready-made. There were two others just like it faced opposite the desk. All three were occupied. Her father sat at the one behind the desk; her mother sat opposite him. To Carissa's surprise, Cameron sat in the third seat, hot chocolate in hand.

"Cam?" Cari asked. "I didn't see you come in."

She'd been in the living room so she should have seen him enter through the front door.

"I knocked on the side entrance. Didn't want to disturb the whole house. Your mother let me in." Cam stood, offering Cari his seat. Carissa put a hand out to decline his offer for the chair. She smiled, though, appreciating Cameron's thoughtfulness. He was always the gentleman.

To the right of the door sat a bench of twisted roots. Carissa sat first, with Alden following behind. Cari noted that

Elixirs and Elves

her parents tensed upon seeing Alden, though he wasn't in his specter form. He had been in their home once before, on an especially stressful night.

"Um...you remember Alden?" Carissa ventured.

"The ankou." Her father must've recognized him from that encounter months ago when he'd brought Hela's husband, Fenigar, here to recover from a dark faerie attack.

Cari's mother's eyes moved from Alden to Carissa. It must've been shocking to have the ankou in their home. Carissa could understand their tension.

"Alden, did you...um...you know." Cameron didn't ask outright but considering he was speaking to a reaper of souls, his unasked question was implied. *Did he collect Toffee's soul?*

"Toffee was upset." Alden shifted in every sense—from shuffling his feet to looking all around the room to vibrating out of focus.

Sometimes being friends with an ankou was unsettling. Carissa couldn't help feeling that way as a knot formed in her stomach. She'd spent so much time comforting the sprites, it was just hitting her now that the elfkin she'd met this morning was gone. It was even more disquieting to hear that the ghost of Toffee was 'upset.'

"I'll bet he was," Cam said, sitting on the edge of the sofa. Alden's ankou form was unnerving to him too, Carissa knew well.

Alden continued, "He didn't exactly want to go to the Otherworld."

"You mean there's a ghost just out wandering around Vale?" Cam's alarm was audible.

His eyes nearly popped out of his head. Both her mother and father seemed to flinch a little, too. Carissa had to admit she was uncomfortable by the notion of Toffee's ghost, but mainly because he must be feeling scared and alone.

Alden's next sentence was said in a strained, gruff voice. "I tried to stop him, but he said he had 'unfinished business.' I swear I'm not good at this."

It was a little surprising to Cari to hear him speak like that. She knew Alden had been human and therefore was bound to have emotions, but every time they'd met in the past, he'd been enigmatic. She'd come to think of him as stoic and unemotional.

Sinking into the chair with his hands on the arms, his eyes downcast, lips tight, face pained, Alden seemed every bit the lonely boy he'd been in high school. When Alden was alive, though, he at least had the hope of a future. Now, what was he? He was lamenting his inefficiency as an ankou, but a reaper didn't seem like an occupation one should want to be good at anyway, did it?

"You'll find him," Cari tried to comfort him. Alden looked up, his eyes widening. His mouth opened at first as if surprised at the encouragement. His lips curled in gratitude. Carissa's first thought was to wonder whether his father, the stern Mr. Everly, had ever bothered to boost his son's confidence before.

"The question is, did the elfkin say anything about his death?" Carissa's father said.

"Did he see who murdered him?" Cari's mother asked.

Alden leaned forward, resting his elbows on his knees. "All he said was that he would make Fudge miserable if the elfkin didn't make amends for all the wrong he'd done."

"Wrong like killing him?" Cam asked.

Alden shrugged, and Cari's parents tensed. Carissa wished she could tell them to relax. Alden was no threat to anyone—not even the dead. He was just trying to help Toffee. The elfkin was probably just scared. Scared, hurt, and angry, not a great combination in a ghost wandering around Vale and possibly Moss Hill.

"Did he say who it was he was after?"

"Yes," Alden said, "but I can't imagine that he could've killed Toffee. At least, not without an excellent reason."

"What do you mean?" Carissa asked.

"Why?" Cam asked simultaneously.

Elixirs and Elves

"Because," Alden put a hand to his mouth and sat upright, as if deciding whether he would admit what he was going to say, "he said it was Fudge."

"Fudge?" Carissa whispered. She couldn't have been the only one who heard the argument between the two elfkins.

"Not possible." Cam shook his head.

"Well, he didn't say it outright, but he was adamant about not leaving until he 'made Fudge confess.'"

"Confess about the murder?" Carissa asked.

Of all the people in the room, Carissa knew the least about Fudge. Alden had grown up with him and even he was not shirking the idea of Fudge as a killer. Cameron, who had been to the Everly's home many times, had a different opinion.

"It couldn't be," Cam reiterated.

"I didn't think so either," Alden agreed, "but when I asked Toffee directly if he'd been killed by Fudge, he said that I didn't know Fudge as well as he did or that Fudge had a big secret Toffee needed to uncover before he moved on."

"Maybe we ought to ask Fudge," Cari's mother suggested.

"It doesn't usually work like that, Kaley," Cari's father said. "He won't come right out and admit it."

"There's nothing to admit. I'm telling you, I know who the killer is," Cameron burst out.

All eyes went to him, waiting for his revelation.

"Who?" Cari's father asked.

"Parker," Cam answered.

He looked quite pleased with himself, but Carissa disagreed.

"Why would Parker want to kill Toffee?"

She couldn't help but enunciate the ridiculousness of the statement.

"Obviously," Cam stressed, "he thought the elixir was for the mayor, and he poisoned it."

Carissa crossed her arms. He couldn't condescend to her like that. She turned it on him. "How did he even know the royals were going to give an elixir to the mayor?"

Cam shrugged. "He's well connected. He knows the Everlys. Maybe he heard something."

"It's a bit of a stretch."

Carissa kept the skepticism in her tone but thought about the comment Parker made to Fudge about the Everly's present. She held off on adding ammunition to Cam's arsenal against Parker, though. The two events were probably unrelated. Just in case, she'd have to find out which present the Everlys had intended to give the mayor. She didn't say all this to the group but came up with a plan to which they could all agree.

"Let's not jump to any conclusions. We'll talk to Varick tomorrow and see what he's discovered."

Chapter 5

Merry Matchmakers

Since the sprites and alvens had taken so long to fall asleep the night before, they woke late the next morning. Carissa had no work today, but she had to wake early if she wanted to make it to church on time. Father Quinn was understanding about most things, but not of those who made it late to church on Sundays. Usually, she dressed in her best, but since she hadn't planned to stay over last night, she had to choose from the old clothes her parents had kept of hers in her old room. There was no dust in her closet in the Otherworld, but neither was there anything of modern style. She really needed to update this wardrobe if she ever stayed over again. She picked out a green sweater and a long pink skirt. They might not be the best match, but they complemented each other nicely enough. She packed up her dress from last night in a large purse she found on the closet top and headed downstairs.

In the living room, she tiptoed past the sprites to make it into the kitchen where she found her parents already preparing breakfast. Her father had just finished setting the table, which looked like a layer of polished redwood bark sprouting from root-like legs curving inward at the center. He looked up just as Cari entered.

"Good morning, my dear." Her father kissed her on the forehead.

"Good morning," Carissa replied to both of her parents.

Her mother stood by the old wooden-burning—or in this case, magically heated—stove, mixing up something for

43

breakfast. Upon seeing Carissa, she reached to the counter beside the stove and handed Cari an empty strainer.

"Would you mind going outside and asking the nature faeries for a dozen raspberries?"

"It's the middle of winter, and you've been gone for months. Are you sure there even are raspberries growing in the garden right now?" Carissa asked.

"Of course. The faeries always tend the garden, whether we're here or not."

She brushed off Carissa's hesitation and shook the strainer in her left hand while mixing with the right. Cari had no choice but to take it.

"Remember to ask, be specific about the number, and thank them," her father warned. "Anything you take from the garden is theirs."

"I know," Carissa said.

She knew how it worked in fae territory. The nature faeries lived outside, traveling from garden to garden, and the fae respected that the world outdoors was their domain. So did Cari.

She turned toward the side exit that led from the kitchen to the garden. As she passed by her father, he grasped the back of one of the kitchen chairs and his face twisted in that thoughtful look he made when he was about to share his sage advice. Cari took a shawl from the hook beside the door and wrapped it around her arms, subconsciously bracing herself for whatever he was about to tell her she was doing wrong.

"Carissa, you're far too attached to the nature faeries from your garden. I understood about Chaos; she was adjusting to Moss Hill, and it was kind of you to take her into your home. But nature faeries should be free. It's not healthy for them to stay indoors."

"Leave it be, Dorian. It was just one night, and they were scared." Her mother kept stirring while cautioning her father to simmer down.

"Yes, but they would not have been scared if they were not at the party, misbehaving, if I may remind you."

Elixirs and Elves

"The alvens were there, too," Carissa pointed out.

She hated to argue. Sometimes she still felt the same way she had when she was a child. Back then, she saw her parents so rarely that when they were together, she never so much as disagreed so as not to lose any precious moment in anger. Of course, it was easier not to disagree with someone when you knew you'd only see them a few months out of the year.

"The alvens journeyed with us, of their own accord. This land is new to them. The royal family allowed them, graciously, to attend this event."

Cari bit her tongue and tried not to show frustration. The nature faeries had been there for her since she was little, in Moss Hill, in Vale, even in college. They had been a constant support in her life, especially when her parents weren't there. Naturally, she was attached to them. And why shouldn't they be allowed to attend this event just as the alvens had done?

Taking a deep breath, Carissa stepped out into the morning air. The winter chill nipped at her ears and nose. It seemed colder today than it had been so far this season. It was so cold, in fact, that she could see her breath. She quickened her pace and held the shawl tighter.

The stone pavers led her through the center of the garden to where there was a circular medallion patio with a fountain in the middle. *Where were the raspberry bushes?* Cari's eyes slowly surveyed the full circle.

There, just to the right of the fountain, she recognized the snow-covered bush. She stepped toward it, stopping to peer right over the plant. The plant, while alive, was covered in a light layer of snow. There was no visible sign of berries of any color. Cari couldn't imagine there were any berries hidden inside. Still, Carissa cleared her throat and held the bowl in front of her.

"Excuse me, good sprites, may I have a dozen raspberries from your bush here?"

She felt ridiculous. Part of her knew that this was how it worked here, but back at Nan's, she would never make such a formal request of her faeries. She waited almost a minute before the bush began to shake. Slowly, tiny dots of frost colored berries peaked through the green leaves. More than that, the red specs were moving.

Carissa gasped when she realized that it was the sprites, in cute, little raspberry hats and leaf clothing, waking at her request. The nature faeries floated to her face and squinted as if examining her sincerity. She kept her hands out, holding the bowl, and the sprites dove back into the bush. It rattled. Then, one by one, a steady line of sprites plopped berries into the container until it was overflowing. She had been specific about the number, but they didn't stop at twelve.

"All right, that's enough. I have plenty now, thanks!"

The sprites ceased their work. They looked at each other and then at Carissa. They were waiting, *for what?*

"Thank you for sharing the berries with me," Carissa repeated her thanks more formally.

To this, they seemed satisfied. The tiny faeries settled back to their places on the bush, snuggling back to sleep. Their little gestures were unlike anything Cari had seen before. So regal, they were, with their delicate hands signaling almost royally that she was excused from their presence. Their clothing of leaves and berries was something else entirely.

For years, on every gift-giving holiday, Cari bought little outfits for the sprites, thanks to Barnaby's impeccable sewing. She'd already ordered the Christmas batch this year. But these sprites were dressed by Nature herself, and she was not a poor seamstress. As unusual as their clothing was, Carissa mused the whole way back inside at how her little sprite friends would look if they lived the way these nature faeries did. She found the thought hilarious.

Closer to the kitchen, Cari frowned. She wondered whether her father was right. Perhaps Carissa was keeping her tiny fae friends from the life they ought to be living out here in nature. Was she doing them more harm than good by being so attached?

Indoors, warmth hit her like a balm soothing her tingling skin. The sweet smell of her mother's cooking tantalized her

Elixirs and Elves

nose. She looked into the pot as she handed the berries to her father.

"Rice pudding?" Cari asked.

"Rice pudding with raspberry coulis," her father corrected. He rinsed the berries and poured them into an oversized mortar. Using elf-light on the pestle rigged it to work as good as any blender. The bowl was deep enough to keep the puréed mess from flying everywhere.

The tea kettle whistled, and Cari took it off the stove, pouring the peppermint green tea into the cups her father had set out on the table. At her right, Carissa spied a sleepy sprite floating around the corner into the kitchen. Chaos rubbed her eyes and half opened them. She pointed to the tea in Cari's hands and glided to the table where she plopped into a space at the edge of a plate.

Lazily, the sprite pulled at a napkin. The silverware slid as she slipped the cloth from underneath it. Cari watched as Chaos wrestled it into the collar of her dress and rested her head into her hands with her elbows propped up on the plate. She must not have slept well.

Carissa opened the little cupboard near the pantry and took out a thimble from her mother's sewing supplies. She ignored her father's disapproving, upraised brow as she washed it out and filled it with tea for Chaos. He might have a point about how she was pampering the sprites.

The thought of her mollycoddling didn't stop Carissa from taking another thimble to fill with the raspberry pudding from the bowl her mother handed to her. Chaos took it eagerly, alternating between the pudding and her thimble of tea. Cari's mother laughed at the sight.

"You know," her mother said with a twinkle in her eye, "the prince shares your view on the nature faeries. I'm sure your offer to let the alvens stay with us last night impressed him."

Carissa hated to strike down the stars in her mother's eyes, but she could see through her thinly veiled suggestion and ignored it.

"I'm not saying it's not kind, Cari," her father said, "but the nature faeries have their own independent spirits. It's not natural to try to keep them cooped up in houses."

"Oh, enough of that," Carissa's mother said as she took her bowl and sat with them. "Try the rice pudding. It's a new recipe."

Her mother was always picking up new recipes from every trip they took. It was one of the few perks of their traveling. Carissa picked up her spoon, relishing the sight of the dish before starting in on it. The milky rice pudding under a layer of raspberry purée and topped with mint was a picture-perfect start to the day.

Her mind drifted and even the sweet breakfast didn't help as her train of thought traveled to last night. Alden, who did not require sleep, left shortly after his visit to find Toffee. Alden's first duty would be to guide the elfkin to his life beyond death, but, hopefully, he could ask Toffee a question or two about who might've wanted to poison him. Cari and Cameron had made it their first duty to investigate Fudge.

Cameron was convinced the elfkin was innocent. Fudge had always struck Carissa as a sour sort of fellow. She wouldn't have put it past him to be guilty of such a crime, especially after their heated argument last night. Cam knew Fudge better than Cari did, so perhaps he was a better judge. Or else it made him more biased.

At least he was putting aside politics and helping a friend. That was Cam; despite his latest career ambitions, at his core, he would always be the heroic type. Well, maybe not heroic in the fearless sense, but he was willing to go out of his way to help his friends. Cari knew he wouldn't let Fudge down if the sidhe began to turn their suspicions toward him. He'd never let Carissa down, either. Guilt slid down her gullet as the bite of pudding lost its sweet flavor.

"Are you all right?" her father interrupted.

Carissa broke her trance-like stare out the window. The rice pudding dripped from her spoon. Chaos, who'd perked up a bit from the breakfast, wiped a stray splatter from her

Elixirs and Elves

face. Even she, in her chiding look at Carissa, mixed concern in with her expression.

"Sorry," Carissa whispered to Chaos. To her parents, she said, "I'm fine, it's nothing." She almost added the words except for Toffee's horrible death, but she didn't want to upset Chaos or any other nature faerie who might overhear their conversation.

"Thinking about yesterday?" Her father glanced at Chaos. Even he didn't want to start any of the sprites off again.

"It's hard not to," Cari said.

"I think it was brave of the prince," her mother said, "how he dashed to Toffee's aid. You and he were the first ones to the elfkin's side, may the ankou rest his soul."

As soon as he finds him, Cari thought.

"Kaley." Her father's tone and eyes expressed warning, and he leaned toward her mother to press his point.

"I said nothing." Her mother's hands flew upward. She bent forward and scraped at the dish with her spoon, apparently wanting to say more.

"What is it?" Carissa asked. Her lips curled in amused curiosity. Chaos, too, leaned forward on the plate where Cari's bowl rested.

Her mother shrugged. "Nothing, but, Dorian, don't you think we should tell her?"

"Tell me what?"

Her father ignored Cari's question. "We agreed after what happened last night that now was not the time."

Her mother argued. "But they won't be here for long. We've got the future to think of."

"Excuse me," Carissa raised her voice to get their attention. "If something's going on that I should know about, just tell me. I'm more than capable of handling it."

"Dorian," her mother commanded, lifting her spoon and scooping up a portion of pudding. She gave her father a commanding eye before resuming her meal.

Cari's father's eyes flitted between Carissa and her mother. He cleared his throat and set down his spoon.

Straightening in his chair, he began, "All right. Cari, as you know, if you were full-elf, we would not have this conversation until you were at least a hundred."

It was Carissa's turn to freeze. She exchanged a quick glance with Chaos, whom she could tell understood enough to know the conversation ahead was serious. Carissa's knowledge of her elf heritage may not be complete, but she was aware that one hundred years was considered an elf's coming of age.

"But you're not a full elf." Her mother pushed her bowl aside. She was finished with her breakfast and just starting on Carissa. "And for a human, thirty is more than old enough."

"Yes, thank you, dear." Her father took his napkin from his lap and set it on the table. Apparently, breakfast, along with Cari's hope of a normal day, was over. "Carissa, what we're trying to say is—"

"It's time for you to marry," her mother burst out.

Cari felt the blood rushing to her ears. Her spoon clanged into the dish. Chaos fluttered to the edge of an empty chair, presumably to enjoy the view of the argument she knew was coming. Carissa breathed deeply to reel back her emotions before her elf-light sparked from her heart to her fingertips against her will.

Once she'd regained control of herself, Cari uttered one simple word, "Marry?"

"Carissa, I know the custom is different for humans, but among elves, it's not unheard of for marriages to be arranged between elf families of good standing," her father explained.

The words "*arranged marriage?*" formed themselves into a question on Cari's lips.

"The king and queen would like nothing more than for you to join their family. In fact, it was their idea! But we wholeheartedly agreed."

"You what?" Carissa asked—in far more than a whisper this time.

Her father's hands shot up, and he waved his palms slowly as if to calm her down. "We agreed you'd meet the prince and spend some time with him." Then he continued

Elixirs and Elves

more delicately, "It's your choice whether you'd like to move forward."

Move forward? That sounded more the *"arranged"* part and far less like a marriage. She could hardly process the words.

"He liked you, and you liked him, a mother can tell. You'll be perfect for each other." Her mother's hands clasped together, and a faraway look overtook her face. It was as if she was seeing her daughter's entire future flashing before her. The vision was not one Carissa was ready to entertain.

"Are you out of your minds?"

She'd never spoken to her parents like that before, not even in her teen years, but the words had flown out of her mouth just now. The room felt unnaturally warm, and she realized Chaos was on her shoulder. The nature faerie's minuscule hand rested on her chin. She almost flicked the sprite away but caught herself before she took such harsh action.

It was then that she discovered why Chaos had come to her. Carissa was standing almost as if her legs had acted on their own. If she hadn't caught hold of herself in time, her elf feet might have flown the coop. Her parents talked among themselves while she stood, open-mouthed, heart pounding, being soothed by a sprite.

"Kaley, I told you we ought not to tell her like this."
"She's floundering, Dorian. She needs a push."
"We might've pushed her over the edge. Look at her."

Her parents and Chaos all looked at her like she was the one who'd gone crazy. This was too much. Cari straightened out her hair with her fingertips and retook her seat. Her attempt at composure had no effect on their expectant faces. Her mother set down her spoon as if waiting for her to pour her heart out.

"I'm not floundering," Cari finally said. "I'm perfectly fine and more than capable of making decisions on my own, thank you."

"So, then I take it you and Cameron are in a serious relationship?" her mother asked.

Cari looked at her mother with steely eyes. Subconsciously, she clenched her jaw and balled her fists. Her mother was as direct as Nan but without the compassion.

"No," Carissa said.

Cari was not going to get into her complicated relationship with Cam with her parents—not today. Maybe she'd never have to if he moved on with someone like Tilly. Carissa brought her napkin up to her lips. It was a difficult task since Chaos was back on the table and standing on the other end of it. Chaos had picked up her thimble and was dunking it into Cari's bowl to get her seconds when the napkin flew out from under her. The sprite lost her footing and ended up face-first in the dish.

Cari winced and picked up the nature faerie, handing her the napkin to wipe the pudding off her. Helping the nature faerie at least offered her something to focus on other than her mother's barrage.

"If you're not in a relationship, then what harm is there in at least getting to know Prince Zephyr?" Her mother picked up her bowl and walked to the sink, turning her back from the conversation.

That was that. From what Carissa knew of her mother, that meant that the conversation—on her part, anyway—was over. Her father was a bit more understanding. He rose and took her hand into both of his.

"We would never push you," he said in a soft, low voice. "We just want to make sure you know what's around you before you realize what you've let get away. Consider it, that's all."

Cari's mother turned from the sink with a look that contradicted her father's "we would never push you" line and added, "It would be very foolish not to at least consider Zephyr, Prince of Elves and Sidhe, for a husband."

Since her parents were obviously finished, and since Chaos had ruined the pudding for Cari by landing in it, she

Elixirs and Elves

picked up her bowl and helped clear the table. She said nothing as she left the kitchen to pick up her dress from her room. Chaos zoomed to her, apparently not wanting to leave Cari's side. Entering the living room, she saw the sprites and alvens were just waking. She noticed that Chaos whipped around to her left hand, out of sight of the other faeries. She tugged at Carissa's hair as if to say "keep going."

Up the stairs, she urged Chaos to let go.

"What's wrong?" Cari asked.

Chaos drew a circle around herself. Then, she tapped her finger as if tapping on someone's shoulder and opened and closed her mouth as if to mimic someone talking. Carissa thought she had come to understand Chaos completely, but now she was at a loss. Finally, Chaos pointed downstairs and made a face, sticking out her tongue. Cari tried a guess.

"Is that alven bothering you?"

Chaos nodded.

Carissa smiled. Based on how he'd been acting at the party, the alven who'd accidentally pushed Chaos out of the tree had apparently tumbled head over heels for her. Carissa wanted to laugh but didn't want to hurt the little sprite's feelings. She opened the window instead.

"All right, you don't have to see him. I've got a task for you, anyway. Think you can summon Alden and find out if he's gotten anywhere with Toffee?"

The sprite nodded eagerly.

"Tell him to meet me back at the apothecary shop after church, will you?"

Chaos saluted and zipped out the window with gusto. Cari watched her swing around to the side of the house. Chaos was bright enough to choose a safe place out of sight to summon the ankou. With that done, Carissa grabbed the large purse with her dress in it and walked back downstairs.

The sprites in the living room, now awake, flurried to her like a cloud in the air. The alvens in their bubbles added a sheen to the cloud of faeries that made them seem more magical somehow. She couldn't help the giggle that erupted from her lips.

"Good morning," she said. She explained to the nature faeries that she'd be home in Moss Hill in the afternoon. To the alvens, she said, "I'm sure the royal family will be ready for you to join them at Head Elf Rolin's today. One particular alven floated near her face, holding his hands up questioningly. She recognized him and knew what he was asking.

"Sorry," she said, "Chaos already left."

He pouted, and Cari bit her lip to hold back her smile. It was too cute not to tug at her heartstrings and pull at the corners of her mouth. Taking her father's advice, she instructed the sprites that they could come home at their leisure. But then, since Cari couldn't just leave them with that, she added that they were welcome to some freshly made rice pudding in the kitchen.

She looked back at the kitchen entryway, to which the sprites and alvens were darting. As much as her parents had upset her, she still called out a goodbye as she left for town.

"Cari." Her mother peeked her head from around the corner. "Take the shawl." She held one out to her.

Carissa took it and replied with a "thank you."

This was not the warm, thick shawl she'd had on before, but a lighter gold one. It shined in the sunlight when she stepped outside. It was perfect for church and even complemented the green and pink she was wearing.

Her parents had always been a mystery. Up until now, they'd been hands off, showing they cared in small gestures, like this shawl, but leaving the details of her upbringing to Nan. Gone one day, arranging her marriage the next, this was just more proof that she would never understand them.

She mused on this, or maybe stewed about it, as she walked down the dirt path out of Vale. She'd walked yesterday with the sprites for company and had intended to ride back with Maren. Cam had offered her a ride home in the late evening, but she'd stayed overnight. She probably could've

Elixirs and Elves

asked him to pick her up in the morning, but Vale was out of his way, and she had her elf-light to help speed up the journey.

She might have used it, too, but not long into her journey, she saw none other than Prince Zephyr himself, headed toward her from Rolin's home. She smirked.

Now she understood about the shawl. Her mother must've known, or at least suspected he'd be out this morning. Or had they conspired for him to meet her today? She had a sneaking suspicion this was no chance meeting.

Chapter 6

A Christmas Courting

"Good morning." The prince's voice flowed like a harmony of flutes and beating drums.
The drums might've been Cari's own heartbeats, growing louder as he stepped closer. He was as tall, if not taller than Cam, and his eyes were an ocean of blue to Cam's brown. The beam of his smile and shine of his golden hair were almost blinding. Cari broke her gaze as if the sight of him had cast some kind of a spell over her. She bowed, as she thought was customary to do.

"Are you going to the human town?" the prince asked. He came right over to her, ignoring the bow.

Cari turned to the road and kept her eyes fixed ahead. "Yes," she said, more curtly than she meant.

"May I walk with you?" he asked.

She couldn't help but look back up at him. Still handsome, the Adonis's face held no air of superiority, no charming smile, no shy anticipation, no outward sign of trying to garner her favor. There was only a good-natured, friendly curl of his lips, and an earnest questioning gaze in his eyes.

"Of course, Your Highness," she said.

He accepted the invitation by turning with her so that they walked in step.

"How is it, living in a town with humans?" he asked.

Carissa studied the side of Zephyr's face. He was looking far down the mountain, seemingly trying to catch a glimpse of the town.

Elixirs and Elves

Cari shrugged. "I don't know, it's normal for me. Humans are less formal than fae folk."

He nodded. "So Toffee said."

She looked at him with one eyebrow upraised. He met her eyes and looked away.

"Before he died," the prince clarified, holding his arms behind him as they walked side by side, each with their eyes on the road. "Toffee lived among humans for a while and even visited Moss Hill before, years ago."

There was a melancholy sound to the prince's words, but not the deep sorrow Cari imagined he should feel at the loss of a friend.

"I'm sorry that he's gone," Carissa said.

"As are we." The prince's brow fell heavier over his eyes as he continued. He walked with his back razor-straight and his eyes aimed at the road. Carissa could picture more sidhe in him than elf. Even talking with her seemed more out of duty than interest. Or was that her feeling toward him? A part of her wondered.

The night before, she'd only seen him for barely an hour. He'd seemed less solemn last night, though still refined. He had smiled more, laughed once even, and the twinkle in his eye she'd caught once was definitely like that of an elf. Now, he was silent, mourning like a sidhe—with little outward emotion. Cari searched for a change of topic, but he surprised her with his own.

"I'm told that you are an herbalist?"

Cari twisted the string on her purse. "An apothecary. I have a degree in herbal medicine," she said. She hated explaining. Whenever she said she had a degree in herbal pharmacology and was technically a full-fledged pharmacist, people assumed they needed to call her Doctor Shae. Or, strangely enough, they sometimes assumed she was less connected to the natural medicine, although she'd literally started in natural medicine before earning her pharmacy credentials. The titles meant nothing to the faeries and were even less impressive to the sidhe. To the humans, it was distinguished, as it should be, but sometimes distinguished meant intimidating. She preferred to keep things simple. Moss Hill had always had an apothecary of some sort, so the title continued with her.

Strangely, she had thought that the prince would be daunting to speak to, but he didn't seem that way in person. She found herself relaxing into conversation.

"Ah, you're well-trained," the prince said. "I suspected as much. You do not hesitate to help those in need of healing. That is admirable."

She hadn't really helped him so much as rushed toward him in curiosity to see what had happened. She'd felt she did more harm than good. The sidhe had pushed her out of the way as they tried to heal him. With her lack of ability regarding the elf-light, she couldn't have done better than the guards.

"I don't think I really helped last night."

The prince disagreed before she could undo his compliment. "Not just with Toffee. You tried to help the Morrigan as well. You're much praised for it in Tir-Na-Nog."

Carissa looked down and swallowed. She was praised in the country of the King of Sidhe and Elves? Cari could feel her cheeks turning red. The sidhe here might disagree with that praise. Miss Morgan hadn't made it. It hadn't exactly been Cari's proudest moment. She blamed herself for not having the skill to counteract the poison that had killed the protector of Moss Hill. Of course, she couldn't have known at the time that the poison had been mixed with hobgoblin magic.

"I've upset you." Prince Zephyr stopped walking. "I'm sorry."

"No," Cari responded quickly. She took a breath and turned to face him directly. "I'm fine. It's just...." She shook her head, not finding words.

Zephyr watched her intently. Cari hadn't expected such concern in his eyes or his attentive silence as he waited for an answer. She didn't usually voice her feelings, much less explain

Elixirs and Elves

them. He wasn't saying anything, though. She had the impression he might wait forever to hear what she had to say.

"There's been a lot of loss this year and with Toffee last night...."

Apparently, he wasn't used to her way of speaking. Usually, Cam, Maren, her parents, or even Nan at times, would jump in if she left her sentences unfinished. The prince was different. If the statement didn't sound like it was going to end, he said nothing at all. She didn't like it. It forced her to finish her thought.

"I just wish all these losses weren't happening," she finally finished off the thought.

The prince looked away. She couldn't see his downcast eyes, but the creased eyebrows and long face portrayed a deeply thoughtful expression. He wasn't like a sidhe, Cari realized. There was emotion there. There was the start of a storm in his ocean blue eyes, and he allowed the feeling to show even as he looked at her.

"I'm sorry Moss Hill has had so many losses this year. If I could undo it, I would."

"It's not your fault," Carissa said. "No one can change the past. We can only do our best here and now."

The look the prince gave was so subtle she almost missed it. The tension in his forehead relaxed, the lips eased, and the faintest impression of a dimple appeared for only a second. It wasn't happiness precisely, but gratitude perhaps that he was showing. He looked back at the road and resumed walking before she could name the expression.

The silence was difficult, especially when he offered her his hand walking down the rocky steps of the mountain. At that moment, she thought of what it would be like to hold his hand while dancing at one of the elf parties. The next minute, she thought of Maren and Cam. Maren, she hoped, wouldn't be too jealous of her as she wrapped an arm in the crook of Prince Zephyr's elbow. Cam, she wished, would be a little off-put by her being so close to another man. Almost by reflex, she pulled away. The prince let her go. The sidhe in him portrayed no emotion about it. An elf might have asked her outright if something was wrong. Prince Zephyr's eyes kept to the road.

Carissa bit her lip, wondering how she'd let her thoughts get away from her like that. She ought to be focused on other things, like the fact that the prince might know something more about the elfkin's murder. *But should I ask?* Carissa felt that she had upset him with the mention of it before. She would have dropped it, but she just had to know if they'd made any progress on determining who might've poisoned the elixir. They walked a few more paces before Cari ventured to ask.

"Have the sidhe discovered what happened yet?"

"No," Prince Zephyr said. This time he seemed unaffected entirely, except that Cari happened to notice the flinch of his fingers. They had almost balled into a fist but settled back down in a quick motion. "The head of the sidhe guard, I'm not sure of his name, is working with our security advisor. They should have some news by midday."

"Do they have any leads?"

"My role as the magistrate in the case prevents me from answering, but I'll know more after the briefing this afternoon. Have you spoken with the sidhe guard?"

Carissa's eyes reflexively widened, and she looked at Zephyr. "Varick? No, not since yesterday. Why?"

Zephyr's eyes shifted back to the trail. "I know you've worked with him closely in the past, but I'm afraid my father wants the matter strictly handled in confidence. I'm sorry that he will not be able to share any details on this matter with you. He's under orders."

Carissa couldn't understand why he felt the need to say that or how closely she thought they had worked before. Had Varick been reprimanded for sharing too much with a non-sidhe in the past? The king was an elf, though, so perhaps it wasn't that she was not a sidhe, but that she was not a member of the guard. Either way, it wasn't right for him to get into any trouble on her account.

Elixirs and Elves

"Varick has never shared information with me about his duties unless it was necessary to the case or part of his instructions from the council. I can assure you, he's a model of a sidhe guard captain."

"I'm sure he is," he said. His tone was gentle, but the sentence was a bit drawn out.

Cari got the sense that there was either something bothering him or something he wasn't telling her. She wasn't sure what to say next, so she looked ahead on the path and said nothing. They were near the end of the trail and could see Greenfield road now. Carissa wondered how far he would travel with her or if he would come to the church. She thought of him sitting in on the sermon with her—every eye would be on them.

But no, when they reached the end of the path, he bowed. She curtsied to follow suit. Then he turned, presumably to make his way back to Vale. She stood, puzzled, watching him. A few steps in, he stopped and spun back around.

"Carissa," he said her name like a question, "Rolin is having a dinner tonight just for the sidhe and elves. It will be a small gathering. I would be honored if you attended it with me."

He looked at her intently. Her eyes skirted the ground; she felt torn. A fleeting image of Cameron popped into her mind while her mother's words rang in her ears: "*What harm is there in at least getting to know Prince Zephyr?*"

The imagined picture of Cam was replaced by the real vision of the tall, broad-shouldered, golden-haired, handsome prince standing in front of her now. She recalled another of her parent's arguments next. The line "*You'd be perfect for each other*," echoed loudly enough in her elf ears that she could not ignore it. She owed it to herself to see if it was true, didn't she?

She nodded.

She swore the sun reflected in the prince's perfect smile. He bowed again, and she curtsied as she was expected by custom. Then, both she and the prince turned and headed in opposite directions. She smiled all the way down Greenfield, until she turned toward the church and found herself doing as she did every Sunday. Without even thinking, her eyes glided over the congregation, trying to catch sight of Cam.

***

FATHER QUINN, WHO had attended the party the night prior, gave a stirring homily on the preciousness of life and importance of living well. Carissa took the words to heart. She was especially moved by his discussion of life choices, though hers at the moment were less of a right vs. wrong and more of a question of how to listen to her heart and know with absolute clarity what it was saying. She was not the only one so profoundly affected by the priest's speech.

Maren, sitting with the choir as she always did, held back a gasp with her hand when Father Quinn explained the peril of our ignoring one's conscience. Cam, sitting a few spaces down from Carissa, bent forward in his seat with a pained expression at Father Quinn's mention of regret. Could he be thinking about her? If she should marry the prince, would Cari regret not giving her relationship with Cam a chance?

It was only when Carissa felt Nan's fingers pinching the skin above her elbow that Cari realized Maren and Cam were not reacting to the sermon itself. Chaos was pinching and poking her friends to get their attention. Eventually, the sprite flew down into Cari's lap. Carissa cupped her hands to hold the nature faerie and bent over in the pew, trying not to cause a disturbance.

Chaos held her hand out, pinching her thumb and finger together as if holding something. She swirled the imaginary item in her hand and then drank and promptly fell in Cari's palms. She was reenacting the murder from the night before. Then she pointed to her head and stood back up. She held her wrists together in front of her and took two steps, then stopped and looked at Cari to see if she'd understood.

She did. The sidhe had arrested someone for the murder. Carissa gave a slight nod. Chaos pointed outside. What was

Elixirs and Elves

outside? The sidhe? It was more likely Alden, waiting to tell her the news.

She glanced up at the pulpit. The homily had ended and the second part of Mass was just beginning.

"Wait now, just a little while longer," she whispered.

She tried to concentrate on Mass, but her mind went to all different places for the rest of the time. Once or twice, she caught looks from both Cam and Maren. Chaos, however, had fallen asleep in the pew beside Cari. She had to be careful not to sit on her accidentally, but at least the sprite was catching up on her sleep.

When they finally said their final thanks and the Mass had ended, Carissa scooped up Chaos, accidentally startling her awake. Cari, Chaos, and Nan were among the first to leave. Chaos guided them around the church to the adjacent cemetery and then flew back to the church, possibly to get Maren and Cam. On this side of the building, Carissa was surprised to see Alden standing near a back wall.

The Grim Reaper was on holy ground.

But why shouldn't he be? Cari realized she shouldn't have been too surprised. Alden wasn't an evil spirit, even if his role as ankou was feared. He was actually a gentle person by nature, and he took his duty as ankou as one who helped ease and comfort those passing to the world beyond. She wondered if the previous ankou could've walked on the sacred ground so easily.

Thankfully, Alden was in his human form, so if anyone saw him, they might question the black attire, but not suspect he was a spirit instead of a living person. Cameron and Maren joined them almost as soon as Carissa and Nan made it to Alden's side.

"Alden!" Cam said too loudly.

This warranted a shushing from Cari and a raised eyebrow from Maren. Cam lowered his voice but kept the surprised inflection.

"Why are you peeking into the church windows during Mass? Do you know what could have happened if anyone saw you? You'd cause a panic to the whole congregation!"

Maren raised a hand like a school girl. "Why would he cause a panic? Wait a minute." She peered at Alden with a finger to her lips. "I know you." She tapped her cheek, thinking. "You're that druid, aren't you?"

Carissa glared at Cam.

"She doesn't know?" Cam whispered.

"Know what?" Maren asked. Her attention didn't linger on the question. She turned back to Alden. "I don't think I ever thanked you for saving us from that hobgoblin."

"Don't mention it," Alden said.

The others were keenly aware of how he meant that—except maybe Nan. Carissa hadn't specifically told her, and Nan never said anything, but she knew Jane well and had to know what Alden Everly had looked like.

Carissa shook her head and cleared her throat, going along with Maren's false belief. "Right, a druid, he's a friend of Cam's."

"See that, Cam? You're worrying for nothing," Alden said.

"Why would he worry? What was that about a panic?" Maren asked.

"Um...." Cam scratched his head. "Well, he, uh—"

"It's a personal matter," Alden said. "I have family in the church with whom I'm...estranged."

The look in Alden's eyes was heartbreaking. His gaze drifted to the church wall. He was close enough to touch the stone, but in his eyes, he was so far away it seemed unreachable.

Carissa stepped in, literally moving toward the ankou and resting a hand on his upper arm. Maren, no longer interested in a druid's family matters, started in about Chaos's actions in the church.

Elixirs and Elves

"Did you have to pinch me?" Maren asked the sprite, who put her hands behind her back and drew her knees together while floating in the air.

"Oh, don't look all innocent," Maren continued. "You're too cute when you do that. Just don't do it again." She rubbed her arm for dramatic effect.

Carissa focused on Alden. She let go of his arm. His eyes drifted to where her hand had been and then up to her. Cari might've imagined it, but Cameron seemed to sway a little closer to her and Alden took a small step back.

"What did you find? Who did the sidhe arrest?"

"Parker," Cam said.

Everyone looked at him, including Alden. Chaos crossed her arms and her head cocked to the side. Sometimes she really reminded Cari of a surly teenager. Cam's hands flew up defensively.

"I'm just guessing. It's only logical. The mayor was the target and who wants the mayor gone? Parker."

"Hey! That's my friend you're talking about." Maren put her hands on her hips.

"Do you have any proof?" Carissa asked.

"Well, no." Cam's open palms dropped to his side.

Even Nan chided him after that. "Don't speak ill in speculation. Have you forgotten you're in church?"

The old woman patted Maren's arm with her gloved hand. The younger woman nodded, accepting her support. Cam, very much like himself, scratched the back of his neck and shrugged.

"Sorry," he said. "I know he's your friend, Maren, but I'm not just speculating. Even Mayor Belkin suspects it. We don't have any proof yet, but—"

"But you hate Parker because he wants your job," Maren said. "You're willing to believe he's so awful he would murder someone just because he's ambitious. Well, he's not a killer. He was with me all night, and he never touched any elixir of any kind." She crossed her arms and turned away from him,

65

giving him the cold shoulder. "I never would've expected this from you, Cameron."

Maren never called him by his full name, which only showed how upset she was. Nan put an arm on her shoulder and looked at Cari as if to say "fix this, now." Carissa put her hands up between the two, both red-faced and still steaming.

"Listen, Chaos told me they've caught the killer already. Alden has the news, I think we should hear him out."

Chaos drifted to Alden's shoulder. Her arms were still folded, and now she was boasting an I-told-you-so look. Alden, who really could have said something earlier, snapped out of his blank-faced stare. He seemed confused about the argument, and Cari did not want to fill him in on their conflicting feelings about a certain greedy man of privilege. Well, greedy was Carissa's opinion.

Alden said, "It's not who you might think."

"It never is," Nan replied.

This was one moment where she wasn't helping with her tidbits of wisdom. Alden glanced between all of them, and Chaos sat down, patting his shoulder for support. Whoever it was, it was hard for him to say it. A pit grew in Cari's stomach. She braced herself to hear that it might have actually been Fudge.

"Varick was able to trace the poison to its original source, and it wasn't the mayor's elixir. The elixir the king gave to the mayor was not contaminated."

"Then where did the poison come from?" Maren asked.

Carissa was nearly convinced that it was the Everly's butler. If the poison wasn't meant for the mayor, Toffee might've been the actual target. If he was the target, then Fudge might be the only one with a motive. Cari didn't know precisely what that motive was, but, based on their argument the night before, he certainly seemed to have one.

Alden took a breath. "Varick had his own vial of elixir. He confessed to the guard just now that it was his vial that contained the poison."

Elixirs and Elves

A sick feeling traveled from the pit of Carissa's stomach to her throat. Varick had a vial of elixir. She's not only seen him with it, but she might've given him the ingredients. Still, it didn't make sense. Why would he try to kill the mayor or an elfkin? Or was someone else his target—like the king, maybe?

Carissa could feel herself physically waver. She'd just defended Varick to Zephyr. The prince had seemed to be holding something back. Had he known about Varick's guilt? Worse: Was Varick actually guilty?

Carissa felt Cameron's arm around her shoulder. She steadied herself and put a hand on his forearm. Nodding, Cari smiled at him, trying to convey that she was all right. She wasn't going to faint or anything, but she had been a little shaken for a moment. Now, she brushed off the thought. Varick was all about honor and loyalty to the sidhe. He wouldn't commit murder.

She wasn't successful in convincing herself of that fact, but she tried to believe it. For Alden's sake, she would give him the benefit of the doubt since she knew Alden's sister had a fondness for the sidhe captain. She looked up at Alden, who had concern in his eyes.

His hand was reaching forward, though he hadn't actually touched her when she'd swayed. He straightened and dropped his arm when Cam let go of Carissa. Maren leaned into her line of sight between her and Alden.

"Are you okay?" she asked.

"Yes, I'm fine," Cari said. She caught sight of Nan, who was the only one in the group looking at her less with concern and more with a raised eyebrow that said "get a hold of yourself, girl."

She did just that.

"What did Varick say?" she asked Alden. "Did he actually confess to the poisoning?"

Alden shook his head. "He said nothing more than that the poison had been in the elixir he had in his possession earlier last night. He wouldn't say how it came to be there."

Astoria Wright

Maren hugged herself as a gust of wind passed over them. Cari bit her lip and brought her a hand to her reddening nose. Nan spoke up in the silence.

"The question is, what do you all believe?"

Carissa studied the ankou's human face. "You don't believe he's guilty, do you?"

Alden's lips pressed together. "No. I don't think so." His voice was firm when he said it.

"Neither do I," Cam said.

Carissa suspected his conviction was motivated by his belief in Parker's guilt, but even Maren agreed with Cam now. At least, she agreed Varick was not guilty.

"Then we have to say something." Maren looked at Carissa. "Or actually, you might have to say something since the sidhe probably won't speak to us."

Alden stepped forward. "You're too late. They've taken Varick to the sidhe holding cells in their mounds beneath the Redwood. They won't allow any human there for the trial."

"It's because of the king," Nan said. "They'll treat it as a matter of the highest security."

Carissa didn't even try to guess how Nan knew that. Sometimes her grandmother surprised her with the oddest bits of knowledge about the fae. Other times, Nan had no knowledge at all. It might've been her extensive knowledge as a librarian or her connection with the fae world through her daughter. Either way, she was definitely right this time.

"The prince is acting as magistrate of this case," Carissa said. "Maybe I can convince him to let me speak to Varick."

Cam's head snapped toward Cari the moment she said that. She didn't look at his face, though she imagined his open-mouthed stare as he searched for the words that escaped his lips next.

"How would you do that?" Cam asked.

She hesitated, finally admitting, "I'm going to dinner in Vale with the elves tonight. The king and the prince will be there. If there's anything I can do, I'll try then."

Chapter 7

Frosty Fae

Dinner with elves always meant a joyous time filled with plenty of good conversation and mirth. Dining with the sidhe, however, would be an entirely different experience. On the way to their host's home, Cari's father warned her about the formality involved.

"The host and the guest of honor, the king, takes the first bite. Then the royal family may partake in the meal. Do not begin eating before all of the elder sidhe have begun. You may initiate conversations with those at the table younger than you, but you must be invited into conversations by those older."

"I'm half-human." Cari rolled her eyes and pulled the door to her parents' cottage shut behind them. "So, I'll be the youngest one there."

The three walked down the stone street to the middle of Vale, where Rolin's home was located. Her father and mother walked arm in arm, with the winter snow falling around them.

"Youngest and a human," her mother said, adjusting her white cape around her royal-blue dress, "and yet, somehow, I think you'll be invited into many conversations tonight." She glanced at Cari's father with a mischievous grin and placed a hand on the gold-embroidered wrist of his formal white suit with the long red vest that was customary for only elf councilors to wear.

Carissa stuffed her icy hands into the mint coat she'd brought with her from Moss Hill. Her mauve ankle boots crunched in the snow. Her mother had insisted on an outfit change, but Carissa refused the stress of trying to impress the sidhe or the prince. There were no laws on the regality of one's apparel, and she was already in her Sunday best. Aside from that, Cari reasoned that the boots might come in handy if the prince agreed to allow her into the prison to see Varick. There was no telling what the sidhe prisons were like and she'd rather not trek through new territory in heels.

Carissa's father offered one last piece of advice as he knocked on the tall, arched door of Rolin's home. He did not turn his head from where he stood, almost at attention, waiting for Sal to allow them inside. Instead, he merely added an addendum to his earlier statements.

"Smile much, laugh little, and say only what is necessary to convey your point."

Her father's wisdom had little time to sink into Cari's mind before Sal opened the door. The elfkin's jolly nature usually had a relaxing effect on Carissa, but today he answered the door with a forced smile. The warmth that always radiated from his eyes was not present.

"Welcome," the elfkin said as he stepped aside to allow them indoors. He took their coats without another word.

"Sal, what's wrong?" Cari asked.

Her father's eyebrow raised. Carissa was sure it was half in curiosity about the elfkin's condition and half a warning to her to be careful in keeping in proper etiquette during the dinner.

"It's nothing." Sal tried his smile again. "That's very much like you, Cari, uh Miss Carissa, always so caring. Really, I'm fine, thank you."

Cari frowned. The whole "Miss Carissa" formality was for the benefit of the guests, she knew, but she disliked hearing it nonetheless. He might be Rolin's servant, but he was her friend, and she'd told him long ago not to call her that.

Carissa did not budge from the doorway. "I know you better than that, Sal. Out with it, now. Tell me what's wrong."

Cari's father put an arm on her back as if to gently remind her that they ought to move on to the dinner party,

Elixirs and Elves

but Carissa kept in place. Her mother issued a low "tsk" of disapproval, but her parents would not make a scene.

Sal shifted nervously on his feet and watched Cari's father trying to wave her on. Carissa knew full well that she was making her parents uncomfortable; she didn't care. Something was wrong with Sal, and she wasn't going anywhere until she knew what was bothering her friend.

Finally, Sal stopped fidgeting. He took out a handkerchief and dabbed at his forehead while sighing.

"It's really nothing, Cari. It's just what happened yesterday is all. I didn't even know Toffee but the little bit that we got to talking yesterday. And it shouldn't bother me so much, I suppose."

Sal's black eyes looked straight into Carissa's brown. "An elfkin died yesterday, and everyone here is disturbed by it right enough. They worry about a killer, but they're not sad about his death. No one here so much as shed one tear for Toffee, and today it's like he was just another servant. There are no prayers or funeral planned for him. The king never even said his name."

Carissa's father put a hand on Sal's arm. He was not without compassion. Even her mother's expression turned to one sharing in Sal's pain. Carissa pulled the elfkin into a hug.

"Don't worry, Sal," she said at the end of the embrace. "I'll ask Father Quinn to say something for him, and we'll do what we can to see he gets a proper goodbye."

Carissa thought of Alden at that moment. She hadn't even asked him if he'd found Toffee's spirit to send to the world beyond. For all she knew, the elfkin was still wandering around Moss Hill or Vale. He might even be in the room.

Carissa's father put a hand on her back again. Having reassured Sal that he was cared for, even if Toffee had not been, Carissa walked with her parents to the inner hall. Sal's mood had improved, at least a little, and he used his elfkin magic to set out the elaborate dinner within moments for all of the guests in Rolin's home.

Carissa and her parents were seated near the head of the table. She found that she'd been placed right next to the prince and across from Rolin's wife. It couldn't be a coincidence. Rolin's position near the king was not unusual since he was the host, but the sidhe elders should have come next.

Yesterday, she had thought that a place of honor had been given to her and her parents due to their position in service to the king. Now, she wondered if the placement meant that the royal family was, in fact, very serious about the matter of marriage. Carissa hadn't been nervous until that moment. She had to maintain the outward semblance of calm but inside the thought transformed her to a jumbled mess of nerves. She needed to control her heart rate, or sparks would fly.

Literally, tiny sparks of her elf-light crackled at under her nails once Carissa realized Prince Zephyr stood next to her, holding out his hand to help her to her chair. She curled her fingers on the arms of the chair as she sat.

It wasn't so much an attraction to him, though he was an inarguably attractive person. It was more a heart-pounding fear of every eye on her at the table and the fact that no one surrounding them would have missed the reason why Rolin had placed her there. Hopes and expectations threatened her, and she had to suppress her elf-light from putting up a shield around her whole person as she felt one emanating around her heart.

Zephyr took his place next to her. She kept her father's advice and only smiled in gratitude of him helping her to her seat rather than saying anything. Surely a "thank you" was allowed, but she wasn't taking chances with all the sidhe watching. She was almost glad she didn't have to speak, but then the king graciously invited Carissa into a conversation after Sal had served the first of the courses.

"How is your grandmother?" King Finvarra asked, retrieving his spoon from the napkin in front of him.

Carissa, not expecting the question, began with an ineloquent "uh," complete with the features of a surprised

Elixirs and Elves

face. Touching the silverware as if it grounded her to the moment, she collected herself.

"She's well. Thank you."

"We missed her presence last night, though perhaps for the better given what occurred. Still, she was welcome to attend."

Cari looked down at the table. For some reason or another, Nan had taken a Saturday night shift at the library yesterday. With her status as a retired head librarian, she only worked when and how much she wanted to, so there was no need to take such a shift. It did strike Cari as odd that she seemed to want to ensure she could not make it to the welcoming party. But Nan was strange sometimes, and Carissa didn't ask—not this time, anyway.

"Unfortunately, she was engaged elsewhere."

Cari couldn't add that Nan would have loved to attend or that she would be pleased that he'd asked about her because she wasn't sure that was true. Maybe she didn't like the propriety of these dinners. Carissa found it annoying speaking so formally all the time. Her father had grown up like this, but how her mother dealt with it she didn't know.

She'd said the right thing, though, because the king accepted her statement with an understanding nod.

"Please tell her that I asked about her and that the royal family wishes her well."

Cari was sure her heart had missed a beat, or her ears had misheard his statement. The King of Sidhe and Elves was wishing a human well? Was this the equivalent of a faerie candid camera show or was he serious? Or, was he so serious about Cari marrying his son that he'd ask after a human for the sake of their betrothal? He was an elf, so maybe it wasn't that shocking for him to be so kind toward humans. Whatever the case, Carissa had to close her jaw and say something while she could still appear normal to the royals.

"I will," Cari replied, hoping the frog in her throat hadn't raised the pitch of her voice. "Thank you."

She lifted her napkin, now doubting whether she ought to place it in her lap, which of the spoons to take, and everything she'd learned about etiquette. Finally, she told herself that she was being ridiculous. She lifted the soup spoon and glanced at Hela. In order of ages, Rolin's daughter was third from the youngest. Being only a year or so over a hundred, she still acted much like a young elf. Her recent marriage had matured Hela somewhat, but she still had the same outgoing, spirited personality she'd always had. Carissa was not surprised to see her in full conversation with her husband and a sidhe elder. She seemed as carefree as ever.

It made Cari grin and warmed her spirit. The warmth deepened to a blush when the prince invited her into a conversation with his parents and Head Elf Rolin. He fixed his bright blue eyes on her with the right corner of his lips curved pleasantly as he spoke.

"Carissa, you know both the people of Moss Hill and of Vale. I've proposed that we hold a Christmas Eve party for both towns to make up for the gathering that ended so terribly last time. What do you think of the idea?"

Cari looked across the table to where Sal was entering with the second course. His words were still ringing in her ears. She smiled at all of them, searching for a delicate balance of words.

"I think it's a wonderful idea, Your Majesty. Though, I wonder if it would not also help bring closure to hold a remembrance for Toffee as well."

The queen waved a hand as if shirking off the idea. "The elfkin's family will conduct their ceremony as they see fit. We would not intrude in their practices."

"I do not think she means that we hold the funeral without the family," Rolin said.

"Then we must see what she means," the king said, setting down his silverware. "What are you proposing?"

Carissa straightened her napkin on her lap while she responded. "Nothing that should intrude on the family. Just a few words of remembrance. Or perhaps we could hold the

Elixirs and Elves

party in honor of Toffee and say a few words before the party begins."

"I think he would like that," the prince interjected. "Toffee deserved nothing less."

Prince Zephyrs beamed, and he fixed his eyes on Cari with his head held high. Then, he did something that expanded Carissa's respect for him exponentially. He set his gaze on Sal, now switching out the soups for appetizer plates.

"Sal, was it? If Rolin could spare you, would you mind leading my staff in preparations of the party in honor of Toffee?"

Sal looked between Cari and the prince with his mouth moving up and down as he struggled for words. He set the plate down and bowed.

"I would be honored." The elfkin's voice shook with excitement. His usual joy returned, and his cheeks regained their happy color.

Carissa's lips curled into a wide grin. She felt her previous nervousness wash away as she turned to share a look with the prince and found his ocean blue eyes and radiant smile. She realized a second later that the table as a whole had their sights set on the couple.

She looked down at her plate, waiting for the conversations to resume. The prince continued to discuss several aspects of his experience so far in Vale with her.

"I would like to visit your shop tomorrow, if I may," he said, taking a bite of the mushroom bruschetta.

"Of course," Cari replied between bites, "you're welcome there anytime."

"I'm curious to see human remedies and how they differ from elf and sidhe cures."

"They don't differ much, except for the use of magic."

"That's precisely what fascinates me. Without magic, it would seem nearly impossible to effect cures."

"Not at all," Cari replied. "Magic only intensifies the power that is already in the herbs, the cures still lie in the plant itself."

"Perhaps a little magic lies in everything." Prince Zephyr sipped the elderberry wine with a twinkle in his eye.

A snort from the elder sidhe beside the prince bordered on disrespect for the royalty. Zephyr, Carissa, and a few beside them set their attention on him. Cari recognized him from being in front of the elders in a hearing months ago. His white-blond hair and blue eyes, tinted with a tinsel-silver gleam, were hard to miss.

"Forgive me, Your Majesty, but that is your youth speaking. Magic is far more than the ingredients."

"I don't presume to have your mastery of magic, Elder Tiache," Zephyr said, "but I believe Carissa's human remedies have some merit to them."

"Whatever humans know is little compared to a sidhe's remedies. Yet, they believe they know much," Tiache said.

"Their remedies work for them," another elder said. From overhearing a previous conversation, Carissa knew his name was Lathor.

"And ours for us," Tiache retorted. "As it has for centuries before we mingled with humans."

"Best keep your personal philosophies to yourself," another sidhe warned. Carissa recognized this one as the eldest. Like Tiache, the eldest sidhe's white hair sparkled like a blanket of snow. Unlike Tiache, his eyes were a blue bordering on violet. There were no specs of fiery emotion in them.

"As you wish, eldest," Tiache said.

Carissa's father had told her the eldest's name was never to be uttered. If he had ever told her the name, she'd forgotten it long ago. All she knew was that Tiache's "philosophy" seemed more like prejudice than pure opinion.

The end of the meal was followed by dancing and discussion with spirited elves. Even a few sidhe joined in on topics—from the solstice in Vale to life in Tir-Na-Nog. From the sound of it, the royals' home was a hub of faerie activity, where prominent fae of all kinds regularly visited. Carissa marveled at the thought of formal dinners and wearing

Elixirs and Elves

dressing gowns daily. It sounded as exhausting as it was exciting. It was the most interesting conversation of the night, aside from talk about the party. By the end of the night, ideas about the party had grown from another dinner at Hela's to a party for all of Moss Hill, to be held in Fairfield Castle. Sal's eyes grew to twice their normal size by the end of the night and Rolin had to assure him that he'd have the help of the elves with the party planning.

Overall, the evening passed pleasantly and, if one ignored the occasional raised eyebrow and judgmental sideways glances, the sidhe made a better impression than previous encounters. Nearing eight o'clock, Carissa excused herself, saying that she had work tomorrow and was ready to turn in.

It was too early for her parents and bordering on rude for her to go, but as she'd hoped, the prince agreed to escort her home. This meant that they were followed by a small band of sidhe guards, but that was more than all right with Carissa. If the prince agreed, the guards could act as guides to the prison where Varick was being held.

Prince Zephyr, while helping Carissa with her coat, asked if they could take the scenic route through the garden that he had used this morning to walk to her parents' home. Carissa agreed, though frozen over as it was, the path through Rolin's garden did not seem like it would be an enjoyable route today.

They stepped outdoors and nature faeries swirled around them in a whirlwind of flowery wings. There were dozens, half a hundred or so, bowing before the prince and his companion. The sprites cleared the path of snow wherever they walked, and the plants glistened. The frost formed a radiant sheen as fairy dust fell softly onto the flora.

"I've never seen anything so beautiful," Carissa remarked when she caught her breath and found the voice to speak.

"I could say the same." The prince's eyes reflected her own image, blush included.

It may have been the frost, but Carissa believed she saw a bit of a reddish hue behind the prince's expression as well.

Astoria Wright

He must've been almost two hundred, which meant he had probably gone for moonlight strolls with many others before Carissa. She guessed he had dated several women since his hundredth birthday, quite likely elves or sidhe suitable for a royal title.

So, why did it feel like he was looking at her as if she were the only woman in the world?

She looked away from the prince. Thoughts of Cameron Larke had a funny way of popping into her mind at the most inconvenient moments. It wasn't fair to the prince, but she said nothing about why she walked the path without so much as glancing at him again.

He walked silently beside her for a few steps. Carissa hoped she hadn't hurt the prince by turning away from him. He'd been nothing but kind to her all evening. Throughout the night, she'd felt she had his attention, more so than any other person in the room. Whereas the sidhe might have disregarded her as too young or too human to have anything worthwhile to say, he'd valued her input on what they could do in their short time here to strengthen the bonds between fae and humans. In light of recent events, especially the near poisoning of the mayor, he believed her tie with humans provided valuable insight.

More than anything, she felt he was genuine. She was beginning to think that she could trust him, even with a strange request like the one she was about to make. They came to a bend in the lane and Carissa started a sentence at the same time as Prince Zephyr.

"This garden reminds me of—" the prince began.

"I know that this is much to ask—" Carissa stopped, and so did the prince. They smiled at one another.

"I'm sorry, Your Maj—"

"Zephyr," he said. "Or Zef, if you'd like."

"Zef." Her smile grew. "I interrupted you, I'm sorry."

"But now you used my name, so we're friends. Friends need no apologies. Please, tell me what you were going to say."

Elixirs and Elves

Carissa's grin reached her eyes. Finally, she could see Zephyr's elfish nature showing through his princely veneer. No sidhe would speak like that.

"I had a request to make, though I know it's a bit bold...."

He nodded as a silent sign for her to continue. She breathed deeply. She found that she was not afraid to ask him—not at all, in fact. But she was keenly aware of the sidhe guards standing just a few paces away. She glanced at them without moving her head.

Then, keeping focused on Zef's kind eyes, she said, "Would it be possible to see Varick?"

The prince's eyes lowered. The slight upturn of his lips flattened. She had gone too far.

"I know he seems guilty. I know he nearly confessed. But it just doesn't seem possible. If you and I could just talk to him, I think we'll find that there's more going on than meets the eye."

The prince looked back at her. The same kindness was still in his face, but the mirth in his eyes had faded. His lips kindly curved up and settled back down the way a gentleman might raise his hat to a lady. Then he nodded to the guard.

"Miss Shae and I will be visiting the mounds."

Chapter 8

Worry in a Winter Wonderland

The mounds of the sidhe were like another realm within the Otherworld of the fae. The redwood was the only part of the sidhe territory the rest of the people of Vale had ever seen. While Cari knew that the sidhe also lived in mounds, she had thought that the few sidhe who lived in Vale resided in the tree itself, since it was magically altered to be larger than any other on the island. The reality, it now seemed, was that there was much more to the sidhe's territory than a single redwood tree.

Carissa had never realized that the little rolling hills of the countryside contained an expansive labyrinth beneath the ground. The mound she entered through could easily contain both Rolin's and Hela's living and dining rooms. Like the homes of the elves, the walls, floor, and ceiling were made of all-natural materials. Unlike the rest of Vale, the materials could not have originated from the island.

At first, Carissa thought the floor beneath her heels was marble, but as they walked farther inside, it became apparent that they were standing on a smooth layer of agate rock. The vivid rings—rust red, emerald green, winter blue—spread outward from the center of the room like ripples. The effect of the lighting playing off the ceiling overhead almost made the illusion of rippling waves seem real.

Cari's eye drew upward. Her mouth opened wide and her eyelids with it. Above them were pure white crystals, like

Elixirs and Elves

the inside of a geode. A roof like that outdid any chandelier in the homes of the humans and the elves.

Rather than any door, the round room branched off in several directions. All but one of the sidhe guards remained in the outer corridor. The one leading them continued on. Carissa followed the guard and the prince a bit slower since she couldn't help but stare in wonder at the sights.

The halls linked with each other in a matrix of connected rooms. There didn't seem to be any doors, but short corridors connecting them. Deep inside, Carissa couldn't tell if they were in the center of the complex or not. They came to a dark room with several concentric circles inscribed on a stone floor. Unlike the other rooms, the floor, ceiling, and walls were all a cold, cement-like structure. There seemed to be only one light, and it was placed above the midpoint of the rings.

The guard led them to the center of the eerie room. Once inside the innermost ring, Cari felt a rush of chilling air. It seemed impossible from the depths of the underground. The winding currents, Carissa soon realized, were actually a warping of the air. Much like stepping into the Otherworld, Carissa found they were transported somehow. Whether they had traveled between dimensions or farther underground, Cari did not know, but this room was even more unnerving than the last.

The narrow walls and long, dimly-lit cinderblock hallway were cold. Their footsteps echoed against the gray, lifeless slabs of stone. Cari longed to wrap her arms around herself for warmth, but she held them to her sides. She would not show weakness among the sidhe.

Darkness enveloped the room until they were right in front of it. Then, illumination from an unknown source blasted overhead, and a form appeared before Cari and the prince. A simple bed backed against the wall supported the razor-straight frame of a former captain of the sidhe guard. Varick of Vale raised a hand above his eyes while his pupils adjusted to the brightness. He rose to a seated position. His back was straight, the sidhe broadened his shoulders, and a steely disposition remained infused in his expression. He seemed not to be diminished by his incarceration, except for one feature. His eyes came to the floor at their feet, but no higher.

He must not be permitted to look at them, Carissa concluded. Whereas yesterday he was in the attire of a guard of high standing, today he was dressed in all black in a plain, long-sleeve shirt and pants that couldn't have been more generic if one tried.

"His Majesty, Prince Zephyr of Tir-Na-Nog," the guard announced.

Varick stood, taking his time. He was duty bound to bow to the prince, but apparently at his own speed. *It's pride that's slowing him down*, Cari thought.

"And Carissa Shae of Moss Hill," the guard added in his announcement.

Varick's eyes flicked upward. For one split second, he looked right at her. Then, he looked back down at the floor. Whether the guard noticed the violation or not, he made no reprimand.

The prince held up a hand. The guard bowed and exited down the corridor. The three of them remained. Prince Zephyr broke the silence.

"If you have any defense, or if any misunderstanding has occurred, speak now."

Carissa held her breath. She hoped Varick would take the opportunity. It was not likely to be repeated. But the sidhe remained silent with his eyes fixed in place. Cari turned to the prince.

"May I question the prisoner?" she asked.

The prince stepped back, allowing her to move closer to the cell. Taking a spot as close to the bars as she could, she said, "I've made a plea for your innocence. If you're guilty, say something now, or you'll lose the chance."

Varick's eyes ventured up the bars halfway, stopping at her clasped hands.

"Will you say nothing?" the prince asked.

Elixirs and Elves

Varick remained motionless. "There is nothing I can say, Your Majesty."

Cari knew Varick well enough to hear the subtle inflection in his tone. There was nothing he could say—not to the prince. If only she could speak with him alone, she might get more out of him than he was saying now. It broke every protocol but would be permissible, if the prince allowed it. Even asking would be a risk. She may have gained some favor with the prince, but enough to grant a private audience with a criminal?

What was the worst they could do for asking? She didn't want to think about that. This was a group that demoted officials for speaking out of turn. But the prince was half-elf. He might be more understanding.

She thought of how Varick had trusted her months before when searching for a ban sidhe. She pictured Jane and the turmoil of their burgeoning relationship. She recalled that Varick had lied once to keep Alden safe, even though he was the ankou, a being for which sidhe generally had no love. In his own way, he was a friend to all of them. Given all that he'd done to protect them, she had to try and help him now.

She turned to the prince and bowed. Prince Zephyr's arms outstretched, gesturing for her to rise. She made her request.

"Majesty, may I have a moment to speak with the prisoner alone?"

She was hoping it would sound like a request to say a few last words to a friend before his trial. She couldn't say more or less than the single sentence for fear of making it seem that Varick was not being forthright or that she had some involvement in his actions. She'd already defended him, which might be seen as suspicious enough.

The prince said nothing for much longer than Carissa had expected. His eyes widened and narrowed before settling back to study her face. There was something in his look, then his gaze broke away. With painstaking deliberateness, he gave a slow nod and turned to walk down the hall. She listened to the clack of his boots as he receded from view. She couldn't help but feel that she'd hurt him somehow. Then, she wondered if her request had made him doubt her. Would he think she had some involvement in the crime itself? She looked away from the empty corridor. There would be time to worry about that later.

Carissa stepped up to the cell and placed her hands on the bars, disregarding sidhe protocol altogether. Now that they were alone, and since the situation was dire, she dropped any thought of formality.

"For goodness sake, Varick, they'll prosecute you for murder. The prince is trying to help you, and so am I, but we can't do anything unless you say something."

"Stop speaking and I will," Varick growled through his teeth.

Carissa let go of the bars as he stepped closer. The angry tone wasn't as much of a surprise as the hushed urgency that followed.

He took a deep breath and whispered, "The elixir I had wasn't made by me. Elder Tiache created it and gave it to me just before the dinner began. If he is responsible for the poisoning, the proof must be irrefutable, or it would be treason to accuse him."

"But why would he want to kill the mayor?"

Varick leaned forward so that his face was nearly pressed against the bars.

"Belkin was not the target," he whispered.

"Who was?" Carissa inched closer, matching the whisper.

Varick released the bar and paced the cell. His head hung low. Then, returning to the space in front of her, he gripped the bars as if steadying himself.

"The elixir was one of immortality. I requested it to be made. I meant to give it to Jane."

Carissa shook her head. "Jane? Why…?" Even as she started to ask, realization struck her. Suddenly, their argument over the last few months became clear.

Elixirs and Elves

"You're immortal. Jane is not. You wanted to be together."

His arms folded in front of him. When he spoke, it was emotionless, yet Cari felt every word was layered in pain.

"The sidhe do not mingle with humans. We are not like you. You fade to dust. You die."

He stood with broadened shoulders and his face held a steely resolve. Whenever Carissa had seen a look like that, she had attributed it to sidhe pride. Now she wondered: Was it pride? Or did the sidhe distance themselves for fear of pain? If they befriended humans, the humans would inevitably die. The pain of loss must weigh heavy on the shoulders of the elders especially.

But this begged the question: Why would an elder wish to kill a human? What benefit could there be from killing Jane? Carissa could not think of one reason for the action.

"Why would Elder Tiache want to murder Jane? She isn't immortal, and she's never threatened the sidhe—"

"Jane is more than she seems." His eyes flared with gold as he spoke.

"I know that Jane is a druidess, that she had a sidhe ancestor...." Cari searched for reasons. In Moss Hill, having magic or fae ancestry wasn't uncommon.

Varick shook his head. "It's not only that. She's a powerful druidess, and, with her training from Macara, she may become one of the most powerful ever to have lived. Jane could be the sidhe's greatest ally or a terrible threat. Many sidhe would consider her dangerous. I would not have believed it of Tiache, but my request for the elixir may have prompted him to take action to stop her before she grows powerful."

Cari bit her lip. Did that mean that Jane was in danger? If so, she had to warn her or at least tell Alden of the threat. She looked down the corridor. Varick's eyes followed hers.

"Say nothing to the prince. I do not know how much he is aware of Jane's powers, but I dare not draw more attention to her as things stand."

Carissa nodded. "I won't."

"Give me your word."

She looked him right in the eye. "I won't tell the prince, and the real culprit will be brought to justice. I promise."

***

ALL THE WAY home, the prince strode silently beside her. Something had changed in his mood from the moment Cari had requested to see Varick, and it only intensified after she'd asked to speak with him alone. At her doorstep, Carissa felt she had to say something before ending the night on a sour note. Grasping the doorknob for support, she faced the prince.

"Zef," she started.

His eyes finally met hers at the sound of his name. He searched her face. For what? Maybe for any trust that she'd lost by colluding with a criminal. Carissa winced at the thought.

"I know how this might have appeared, but—"

He raised a hand, stopping in the air just short of her lips. "I already know. I saw you and him together the night of the party."

Alarm bells went off in her mind. Oh no, the panicked thoughts trickled from her brain to flood her heart with elf-light. Did Zef think she'd conspired with him in the poisoning? She tightened her grip on the doorknob, trying to keep the flow of magic from her pumping veins in check. But if he did, why had he let her see Varick tonight? In all her racing thoughts, she almost missed the prince's next words.

"If you love him, I will not come in the way. For your sake, I hope he is innocent of the charges against him."

Carissa let go of the door and straightened. Her elf-ears twitched. *Love him?* She brought a hand to her forehead. *Of course*, she realized. It was understandable to her how the situation could've been seen in that light. She felt silly that this obvious interpretation was only just occurring to her now.

Elixirs and Elves

"No." She shook her head and smiled. "No, I don't feel that way about Varick. Not at all." She stepped away from the door to face him fully. "I do believe he's innocent and that he is an honorable guard. I've even come to think of him as a friend." She paused, it was true enough that she considered him a friend. She wasn't sure Varick would admit it, but she liked to believe that he thought of her the same way. "But *love?*" She almost laughed out loud. "No. He's in love with...someone else and she, I think, loves him too. She's a friend of mine and I would do anything to help them both."

The prince's smile returned. He stepped closer to her and reached for her hand. She gave it to him. He stood, clasping her palm between his. The moonlight shone over his face, illuminating newfound hope in his eyes.

"I had felt there was someone else. I'm glad to hear that I may yet have a chance to earn a place in your heart."

Carissa felt the heat rising in her cheeks. She looked away. Zephyr had a chance for a permanent residence in her affections—undeniably. Each moment with him she felt more and more swayed into thinking he might be the one for her. Though, that feeling was complicated by expectation, propriety, and a host of considerations she'd never thought about before. It wasn't like her comfortable relationship with Cam. That was based on friendship; this was more like what she thought the picture of romance looked like. Maybe she could have a future with the prince. But, the thought alone of Cam at this moment was evidence that there was still someone standing between them.

She bit her lip before saying, "It's late. I should go inside."

A brief glance at him showed a wavering smile. Yet, the glow in his eyes remained in the end. The blue turned to a gleam of silver much like a sidhe's eyes in that the emotion was conveyed in a metallic shine. He let go of her hand and bowed.

"Until tomorrow."

"I look forward to it," Carissa responded before heading indoors. Once the door closed, she lingered there with her back against it. Her head rested on the door a minute as she closed her eyes. She smiled, admitting to herself that she really was looking forward to seeing him again.

Not one second later, she heard a knock. She opened her eyes and turned, sliding open the circular peephole. Through the wood lattice, she saw a familiar yet unexpected face. She opened the door hastily.

"Alden?"

"I thought I'd use a door this time so as not to scare you," Alden said.

"Come in." Carissa stepped away from the door.

"So, everything seems to have gone well with the prince tonight." His voice was flat.

Carissa stared into Alden's ice-blue eyes. "Were you watching us?"

He didn't flinch or look away. "I was waiting for you, so you could tell me what you learned about Varick. That was the plan, remember?"

Cari turned and walked farther into the living room. She felt a bit too warm suddenly, and it wasn't just the perpetual faerie fire burning to her right. She didn't know why she had interpreted his comment as jealousy. Her mind didn't usually work that way. Now she could see that he was referring to her task of swaying the prince to help her with Varick's case.

Carissa took a seat on the recliner, and Alden took the sofa chair opposite her. The fire crackled between them. She looked toward the kitchen. Her parents still didn't seem to be home, which worked well for her as she knew they were uncomfortable around the ankou.

"Have you been able to find Toffee?" Carissa asked.

She'd get around to Varick, but not just yet. She had to find a way to delicately tell him that his sister might've been the target.

"Yes and no." Alden rested his arms on the chair and brought one hand to his forehead. "He keeps slipping away from me. Those elfkins are spry."

"What do you mean?" Carissa nearly laughed. "It can't be that hard to catch an elfkin."

Elixirs and Elves

"Oh, can't it? He's using some kind of magic to make himself invisible even to me. I've always thought that Fudge's magic was different than the other fae, now I know it's true. Toffee is quite possibly the most difficult quarry I've had to collect."

Carissa cringed. No matter how much time she spent with the ankou it was not easy getting used to his talk of collecting souls or referring to the dead as "quarry." Alden caught her eye by dropping his hand.

"You're stalling," he said. "What happened with the prince? Did you learn anything about Varick?"

Cari nodded slowly. "It's not good news, I'm afraid. Varick had a second elixir, and it really was poisoned."

"But not by him," Alden's tone was certain.

Carissa agreed without hesitation. "But," she added, "an elder sidhe may be responsible."

She revealed that Elder Taiche may have created the elixir to eliminate what he thought might be a formidable threat to Vale. Next came the very same question she had asked Varick in the cell.

"Why would a sidhe elder want to murder the mayor?"

"The mayor might not have been the one they were after," Cari revealed.

Carissa sat at the edge of her seat, garnering the courage to explain. Taking a deep breath, she finally spoke.

"The target may have been your sister."

"Jane?" An upset ankou didn't change eye color like a sidhe, apparently. Alden's face shifted slowly to his full spectral form.

"Alden," Cari tried to put her hand on his shoulder to stop the transformation.

He pulled back. "What do you mean Jane might've been the target?"

Carissa took a breath and tried to give a quick explanation that might calm him down. "All Varick said was that a sidhe elder prepared the elixir. He was speculating that the sidhe might think she's a threat because she's a druidess. Alden?"

The ankou turned full skeleton and disappeared. Carissa wondered what she'd just done. No good could come to a town with an angry Grim Reaper afoot.

Chapter 9

The Proof in the Pudding

For the second day in a row, Carissa had spent the night at her parents' home in Vale. She rummaged through the closet. She took longer than usual choosing what to wear, whether that was because of the selection of apparel or who would see her in them today, was not something she cared to ponder.

Throwing on a red sweater and jeans, she headed downstairs where she decided she would eat a quick breakfast and leave straight for work. When she reached the end of the hallway, she could hear her parents speaking. While she usually never eavesdropped, Carissa overheard her name. She couldn't resist listening in.

"She's partly elf, though. You can't apply the same logic to her as a human."

"She's always been mature for her age compared to other humans."

"In other matters, possibly, but matters of the heart are different. It's not something an elf thinks about until much later in life. At her age, I was interested in mysteries and adventures."

"Cari is interested in mysteries, too, it seems. But in this case, those mysteries are murders and," her mother lowered her voice, "matters not befitting a young lady."

"But that is very much like an elf," her father said. "Elves are naturally curious, a bit reckless, and very light-hearted.

Young elves are especially mischievous. I've always said you can tell an elf's age by how serious he is."

Carissa cleared her throat as she entered the kitchen. Her parents quieted down. Not one for awkward exchanges, Cari answered the question of whether or not she'd been eavesdropping by diving right into the conversation.

"Rolin must be a millennium old by your reasoning, Dad. He's as serious as any of the sidhe."

Carissa took a plate and helped herself to the fresh fruit on the table. The grapefruit smelled sweet and inviting. The juicy sweet and sour fruit tingled on her tongue.

Her mother frowned. "Carissa, tell me you did not lead the prince to the sidhe dungeons to see Varick."

"I didn't." Carissa gave her best impish smirk. "The sidhe guard led us both there."

"Carissa Shae, this is serious." Her mother stood, both to clear the dishes and probably to appear more intimidating. "You may ruin your chances altogether with the prince."

Cari noted that her mother knotted her hands together as she spoke. It was gut-wrenching to watch her mother twisting into a bundle of nerves about her marriage, or the possibility of losing the chance to marry the prince.

"I doubt it," her father said. He wiped his mouth with his napkin and set it on the table to indicate he was done with his meal. Then, reaching an arm across the table, he patted Cari's hand. "Don't forget: the prince is half-elf, too." He winked.

"Part elf or not, Cari, he won't continue to take an interest if you're cold to him."

Carissa's mother lifted the fruit platter in one hand and raised one finger on the other. "At least you have one opportunity to impress his majesty. We've brought many items from our travels so that you can choose one to give as a gift at the Christmas party."

The Christmas party, Carissa hadn't realized before, but it was a gift-giving holiday and it made sense that they'd be expected to exchange gifts with the royals. She'd already

Elixirs and Elves

shopped for Sal and Hela. In fact, all her shopping was done, except for Cam. That was a whole different problem.

"Kaley, you can't just pick a gift like that. This is the royal family. Whatever she gives must be really special."

"What about the spider silk from Anansi? Or the rare dragon's blood sapling gifted by the faeries of Socotra?"

"It's technically a succulent plant," her father corrected. "And the king already has one and an actual dragon, too, I would think. No, Carissa has to think of a gift on her own. It has to be something special with meaning to her."

Carissa nearly choked on the juicy grapefruit. She swallowed it down quickly. "How am I supposed to get something like that in Moss Hill?"

The items her parents were referring to outdid anything she'd seen here, except maybe in the sidhe mound, and she doubted she could waltz in there and ask for the gift shop.

"I'm sure you'll think of something," her father said.

"Don't worry," her mother added, "whatever you give, I'm sure the prince will *love* it."

Carissa patted her napkin to her lips and set it on the table. "Don't be too hopeful. He's only in town a few days, and I'm not committing to anything unless I'm really sure it's what I want."

Her mother set the dishes in the sink with a clang. The noise made Cari jump. She and her father exchanged a look. Her mother ignored their open-mouthed stares.

"Didn't you think he was wonderful?"

Her mother's furrowed brows insisted on only one answer. Anything less than an agreement was sure to cause steam to shoot out of her ears. Carissa stood up.

"I'd better be off for the shop."

Cari kissed her father on the top of his head and hugged her mother goodbye. Exiting the kitchen, she grabbed her mint coat beside the door and walked out into the snow.

The day was a sunny one, with a brilliant shine reflecting off the ground. It was still cold, but at least not snowing at the moment. Her eyes darted down the lane toward Rolin's home.

She half expected Prince Zephyr to appear on the path, but there was no such luck this morning. Carissa wondered if the head elf was still hosting the royal family or if they'd move to sidhe territory today. Either way, she had to move on. She walked to where the path became steps and down to the edge of the mountain. There, she shifted to the human world.

She'd had enough sense to bring Nan's car this time. Much as she didn't like to drive, in subzero temperatures on long walks, she'd rather not expend the energy of her elf-light to keep herself warm. The gray vehicle came into sight. There was still no sign of the prince. She found herself sighing and looking back up the path to Vale before she could catch herself. Shaking her head, Carissa chided herself and sat inside the vehicle.

The ride to Moss Hill was short. She drove on the dirt path, passed the castle, and pulled around the corner of Greenfield and Gorse. The bakery on the corner next door to her store was already bustling with customers. To Cari's surprise, someone was waiting at the apothecary shop when she arrived.

For a moment, she assumed it was Cameron Larke. The man had a long, wool coat like Cam's, and she spied a scarf at the collar. The earmuffs were really not his style, but it was the wisp of red hair she spied when she pulled the car to the side of the shop that gave her a hint to who it might be. She also noted the glasses. There was no camera around his neck this time, but Carissa recalled the freckled face of Reginald Smith the moment she saw him.

"Reg?" she asked, getting out of the vehicle.

"Carissa!" Reginald greeted her with a grin. "It's good to see you again!"

"Well, this is a surprise." Cari swung the tote across her shoulder and unlocked the shop door.

Reginald followed her in, taking off his gloves and breathing into his hands. They had to be ice cold. He followed her to the counter.

Elixirs and Elves

"What are you doing in Moss Hill?" Carissa set the tote down and turned up the thermostat.

Reg loosened the scarf around his neck.

"I was sent by my boss. I think you know him."

"Yes, I remember." She was half annoyed and half smiling at his boastfulness. Then again, it wasn't bragging since it was true that he worked for a very powerful man.

She recalled Mr. MacLir, the mythical man of the Tuatha de Danann, a race far older than any faeries Cari had ever known, was posing as a human running a real estate investment company in Scotland. He was currently investing in rebuilding Moss Hill's aging infrastructure. Reginald Smith, the nosy tourist eager to learn the secrets of the faerie people of Vale, had worked hard to expose the fae folk on the island and promptly been rewarded by MacLir with a position in his company. Carissa had thought it a strange move, but who was she to question the ancient god of the sea?

"What does MacLir want you to do here?" Carissa asked as she started up the tablet, which was the shop's register and accounting system.

"That's confidential." Reginald showed every one of his teeth in the enormous smile that formed on his face.

Far be it for Carissa to judge, but Reg's hubris was possibly the silliest thing she'd seen in her life. Cari issued a silent thanks when the bell chimed at the front door. The moment Maren Raines walked in, Carissa revoked the gratitude as having been given too soon.

"That horrible, awful, selfish man!" Maren stomped up to the counter in a huff.

"Uh oh. What's wrong?" Cari asked.

"Parker Greer came into the bakery today with two ladies around him chatting away about how wonderful he is." She held two fingers up, turning them into a little talking mouth for a visual. "They're flirting right in front of me, and when I confront him about it, he says, 'Maren, we're not exclusive. I'm sorry if I hadn't made that clear.'"

"Ouch, Maren, that's tough." Carissa didn't know exactly what to say. Rather, she knew exactly what she wanted to say, but she thought it a bit snarky to say, "*You knew that was what he was like*," when her friend was already feeling hurt.

Maren, still in a huff, ignored Carissa's sympathy. "What does that even mean, '*exclusive*?'" She turned to Reg. "Would you use that line with someone you'd just started going out with?"

Reginald was taken aback. His eyes were wide as could be, and his mouth hung open as he shook his head in response to Maren's question. Eventually, he found his voice.

"Uh, no, I, um, no I wouldn't," he said.

Maren sighed. She closed her eyes and pressed two fingers on either side of his temple. "Now I have to go back in there," she whined.

"Is he seated at a table with them?" Carissa squinted her eyes in a wince as she asked.

"No," Maren said, her voice strained. "I'm sure he's left by now."

"Well, that's good, isn't it?" Carissa asked. "You won't have to see him or even think about him the rest of your shift."

"Mmhm." Maren's eyes drifted downward. "If I still have a job."

"What do you mean?" Cari folded her arms on the counter.

"I might've thrown a pie in his face," she admitted.

Carissa couldn't help but laugh. "Oh no, Maren, you didn't?"

"Plum pudding pie," Maren confirmed. They both started laughing. Even Reg joined in with a nervous chuckle. Maren wiped her eyes.

"You're right, Carissa, I'll go in with my head held high and not think about him. If I'm fired, I'm fired, but I'm not going to stay here crying about it." She straightened herself up and spun around, standing tall before walking back toward the door.

"I'm here if you need me," Carissa called out behind her.

Elixirs and Elves

The chime of the bells announced her departure and Cari turned her attention back to Reg. His eyes lingered on the door. Apparently, Maren had captured his attention, and he wasn't ready to let go. Carissa cleared her throat.

Reg seemed to snap out of it as he looked back at her. "What? Right, um, you were asking about MacLir." He broke eye contact with her for another glance at the door. "Who was that?"

Carissa smiled at his lack of tact. "Maren Raines. She's the assistant here and a good friend of mine."

"Assistant here?" Reg asked. "But she works at a bakery?"

"Next door. That's just part-time for the holiday."

"She's a baker and an apothecary assistant?" Reg seemed to be unable to take his eyes off the doorframe.

"Reg, was there something you needed from me?" Carissa tried in a patient voice to move the conversation forward.

She was due to open soon, and he was taking up the time she generally used in the morning to check that everything was ready for the day.

"Yes, uh, I do. I need an audience with the king. I can't announce myself in Vale, and I've heard you're close with the prince."

Cari hesitated. She wasn't used to talking with Reg openly about the fae folk. Obviously, MacLir had trusted Reginald with knowledge of the people of Vale. She supposed she ought to do the same. She would, but not without questioning him first.

"What do you need an audience with the king for?"

Reg held up a finger. "Nice try, but that's between Mr. MacLir and King Finvarra. Now, can you get me an audience with him?"

The bell chimed again. Reg snapped around as if expecting to see Maren again. Instead of the average height brunette, a short-statured, red-headed bean tighe appeared in the doorway. She was accompanied, quite happily, by a leprechaun.

"Barnaby, Holly," Carissa called out with a smile. "What are you two doing here?"

"Just here to get a few items for Macara's dinner with the Everlys," Holly replied.

"And I'm only accompanying the lady." Barnaby's voice still sounded a little scratchy from his cold.

"How are you feeling?" Carissa made her way around the corner and folded her arms at the chill in the air that had followed the pair inside.

"Right as rain, now that Holly's been taking care of me." Barnaby smiled at Holly, who blushed.

Carissa beamed. Seeing the pair so happy warmed her. Reginald ruined the moment.

"A bean tighe," he whispered, "and you're the leprechaun I saw before at the pub."

"Ah, who are you?" Barn retrieved his signature emerald-colored hat and scratched his head. "I don't recall meeting you."

"We haven't officially met before." Reginald thrust out a hand and leaned down. "Reginald Smith."

Barnaby shook reluctantly. He glanced at Cari as he did so. She could only shrug. It was too much to explain here and now. Holly, on the other hand, was not looking perplexed so much as intrigued. She didn't shake his hand at first but put a finger to her lips.

"Yes, I suppose she would want you to attend. Why that's settled." She dropped her hand and finally shook his. "Reginald Smith, you're invited to dinner tonight at Macara's cottage. It'll be at 7:00 p.m. sharp. Don't be late."

This time Carissa exchanged the look with Barnaby. Holly instructed Reg on directions to Macara's home. Carissa stepped closer to Barnaby.

"Does she usually go around inviting strangers to dinner?" she whispered.

Barnaby tilted on one foot, so he was close enough to whisper back. "Her heart's in the right place, but she's always been a little pushy."

Elixirs and Elves

Holly's eyes moved to Barnaby. He shifted back to two feet. "And I love that about her," he added at a louder volume.

"You're all invited," Holly said when she was done directing Reginald.

Reg held the napkin on which she'd written directions and floundered, "I, um...I'm not sure that I can make it."

Holly ignored him. "You had an assistant too, right?"

"Yes, Maren," Cari said.

"Splendid. Invite her, too. Hate to leave anyone out."

Reg perked up at the possibility that Maren would be attending. "Yes," he said as if to himself. "Yes, now that I think about it, I should be able to attend."

"Good." Holly opened a cloth bag she'd brought with her. "Now then, Barn, shall we pick some herbs?"

"Absolutely." The leprechaun was on his toes and at the back barrels in seconds.

Since Carissa hadn't taken the herbs out of the freezer yet, she had to excuse herself to retrieve them.

"Only the freshest ones," Carissa could hear Holly calling out. She wasn't sure if the bean tighe was talking to her or to Barnaby, but she lugged the basket of herbs out of the freezer either way.

"Carissa," Reg followed her from the wall of freezers to the back of the room where the empty barrels awaited stocking. He absentmindedly reached to help her set down the herbs as he spoke. "You have to either get me an audience with the king or introduce me to a fae who can."

"It would help if I knew what it was about," Carissa said.

"I swore an oath." Reg held a hand up to his chest, resting a palm on his heart. "I won't break it."

Carissa narrowed her eyes, but even under her stare, he wouldn't budge. Based on her previous experience with Reg, Carissa was inclined not to take him seriously, but Holly seemed to think Macara would want to see him. Given that he worked for MacLir, Reg probably did have something important to share with the king.

"All right, I'll talk to Prince Zephyr about granting you an audience."

"Thank you." Reg actually bowed.

Having never been bowed to before, Carissa wasn't sure how to respond. She tapped Reg lightly on the shoulder.

"Okay," she said, "that's enough of that. I'm not royalty myself, you know."

Reg stood back up with a telling smile. "I think you'll find very soon that that is not true."

Reginald replaced his earmuffs and walked out of the shop with his head held high. Carissa heard the chime of the bells as she went back to her work. Holly and Barnaby dove into the herbs, sifting through them for the freshest ones.

"I've been to two farms and the large grocery store on Lemon Street, but your herbs are the best, Carissa," Holly said.

"I second that," Barnaby added.

Carissa thanked them. Barnaby was clearly smitten, so he'd probably agree with anything Holly said. In this case, though, even Cari agreed. She was sure her herbs were the best in town. Her secret was the nature faeries. Especially since Chaos had arrived. The little nature faerie insisted on coming with her to the shop at least once a week and she kept the herbs fresh with her magical touch.

Cari walked back to the freezer for the second basket. The chill of the air struck her as even colder than before as she grasped the second barrel from storage. She felt the door to the freezer widen, and she wobbled. A hand reached for the edge of the basket to stabilize her. Cari noted the red polish on the fingernails.

She looked up to see Jane, dressed stylishly in a white winter coat and red dress pants. Cari couldn't see the blouse but imagined it was the height of modern fashion. Jane made it seem frustratingly simple to keep track of the latest trends all without ever appearing to take an interest. Her family's wealth might've helped with that. She was among the wealthiest

Elixirs and Elves

Mossies on the island, but Jane wasn't the snooty type, which made it impossible to hold that against her.

"Sorry about that, Carissa," Jane said meekly as she let the basket go.

Despite her flawless makeup, Cari could see Jane's eyes were puffy. Carissa wouldn't have been surprised if she'd been up all night worrying about Varick. Carissa smiled softly.

"How are you, Jane? I didn't hear you come in."

She walked over the second barrel and wrestled the basket of herbs into place. Jane slipped off her gloves and removed her sleek, black sunglasses. Placing her accessories into her coat, she walked with Carissa back toward the center aisle.

"I'm all right," Jane said in a wavering tone. "I think you might know why I'm here."

Carissa's would've given her a sympathetic embrace, but she wasn't much of the hugging type and from what she knew of Jane, neither was she. Instead, she placed a hand on Jane's shoulder and squeezed.

"I've spoken with Varick."

A sheen came over Jane's eyes. "Is he all right?"

"He's fine for now."

She wasn't sure what to say, especially with Barnaby and Holly standing so close by. She released Jane's arm and walked behind the counter. Jane stood opposite her, turning around when the bell to the store rang.

Carissa tensed upon seeing Jane's butler. It was instinctive. Her fingers tingled as if frostbitten. She recalled an instant picture of Fudge arguing with Toffee the night before. She calmed her elf-light, reminding herself that she'd seen Fudge many times now and had no reason to think he'd commit murder. People argued—it was natural.

The unnatural way in which Fudge kept glancing over his shoulder didn't make him seem innocent. His bowler hat was pulled down low on his head. The coffee in his hand, clearly marked Gooseberries, spilled a little as he nearly bumped into a shelf. He grumbled something while shaking the hot liquid off his hand. Jane took the drink with a "thanks" when he finally reached the counter.

Fudge eyed Carissa, letting out a sharp grunt.

"Your friend is a crotchety one today," he remarked, pulling off his hat.

If that wasn't a teapot calling a kettle black.... Fudge was a scrooge if ever a Mossie saw one. If he wanted to call someone cranky, he ought to look in a mirror. Carissa had plenty more thoughts like that, but she kept them all to herself. She opted for a more polite, straightforward response.

"She's had a bit of an argument with Parker," Carissa said.

Jane shifted uncomfortably. Fudge's eyes met Jane with an I-told-you-so expression.

"I have no doubt of it," Jane finally said.

"Is there something I'm missing?" Carissa asked.

Jane winced. Since she wasn't saying anything, Fudge spoke up. He held his hat against his chest like a gentleman while revealing what he ought to have allowed Jane the courtesy to do herself.

"He was up at the house three days ago asking Miss Jane for a date to the very party to which I believe he invited your friend first."

"I don't think he was interested in me at all."

"What do you mean?" Carissa asked.

She could easily assume Jane meant that he was interested in the Everly fortune, but something in Jane's eyes told her there was more to the story. She was looking away. Her eyes thinned as if remembering something specific.

"I don't know, exactly. Parker said he'd come to see me, though we've never talked before. Then he went on about a dozen things with Father. It was mostly business deals, advertising for more tourists, things like that. Then he left without another word to me."

"He was asking about the Everly's gift to the mayor," Fudge used his hat to point to Cari as he said it.

Elixirs and Elves

She could see in his eyes he was trying to tell her something, but she didn't understand what.

"Yes," Jane said. "He told us what he'd gotten for both the mayor and for the royals for Christmas—asking my father if he thought it was enough. Normal enough things, but—"

"But it seemed strange?" Carissa asked.

Jane nodded.

"What was the gift you gave the mayor?"

It felt odd asking, but Carissa felt every little clue might help her prove Varick's innocence.

"Just a tie pin," Jane replied. "It was enchanted by Miss Morgan as a good luck charm. It hardly matters now. Poor Maren."

The shadow of a cloud hung over Jane's pale-as-snow face. It was like winter had decided to direct its flurries toward one Mossie in particular. Carissa knew it wasn't for Maren that Jane looked so drained of holiday happiness.

"You must know Varick is not guilty," Carissa reassured her.

The businesswoman let out something between a laugh and a sob. "I know that. He would never do anything dishonorable. But I need to see him." Her lips quivered like a struck chord. "I don't know why he would confess like that. It's not like him."

Carissa's thoughts took on the same tune Varick had harped on the night before: keep Jane away from the sidhe. She knew Jane would ask to see him.

Her eyes shifted to see that Barnaby had inched closer to the counter. With the abrupt halt to the discussion, the leprechaun's eyes shifted to the pair and caught Carissa's frowning expression. She turned her head toward him, not hiding the fact that she'd caught him eavesdropping.

He cleared his throat. "Oh, um." He took out a handkerchief from his breast pocket and dabbed at his forehead. "I'm still not feeling well."

"Stop that, Barn," Holly didn't even look up from the herbs that she'd gathered as she said it. "You should know when you've been caught."

The bean tighe put the herbs onto the counter and took out a small change purse from a pocket in her dress. While Cari rang up the items, Holly lifted Jane's fingers, dangling at her side.

"Have faith," Holly said. "You know your man is not guilty, and the council will discover the truth, I'm sure of it. In the meantime, Macara will expect you for dinner tonight at 7:00 p.m. with the rest of you." She looked at Carissa.

It took Carissa a second to realize the expectant look on Holly's face was her waiting to hear the amount due. She looked at the number on the tablet and called out the amount, taking Holly's money. Unlike quite a few of the fae shoppers, there were no arguments with her new customer about what constituted legal tender.

"I'm not sure I'm in the mood for dinner parties, ma'am," Jane replied.

"But that's exactly when you need to attend one the most."

Holly scooped up the bag with one hand. Jane's eyes pleaded with Cari for help.

Carissa noticed Fudge was conspicuously absent. The elfkin had disappeared somewhere within the store shelves.

"I need to see Varick," Jane said. "The last time I saw him, we fought. I couldn't bear it if that's the last I'll see of him. Please, Carissa, both Rolin and the sidhe wouldn't hear me out yesterday. I thought maybe you could speak with the royals about letting me talk to him."

Carissa couldn't agree. With what Varick said, Jane might be in danger if she went anywhere near the sidhe. Alden hadn't taken the news well yesterday. If she hadn't caught his arm, he'd likely have transported straight to the sidhe mounds himself, which would've been disastrous. She persuaded him not to do anything except watch over his sister. For all she knew, he was in the room now, listening to this very conversation. Cari didn't want to imagine how cross he'd be if she allowed Jane to enter into danger.

Chapter 10

Candy Cane Hearts

Fortunately, Carissa could delay an answer to Jane for a few moments longer as a gentleman walked through the door. The sound of the bell caught her attention after the sight of a handsome brown-haired man. Cameron, in a gray, woolen coat, stepped inside, wiping a bit of snow off his shoulders. A little flurry looked like it was just beginning behind him. He took off his flat cap and ran a hand through his silky hair. Unlike Reg's style, the red scarf flared around his neck and even the newspaper in his hand, as he brought it away from the door, made him look strikingly debonair against the wintery background.

"Was that Reginald I just saw coming out of Gooseberries?" Cam asked.

His eyes glided over the group huddled near the counter. It didn't seem to occur to Cam that he might be interrupting the conversations already underway. He strolled up to the back of the store too comfortably, as if coming home and without much notice that the OPEN sign was not yet lit.

"Apparently, I'm open early today." Cari shook her head as Jane and the others greeted Cam.

As soon as the words were out of her mouth, the doorbell chimed again. Carissa peered around Cam's shoulder. In came a pile of boxes and bags attached to a pair of hands and a pair of long, lanky legs.

"Hello, all!" the cheery voice of the elfkin, Sal, rang with the bell at the door.

Elixirs and Elves

Cameron hustled over and helped him with his cargo.

"Doing a bit shopping this morning?" Carissa called from the counter.

"Did you buy out a small store?" Cam asked as he took a few of the packages.

"Not at all, these are for Cari." Sal grinned and walked to the back of the shop.

"For me?" Carissa eyed the packages in wonder.

Sal wasn't a delivery man, and Rolin was not one to give gifts, leaving Carissa to guess the identity of the sender. Now Barnaby and Holly had left the baskets and wandered over to the center aisle to see what the fuss was about. Barnaby scoured to the packages, picking one up to examine the tags. He nearly dropped the box, catching it halfway down to the floor.

"It's from Prince Zephyr." Barnaby placed the gift up onto the counter.

Sal followed by placing the bags in his hand on the space near the tablet that served as the shop's register. A thud caused every eye to turn to Cameron, who'd roughly thrown down the last of the packages. He hid his scowl by quickly putting a hand to the back of his neck.

"Sorry," Cam said, his cheeks turning the slightest bit red, "it slipped."

Carissa wasn't sure anyone bought the explanation. He was angry about something. Cari didn't want to speculate what it was about. She was afraid she already knew.

Carissa turned to elfkin, diverting everyone's attention. "You brought these all the way from Vale? That was very kind of you, Sal."

"'Twas nothing," Sal waved it off. "I was coming this way anyway." He took a note out of the back pocket of his brown corduroy pants and held it up. "I've got a list of items for the Christmas party."

"And the solstice, I'll bet?" Holly asked.

"No, ma'am, the sidhe are handling that this year," Sal said.

107

"What kinds of presents are these?" Cameron interrupted, peeking into the bags. "There's a bunch of groceries here: vegetables, cheeses." He pulled out a bottle. "The wine's not bad, though."

Carissa grabbed the elderberry wine out of his hand, arguing, "I think it's very sweet."

Sal unbuttoned his coat and pulled at his matching scarf. He dabbed it against his forehead. Despite the cold, he appeared to be sweating from the arduous trek down the mountain.

"The prince wasn't sure what you'd like. There's some jewelry and cloth there, too. The wine was Miss Hela's idea," he said.

Barnaby, nosy as he was, peeked into the box Sal pointed to when he'd said the word "cloth." Carissa could only see into one open corner. It was a red, satin-type of material. There may have been a glint of gold to the edge.

"Oh, Cari, I can make a fine dress out of this!"

"As long as I get the good neighbor discount?"

"Of course."

He snatched up the box with a wink and a nod. He might've walked right out of the shop, except that Holly caught his arm to remind him that they were still shopping.

"Sal," Jane seemed ready to burst after waiting politely for the pleasantries to end, "any word on Varick?"

Sal's grin receded. "Sorry, Miss, I was supposed to tell you," he turned back to Carissa, "that his majesty is held up in Vale today on account of the investigation. I'm not privy to what they're looking for." He leaned in, whispering, "But I gather it's something to do with testing the magic from the elixir."

"Magic?" Carissa asked. "Wasn't it poison?"

Sal shook his head. "No, it was magic that made it act like a poison. He's scanning all the fae that were there the night of…well, you know." Sal cleared his throat. "Well, they've already checked mine, though I told them I don't really have any magic—not strong magic, anyway. Which reminds

Elixirs and Elves

me, they'll probably be wanting a look at Fudge," Sal said to Jane.

The squeak of a shoe on tiled floor sounded from the front of the rows to their left. Carissa frowned. Whatever Fudge was up to, she hoped he wasn't making a mess of the items on the shelves. He was an elfkin, so he was more likely to rearrange things than break anything. Still, rearranging her organized inventory was not appreciated.

Sal may have noticed Carissa's disapproving scowl. He glanced at Barnaby and Holly, then back at Carissa and Jane. "I think I've said too much."

Carissa wanted to explain that she wasn't angry with Sal, but Jane didn't let Sal go that easily without an explanation.

"Sal, could you speak to his majesty about letting me in to see Varick?"

Carissa waved her arms in crisscross action. "I don't think it's a good idea for Sal to ask Prince Zephyr that. He might think Sal is overstepping."

"Oh, no, he's more like you, Cari." Sal's smile returned. "I'm sure Prince Zephyr will extend an invitation to Miss Jane for the trial. He's about the nicest person I've ever met."

Coming from the kindest fae Cari had ever known, the sentiment was even more meaningful. The only problem was: Carissa had to find a way to protect Jane if she did go into Vale for the trial. With all the sidhe there, several sets of eyes might be needed to keep her safe.

"Well, that's wonderful," Cari strained to sound normal. "I hope he'll also allow some of Varick's friends, such as myself and Cameron, to attend." She shot a look at Cam so he'd go along with it. He didn't jump in like normal, but he didn't disagree with her, either.

"I'm happy to, but you could ask him yourself if you want. He said he would be in Moss Hill tonight to make up for not being here now."

"Splendid," Holly exclaimed. "The prince can escort Carissa to Macara's for dinner tonight."

Astoria Wright

Carissa had to admire Holly's tenacity. She doubted the prince would miss the winter solstice, given that it was among the most honored holidays of the fae. Though, as far as the fae were concerned, an invitation from a Tuatha de Danann might outweigh even the solstice celebrations. Carissa looked over at Cameron, expecting to share a glance acknowledging Holly's pushiness, but Cameron's eyes were fixed on the counter. Carissa could tell he was waiting for the conversation to end.

Since the prince might not even attend, Carissa thought an evening at Macara's might do him some good.

"Don't forget Cameron," she said to Holly. "You'll have to invite him, too."

"Who?" Holly asked. Her mouth formed a comical "o," to match the shape of her startled eyes. "Yes, of course—"

"That's all right," Cam jumped in. "I'm busy tonight."

"Oh, well, then, that's that," Holly said. "Come, Barnaby, we've got much to do!"

The leprechaun followed the bean tighe to the door.

"I'll have the dress ready for the Christmas Eve party!" he called.

"About the party, Barnaby," Sal said, "hold on a minute, I need a little help."

The elfkin bounded over to them, standing just outside the door and chatting away with Barnaby about party preparations. Jane's eyes shifted between Cam and Cari, apparently deciding that the awkwardness between them warranted some time alone. She walked down the aisles and Fudge appeared in time to open the door for her from wherever he had been hiding. She might've commented on it to Cam, except he seemed too upset. Once Jane and Fudge were out of the shop, Carissa turned her full attention to him.

"What's this about being busy tonight?" Cari asked.

"Doesn't matter." Cameron side-stepped closer to Carissa, standing directly in front of her. "What matters is this."

Elixirs and Elves

He slapped the crinkled newspaper onto the counter. The daily news article titled: "Local Businessman to Run for Mayor."

"I'll give you one guess as to who's already announced his candidacy for the mayoral elections in May," he said.

Carissa picked up the paper. Parker's image was plastered on the front page in black and white.

"Parker Greer," Carissa said, holding the paper up to find out who wrote the article.

It was Tilly Brier, of course. Carissa was beginning to think Moss Hill only had one reporter. One very effective reporter, she had to admit.

"Why is he announcing his candidacy so early?" Cari asked.

Elections in Moss Hill typically ran short, within two or three months, and sometimes less than that. Candidates were announced, paraded around, and voted into office with little campaigning. Mayor Belkin had been elected the last two terms and ran unopposed last time.

Cam smirked, vindicated in his suspicion. "He's practically admitting his guilt."

"Cam, please." Cari dropped the paper and began sifting through the orders on the tablet. "I've already listened to your accusations, and you just heard Sal. It was magic that poisoned Toffee. I doubt Parker has any magic. Now, I've got a lot to do this morning, so I'd rather not hear it again."

"This is Moss Hill, in case you forgot. It's bristling with magic. And if you had heard me out the first time, I wouldn't need to repeat it. Cari, you've got to tell the sidhe to investigate him."

"I can't waste the sidhe's time. There's no evidence against Parker but your blatant jealousy."

"Jealousy?" He flattened his palms against the counter and leaned in. "Of what?"

"He's rich, he's well connected, and he's been after your job for a while. Now, he might soon be your boss." She gestured to the newspaper. Cam's head bent lower and lower as she spoke. Eventually, he seemed to be examining the grain lines in the wood and not hearing her at all. Cari realized how harsh she sounded.

She tilted her head and let go of the tablet. Stepping on the other side of the counter, she leaned in sympathetically and put a hand on his arm. "You really have nothing to worry about, Cam. You've been doing very well as ambassador to Vale. Besides that, Parker's not likely to win. I think you'd have as good a chance of beating him as Belkin does if you ran for mayor yourself. He might have ties to businesses in Vale, but he's not popular among the townsfolk. You have no reason to be jealous of him."

Cam stepped back from the counter. He refused to look at her, bending his winter hat in his hands. When his eyes did lock onto hers, there was such hurt and anger in them that Cari felt her elf-light flicker in her chest. Her eyes shifted between him and the shelves behind him. He'd never looked so severe before. His eyes lowered. She wasn't sure if the anger was weighing him down or if he was taking a moment to weigh her words. When he looked back up at her, the expression was softer.

"You're wrong, Cari. I'm not saying these things out of jealousy. If I were, I'd be accusing Prince Zephyr." With that, Cam spun on his heels and walked out of the door, placing his hat on his head and pushing the doors open like it was best for them not to be in his way.

***

"ARE YOU ALL right?" Nan asked when Carissa arrived at home after work.

It was good to be in their split-level, two-story in Moss Hill after two nights in Vale. Her nan, just sitting down for tea, held a hand to the edge of her glasses to study Carissa's face.

"Yes," Carissa said, balancing two bags on each arm. Thank goodness Mrs. Harbridge volunteered to drive her

Elixirs and Elves

home in her SUV, or she'd never have managed all the groceries on her meek, little bicycle.

"No one would blame you if you weren't."

Carissa lugged the bag of groceries and presents onto the counter. The nature faeries and alvens, who, for some reason had been wandering around their kitchen, circled the presents. Two of them immediately began a tug of war with the fruit. An apple rolled across the floor.

"You heard about Toffee's death," Carissa said.

"This is Moss Hill, dear. Of course, I heard. What I haven't heard is how you are—coping with so many tragedies this year."

Carissa breathed in the spiced air and tried for a smile.

"Just a long day. I'm fine."

She shirked off a real answer. But Nan observed much over the rim of her hand-painted teacup.

"Yes, you look as happy as anyone bringing in so many presents would be."

Carissa picked up the apple on the floor and started unloading presents.

"I really am fine, I—wait, how do you know these are presents?"

By all appearances, Cari was just sifting through groceries to restock the fridge. She paused on the cauliflower.

"The same way I know that you're upset about the murder: Cameron Larke."

"Cam's been to see you?" Carissa asked.

"Of course. He stops in the library to chat sometimes, mostly about you." Nan hid her smile beneath the china.

Carissa let go of the groceries and sat across from her grandmother. Fog steamed over Nan's eyeglasses and faded, but the scent of apple and cinnamon lingered. The aroma from the teapot filled the whole modest kitchen with warmth, both in temperature and feeling. Carissa tried for a smile.

In a rare gesture, her grandmother placed a hand on her arm.

"I'm sorry I didn't say this a long time ago." Nan sighed. "I know I raised you to be strong. I was old, your parents were away often, and maybe my heart was a little…well, that doesn't matter. The point is you don't have to be strong all the time. You can open up if you need to."

"I don't—" Carissa couldn't find the words. "I didn't know Toffee well, and there wasn't anything I could do anyway."

"You see?" Nan asked.

"See what?" Carissa responded.

Nan set down her teacup. "There wasn't anything you could do, but why do you feel that you had to do something anyway?"

"I'm an apothecary. I help people."

"But Mr. Carson is a doctor, and he was there. The sidhe have magical cures, and they were there. You don't have to carry it all on yourself."

Nan waited her out, which was a feat since she indulged her sullen feelings for at least a minute or two.

Finally, Nan leaned across the table. "Cari?"

"Varick isn't guilty," Carissa said. "Cam thinks it's Parker, Varick suspects a…someone else."

She tried being open, but she didn't want to go into detail. There was no need to involve Nan in all of this. Her grandmother sighed. Nan must've realized Cari had shared all she could. She changed the subject.

"Parker?" Nan asked.

"Yes, Mr. Greer's—"

"I know who he is," her grandmother chided. She'd worked with the head of Moss Hill's public library for years. Of course, she would know his nephew.

"Do you think he could have done it?"

"I'd be surprised if it were true. He was a big bookworm in his high school years. From the day his family moved to Moss Hill till the day he graduated, I might've seen him at least twice a week pouring through the books. He was always polite."

Elixirs and Elves

It was too bad she hadn't been as open as all the chatterboxes of Moss Hill. She told Nan about Maren's bad date back in July, but she hadn't specified that it had been with Parker. As much as she disliked gossip, telling Nan news was not the same as spreading idle chatter. She didn't want to get into it now, though, especially after learning Cam was probably wrong. There was no need to shatter her grandmother's image of the schoolchildren whom she still helped at the library three days a week.

Carissa spied a few nature faeries trying to get into the upper cabinets where they kept all sorts of snacks. She walked over and shooed them away. Since she was up, she decided to continue with the unpacking. It offered a more pleasant topic.

"Do you know who sent all of this? It's not just food." She opened more of the bags. "There's jewelry, too, and a dress." Carissa retrieved said items from their bags and Nan twisted in her chair at the table.

"Prince Zephyr seems taken with you."

Nan had that look on her face that always spread across her lips and twinkled in her eyes when she was waiting for the light bulb to switch on in Cari's mind. This wasn't a much better topic than the previous one. She had no desire to discuss her budding romance—if that's what it turned out to be.

"Zephyr is a gentleman."

"And handsome, too, I hear." Nan wouldn't let her off that easy.

Carissa, shutting the fridge, turned back to Nan. "Why didn't you come to the welcoming party? And don't tell me you had to work, you know that isn't true."

Nan shrugged and grasped the handle of the teapot. "I've met the royals before. I'm not much for all their pomp and show." She poured herself another cup of the freshly brewed tea.

"King Finvarra mentioned you."

"Did he?" Nan adjusted her glasses and reached for the paper.

She could try to be nonchalant, but Cari couldn't believe Nan found the conversation boring. Carissa finished putting away the last of the items and retook a seat. This time, she held down the corner of the paper and waited for Nan's attention. Nan looked up. Her glasses had slid mid-nose. It reminded Cari of her grandmother's stern warnings when Carissa had been a child.

"The king asked how you are, said to tell you hello."

"How nice of him." Nan let go of the paper and lifted her teacup again.

"Nan," Cari strained her tone a little, "I just told you the King of Sidhe and Elves said hello to you, and you're drinking tea like it's a normal Monday."

Nan set down the cup. "Cari, your grandfather was the mayor of Moss Hill once. You must know we'd have met the king before."

Cari blinked. Now that Nan said it, it seemed apparent.

"I guess you're right. It just seemed more like he knew you, personally, as a friend."

"We're all friends in Moss Hill," Nan recaptured her teacup and leaned with both elbows on the table. The steam rose up the middle of her face. "I'm more interested in your impression of the royal family."

Carissa set her arms on the table rested her chin in both hands. "They're fine."

"And their son is a gentleman," Nan repeated her earlier sentiment.

"Yes." Cari smiled despite herself. "He's nearly perfect, except...."

"Except?" Nan nudged in a gentle tone.

Well, if she was going to be an honest person, she might as well start with why she didn't think Zef was right for her. The problem was, she couldn't honestly find an imperfection in the prince. He was handsome, considerate, honorable, and even understood her since he was half-elf too. Even his sidhe side was more understandable the more time she spent with him. She was developing a newfound appreciation for the

Elixirs and Elves

sidhe since he had opened her eyes to their world. The more she thought about it, the less Carissa understood why she'd placed the qualifier "nearly" to his perfection.

"Except that you don't love him," Nan ventured a guess.

Carissa dropped her hands and tapped her nails on the table. That could definitely be it. "I've only known him two days. Mum and Dad seem to love him, though."

Nan waved a hand and set the cup in its saucer. "They love you. They only want you to be happy."

"They've made it fairly clear that they want me to be happy with him."

"But you're not?"

"How can I know that in a few days?"

"I don't think you can, dear. After all, it's taken years, and you still haven't realized you're in love with Cam."

A crash interrupted their conversation. Carissa and Nan both sprang to their feet.

The golden chalice given to hear by Manann MacLir had toppled from the uppermost shelf of the cabinet where Cari thought the goblet would be safe. The nature faeries had knocked it down while rummaging for sweets. Chaos, Hiya, and Cynth gathered on the middle shelf, looking everywhere but at the fallen cup. Chaos was doing her best impression of a nonchalant sprite.

"Chaos, how many times have I told you not to invade the shelves?"

Chaos opened her palms upward. Cari shook her head. She was too distracted by Nan's last statement to chide Chaos anymore.

"I'm not in love with Cam," Cari said as she enveloped the cup with her fingers. The gold shattered into three large pieces in her hand. She gasped and let the shards go. They clinked and clanged against the tile.

"Now look at this; it's broken." Carissa gave a sharp eye to the three nature faeries, who took to the air, apparently deciding this was a good time to leave.

Cari scooped up the base and two sides of the goblet. They fit together well enough. She'd only need strong glue to hold them. It was strange, though, that it had broken at all. She didn't expect a gift from Manann MacLir to damage so effortlessly.

"I'll have to try to repair it. I'll take it into the shop tomorrow." Carissa placed the pieces into her tote and sighed. "I don't think MacLir will be too pleased about this."

Chapter 11

Old Acquaintances

Cari heard the doorbell from her room upstairs. Chaos zipped out the window and back inside. The little sprite held her hands together beside her head and blinked, making googly eyes. Cari got the message.

"I do not look at him like that," she retorted.

Just to be sure she was ready to go, Carissa took one glance at herself in the mirror. Chaos exaggerated ladylike steps up to the mirror and pretended to fuss with her hair.

"Stop that," Cari meant to snap at Chaos, but she laughed in spite of herself. "All right, I see your point. You don't have to be that way about it."

She made her way out of the bedroom and down the steps. Chaos zipped right onto her shoulder. Carissa didn't mind. She knew Chaos was at her wit's end with the alvens. After what happened with the goblet, the sprite had certainly had enough.

Tonight should prove to be a harmless party. It was, after all, being hosted by the most powerful woman in all of Moss Hill and the town's current protector. Surely, Chaos couldn't get into any trouble there.

Downstairs, Cari rounded the corner of the staircase to see Nan on the sofa of the sitting room reading a book. Cari stopped and held her hand out to the front door, with her eyebrows raised at Nan. Her grandmother looked up only to turn a page.

"Your prince is here," Nan stated bluntly.

"I hear that, thank you," Carissa said. "And you couldn't answer the door because...?"

"He's your prince," Nan looked up from her glasses. "I'm not one to get in the way."

Carissa murmured a soft "mmhm" under her breath. Nan wouldn't interfere, but she would sit in the front room listening to their conversation. Cari opened the bright red door to reveal Prince Zephyr, dressed in his royal garb.

He wore a long, green cloak over a matching tunic and pants. The clothing was all gold trimmed. The tunic was laced with gold-colored strings. A brown belt was strapped around his waist. His gold hair was tied behind his pointed ears and flowed down his shoulders.

He might've stepped straight out of a storybook. The faerie prince was the embodiment of charming. He bowed low and kissed her hand. Carissa felt Chaos's little hands pushing at her chin to close her mouth. She gently pushed the faerie back onto her shoulder.

She invited him inside, where he saw Nan in the sitting room. Though he had already given her so much, Zephyr pulled a gift from the inside pocket of his robe. It was a small, red box with a gold ribbon.

"For your grandmother," he said.

Carissa looked in on Nan, who gave no sign that she'd heard him. Prince Zephyr stepped down into the room and bowed in front of the sofa. Her grandmother did not get up.

"Nan," Cari said, tilting her head toward the prince and stressing with her eyes that she ought to bow to royalty.

Nan put down the book she was reading. Her eyes scanned Zephyr up and down.

"So, this Finvarra's son," Nan said. "You have an even mix of your mother and father in you."

Carissa was surprised at the lack of formality in Nan's greeting. She had never been one for pomp and circumstance, but Cari at least expected her to pay her respect to fae royalty.

"Mrs. Shae, I am pleased to make your acquaintance."

Elixirs and Elves

The prince reached out to her. Nan allowed him to grasp her fingers and he kissed the back of her hand as he had done for Carissa.

He presented her with the gift that was no larger than a tree ornament but containing something Cari suspected was far more valuable. Her grandmother took it gingerly. She opened it to reveal a metal pin. It had an insignia Carissa hadn't seen before. It was a bird on one side and an arm with a sword on the other.

"What does it mean?" Carissa asked.

The prince looked between Cari and her grandmother. He hesitated to answer.

"It's a thoughtful present," Nan said quickly, "and I thank you and your parents for it."

Nan stood and bowed in her own ladylike way, lowering her head and dipping in something of a half curtsy with her arms in front of her. Prince Zephyr nodded and kept his head down until she was out of the room. Carissa's eyes followed her grandmother and snapped back to the prince.

"Someone will have to explain that to me later," Cari said.

Prince Zephyr offered her his arm, and they stepped up to the foyer.

"I don't believe it's my place," the prince said, "but I'm sure your grandmother will explain when she's ready."

Carissa took one last glance behind her. Nan wasn't in the hallway. Wherever she was, she was acting strangely. There was nothing to do but drop it for the time being, but Carissa would definitely be asking her about it later. Cari let go of the prince's arm for just a second as she opened the red door.

"Shall we?"

The prince held an open palm out in front of him, signaling for her take the lead. Outside, Carissa's jaw dropped upon seeing a horse-drawn carriage with two sidhe guards, one at the perch, and one holding the door open.

Two gorgeous white horses stood at the lead. They were large enough to be Clydesdales. Tufts of fur surrounded the hooves, and thick, luxurious hair grew from the mane and tail of each one. The hair seemed to have almost a purplish hue to it as the silky strands reflected the moonlight.

Carissa, at a loss for words, approached cautiously and stroked the mane of the one closest to her. Chaos flew up and did the same. Cari assumed Chaos's tiny hand would not make an impression on the massive animal, but the horse turned its head toward them at about the same time the sprite touched its soft, shiny mane. The way it nodded its head and neighed seemed like an equine greeting to the little faerie.

Carissa was breathless. Finding her voice, she wondrously declared, "I've seen the sidhe horses, but none are as beautiful as these."

"Elstar and Etania are twice rare: twin mares and descendants of the unicorns of old."

"Unicorns?" Cari shared a grin with Chaos. "They exist?"

Anything was possible in Moss Hill. Carissa supposed nothing should really shock her. Yet, even after a lifetime of magic among her faerie kin, the fae folk still managed to surprise her.

"They existed here, once. They've all gone now."

"They've all died?" Carissa looked at Chaos, who hung on his every word.

"I didn't say that," the prince said. "There are many realms of existence. They're in one, somewhere, just not here anymore."

The prince offered his hand and helped Cari into the carriage. He climbed in after only to find that Chaos had claimed the space between them on the seat. The sidhe guard closed the door and took a place beside the driver. The horses increased in speed steadily. Carissa could only imagine how fast the journey would fly if they were unicorns at the helm.

Legendary creatures aside, the topic of Jane's request to see Varick remained. She wasn't quite sure how to broach the

Elixirs and Elves

subject. It would be a delicate matter trying to ask for her sake and yet sway him not to let her near the sidhe, all without trying to reveal her true nature.

"Zef," she felt odd using the nickname he'd asked her to call him, "did Sal ask you earlier about a friend attending Varick's trial?"

"Yes, Jane Everly. All is set for her attendance at the trial."

Carissa held her breath, "I'm not sure that's wise."

The prince's eyebrows lifted, awaiting an explanation. She repeated the excuse she'd thought of earlier in the day.

"Jane cares for Varick. It will only distress her if the verdict is unfavorable."

The prince looked down at the seat between them. His solemn expression softened upon seeing the sprite looking up between them. He faced her again.

"If the verdict is unfavorable, she may want to say goodbye to him. It might be her only chance."

"Her family is important to Moss Hill. Whether her feelings are reciprocated or not, she cares for Varick, and I believe he is kind enough to want her to be spared any heartache from the ordeal."

This news had an opposite reaction from what Cari expected. The prince's elf ears twitched. He squinted, tilting his head.

"Did Varick make a request for her not to attend the trial?"

The words "oh, no" briefly passed through Carissa's mind. She had thought this through. He wasn't supposed to find that suspicious. It was just the care for the feelings of a human for a sidhe; most sidhe would pass that off as nothing. She thought the prince would dismiss it as quickly. Of course, Carissa wasn't supposed to talk to the prince about Jane at all.

But what if her fear was unfounded? What if Prince Zephyr could be trusted to see the situation with an open mind to Varick's innocence? Surely, he was more understanding than the sidhe.

"Varick said nothing of a trial," Carissa said.

She looked away. She hadn't lied, but the technicality didn't feel right. She hoped Zephyr would simply agree to keep her away from the council and then drop the discussion.

"I must be entirely honest with you." He reached for her hand. "Carissa, the council has asked that I summon both her and you to the trial."

"Me?" Carissa looked up at him with a shock that was soon engulfed in realization. She closed her eyes. "The discussion with Varick. I see."

"I'm sorry, Cari, I have a duty as the magistrate."

She put a hand up. "It's all right, I understand."

The prince squeezed her fingers. "I have never slacked in duty nor broken an oath. I will make a promise to you now that I will not let any harm come to you at this trial—regardless of the outcome for Varick."

Carissa smiled. Chaos flew above them, trying to get a look out the window. The two chuckled. Then, the nature faerie ruined the moment by pulling Carissa's ear and pointing to a cottage as the carriage turned into a long driveway.

"I see it, yes, thank you, Chaos," Cari winced as she spoke. Chaos let go, and Cari rubbed her ear. The prince's hand on her shoulder caused the tinge of a blush on her face. She smiled to show she was fine. Then, both of their eyes turned toward their destination.

Macara's home, up the hill from the Everly's mansion, welcomed them with holiday lights above moss-green bearings of the Tudor-style roof. The fire-red bricks of the cozy cottage seemed like a more appropriate residence for the variety of elves from Santa Claus legend, instead of the home of a Tuatha de Danann. The carriage gently eased alongside the house and stopped in front of the brightly-lit front porch.

Chaos zoomed out the window and to the doorbell before Prince Zephyr could even open the carriage. He exited first, reaching in to help Carissa down. She and Zephyr walked up the porch. The cranberry-colored door with a festive green wreath opened to reveal a bean tighe wearing a

Elixirs and Elves

pink apron and the same ankle-length dress from earlier in the day.

"Come in, come in before you catch your death of cold, my dears!" the short woman commanded with a cheery smile. Chaos floated right above Holly.

Cari stepped in first. The warmth of the hearth in the living room heated her rosy cheeks. Holly took her coat and placed it on the rack to the right of the door.

Carissa thanked her, adding, "Are those sugar cookies and gingerbread I smell?"

"No dessert until dinner," Holly reprimanded as if she were a child. The harsh tone made more sense when Carissa spotted Chaos hovering over to the counter of the open kitchen. Cari shot her a narrowed-eyed stare. The sprite folded her arms resentfully and floated into the living room.

"I think you'll like what she's cooked up," Barnaby said with a wink.

The leprechaun stood behind Holly with a glass in hand. Cari assumed it was ginger ale since she knew the leprechaun did not drink. That might've been on account of his cousin, who had a bit of a problem in the past.

Cari thought of Clancy briefly and, lo, the clurichaun appeared on the sofa in the living room. In reality, he'd been sitting there with his friend, Emony, the whole time.

"Hello, Clancy," Carissa said. "How are you?"

"Fine, fine." The clurichaun cheerfully held up the glass of what she was now convinced was a soft drink. "And yourself this fine evening?"

He was trying to fit the formality, and Cari found the attempt charming. She replied with a tilt of her head and a response befitting his question.

"I'm very well, thank you."

She nodded to Emony. The brownie's kind smile told her that she understood just as well as Carissa that Clancy was trying too hard. Her levity took on a gravity in the next second that bordered on awe.

She popped out of her seat and Clancy let out a short "huh," before changing that to an "oh," and springing to his feet.

"Your, uh, Majesty," Clancy uttered in his gravelly voice.

Holly and Emony curtseyed while Barnaby and his cousin bowed. Prince Zephyr returned a nod in each of their directions. Only after their reactions did Carissa notice that there was a taller woman in a sofa chair directly beside the fireplace: Macara. Prince Zephyr bowed lower than she'd seen him do before.

Macara lifted her chin. Chaos had found her place on the woman's shoulder and was now mimicking her movements, lifting her head as if to examine the prince as well. When Macara lifted her fingers next, Chaos did the same.

"You may rise, Zephyr. Come and join us."

She pointed to the sofa chair across from her. The prince obliged. This left Cari to find a seat elsewhere in the room. The seat beside Emony looked inviting, though Barnaby placed himself there first. The only other space was that of the long window seat, which Cari began to walk toward. The sound of the doorbell caught her attention as she stepped to the window facing the porch.

"I've got it," Holly called out.

Cari could see through the curtain that it was the Everlys, all three of them, and Fudge included. Though, the elfkin was pacing on the porch and fidgeting with his hat. He disappeared from sight the second Carissa heard the door open. Her elf-ears twitched as Holly bellowed, "Hello!"

Carissa didn't need superior hearing ability to listen in on Holly. "Oh, Fudge, glad you came, too. I told you: a sip of my soup, and you'd be all better. Though you look a bit sallow...."

She went on. Carissa though it would prove convenient that Fudge had come. She'd wanted to question him since Varick told her he'd given Fudge the elixir to give to Jane. Varick didn't seem to think he was guilty, but Toffee's accusation and Fudge's sudden illness were suspicious. She'd

Elixirs and Elves

have to find a way to ask him alone, however, which would be difficult in these close quarters.

Apparently, the prince had the same thought. He called a sidhe guard who was standing at attention on the side of the room. Carissa overheard the order to take a sample of Fudge's magic. The sidhe guard was formally polite when he relayed it to Fudge. It was a task sifting through the various conversations in the home while listening with her heightened elf-hearing.

"Sir, if you would come with me—"

"But I haven't done anything," Fudge's voice wavered. He seemed to squeal a pitch higher than usual, but Carissa might have imagined that.

"Just a sample of your magic, sir."

The guard and Fudge passed out of hearing range, which meant they must've gone outside.

"See? Warm and toasty right here," Holly's voice startled Cari as it came closer. Carissa jerked her eyes toward the bean tighe, who was leading Jane and her parents around the corner to the window seat.

Since Cari hadn't yet taken a seat, she did not have to stand to greet them. As usual, Jane looked stunning. She was a little less formal in a simple blue dress, and she met Carissa with a hug.

It was strange that she was a hugging person since her parents were the opposite of that. Mr. Everly walked straight to the prince and bowed. His face was like his son Alden's, but Cari felt his nature was the opposite. She didn't know him well but wouldn't be surprised if he was a tyrannical businessman. Fudge brought him a chair from the kitchen table, and he sat alongside Prince Zephyr.

Mrs. Everly, in a black dress with her brown hair in a bun styled to perfection, said formally, "Hello, Carissa, I hope you're well."

"I am, thank you. Yourself?"

"No complaints." The businesswoman glanced over to her husband. "If you'll excuse me."

She left Jane and Carissa upon seeing the second chair Fudge was bringing in. Cari traced Fudge's footsteps back to the kitchen. No doubt he was offering his assistance to Holly with the dinner.

"Have you asked the prince yet about Varick?" Jane asked, taking hold of Cari's hand for support.

Carissa clamped her lips. She needed to tell her. Since Jane was summoned regardless of her desire to attend the trial, it was best for her to know what was expected.

"The sidhe are summoning you to the trial."

Jane took her hands away and twiddled her fingers in her lap. "I should've known."

Carissa narrowed her eyes. "What do you mean?"

Jane lowered her voice. "Varick did have a second elixir, but it was for me."

Carissa glanced at the prince, who was in comfortable conversation with the Everlys. She knew an elf's ears were sharp enough to hear even the slightest whisper, but only if they were paying attention. She hoped he wasn't at this particular moment.

Jane went on, "He and I had been arguing for a while about it."

"About the elixir?" Cari asked.

Jane shook her head. "About my mortality." The young Everly let out a breath as if she were letting go of everything that had been bottled up these past months. "You know I don't want this, these powers." She glanced at her hands.

Carissa's eyes drifted to the prince again. He seemed to be distracted by some story Barnaby was telling. In a way, Cari wondered what Prince Zephyr's reaction would be if he heard Jane speaking. Jane followed her eyes.

Carissa interrupted Jane's gaze with a question. "Macara's been helping you, though, hasn't she?"

"Yes. Varick was helping me, too. Over time, I came to care for him and he for me." Jane's smile was coated in sorrow.

She stopped, perhaps picking up on Cari's hesitation. She seemed to choose her words more carefully. "I never wanted

Elixirs and Elves

to be the way I am. He made me realize it might be something I could accept. But immortality?" She looked at her parents.

Something in Jane's eyes told Cari that she was thinking of her brother. Jane placed a finger to the outer corner of her eye, wiping away a tear before it could fall.

"I don't want it," she said. "But it's too painful for a sidhe to love a human with a limited lifespan."

Carissa jumped in while Jane struggled to keep composure, "So he made an elixir to force you to become immortal so you could be together?"

She was a bit indignant in her tone. Carissa was ready to dislike Varick all the more, but Jane contradicted her.

"No," Jane said quickly, "I broke it off and I broke his heart. Only, he wanted me to have the elixir anyway for my sake if I wanted it, or perhaps in the hope that I would change my mind; but it would be a choice. Only, I refused to take the vial, so Fudge took it to keep for me."

Carissa pondered for a moment. Could she have broken Varick's heart in such a way that he did poison her? Vengeance for love scorned wasn't an unheard motive among humans. Could it be possible among the sidhe?

Jane wiped away another tear and shook her head. "He wouldn't have poisoned it."

She had responded to Cari as if she had read her mind. Despite being taken aback by Jane's possible psychic abilities, Carissa smiled.

"It'll be all right. We'll find a way to prove his innocence."

Carissa feigned confidence as best she knew how. In truth, she had no idea how they were going to help Varick. She just hoped Jane couldn't see through her bluff.

Chapter 12

Ghost of Christmas Past

In the middle of Carissa's earnest conversation with Jane, Chaos decided to play charades over Jane's head. At first, it annoyed Cari, but then she noted the look of sheer panic on the nature faerie's face. Chaos pointed frantically to the kitchen, where she caught a glimpse of Fudge exiting the room.

"I'm sorry, Jane, would you excuse me?" Carissa asked.

Jane nodded. Her brows furrowed and she looked at the nature faerie. "Is everything all right?"

"I'm never sure with Chaos," Carissa half-joked.

She followed Chaos to the dining room off the side of the kitchen, where Fudge seemed to have disappeared out the back door.

Carissa opened the sliding glass and followed him out. The sudden cold chilled her. She felt Chaos tangle up into her hair. Rubbing her hands together, Cari summoned the elflight from her heart and warmed herself as best she could. Snow fell lightly through the air, just enough to impede visibility. Out of the corner of her eye, Carissa saw a form dashing past a tree.

Cari called out while hastening past the shrubbery, "Fudge? Fudge, is that you?"

"Leave me alone," came the elfkin's reply.

Carissa walked up to a bench overgrown with vines. Fudge was about ten paces farther out and looking all about

Elixirs and Elves

him. It wasn't clear what he was searching for, so Cari approached cautiously.

"What's wrong?" Carissa asked.

Fudge relaxed his posture. "Nothing," he said. The elfkin stuffed his hands between his arms and his torso and began walking back to the house. Chaos found her way out of Carissa's hair and to the elfkin's shoulder. He tried to shake her off, but that was difficult to do.

"Fudge," Carissa hesitated given his foul mood.

Then again, his mood was always grumpy. She took a breath. The question needed asking.

"What happened the night of Toffee's death?"

"How should I know?" Fudge's tone was defiant, but he stopped in his tracks.

"You were there and possibly closest to him most of the night."

"Are you seriously accusing me?"

"No," Cari shook her head, "not accusing, just hoping you could shed some light on what happened."

"Are you a sidhe guard now?" He continued walking.

Cari reddened. "No."

"Then I think you have no business asking me that."

"Fudge, I have reason to believe Jane might've been the target."

He paused and looked at Carissa with eyes as big as walnuts. "Who would hurt Miss Jane?"

"That's what I'm trying to find out."

He put a hand to his chin. He walked back to sit on the bench. "The elixir, of course. It was for Miss Jane." He closed his eyes, rubbing them with his fingers. "But, no, the elixir wouldn't have been made to hurt her."

"You're sure of that?" Carissa asked.

"Of course, given who was giving it to her. I've heard you've even been to see him in the sidhe dungeons." The elfkin shuddered at the mention of the sidhe prison.

"But Varick wasn't the only one who had access to the elixir."

131

Upon hearing this, Fudge wrapped his arms around his stomach as if he'd taken a blow. Chaos's little hands patted his neck to comfort him.

"You can't believe that I would ever hurt Miss Jane."

"Or Toffee?" Carissa crossed her arms. She hated to do it, but she couldn't back down if she wanted to prove Varick's innocence.

Fudge sighed. As if deflating, he sank in the bench. He held one hand over his face. *He's guilty of something*, Cari concluded. Having learned from the prince, she waited patiently for a response.

At long last, Fudge grunted.

"He's haunting me. It was him I saw just now, in the kitchen." He looked up and raised his voice to the air. "I didn't kill you, you know." He softened. "I wouldn't do that."

Carissa ventured closer to the bench. Chaos flew from the Fudge's shoulder to the bench, sitting next to the elfkin. Fudge looked at the tiny sprite wearily. Then, he glanced up at Cari. He looked aged—more so than usual.

He sighed. "Toffee was a friend, a long time ago. Not just to me, but to Sal's parents. Sal and I are not elfkins. There are no elfkins. That was Hela, you know, who made up the name." He paused. "We are Rhys Dwfen, of the Welsh faeries, the Rhys of the Deep. Our home is on a small, peaceful island made invisible to human eyes by the plants that grow there." Fudge's eyes drifted upward, dreamily. "It's a paradise where no hardship is known, and all are happy—the jolliest lot you'll ever see."

"Then why did you leave?"

Fudge's eyelids drooped. The same darkened dreariness returned to his features. "Have I ever seemed happy and jolly to you?"

Carissa didn't like to say. She tugged her lips to one side. There was no answering that without being hurtful.

"Don't bother sparing my feelings. I know myself. The island was no fit for me."

"So you came here?"

Elixirs and Elves

Fudge nodded.

"But how does Sal fit into this?"

"I'm not a jolly fae and Sal is not a handsome one. Oh, don't start with your arguments. I'm not saying it to hurt him. Sal didn't fit in. Neither did I. We left to find a place where we could live without feeling so different. Everyone is different here."

"Sal never told me this."

"No, of course not, how could he? He was just a baby when we left."

"A baby? Who were his parents?"

That darkness returned to Fudge's eyes. "People who were very close to me. They're dead, and I don't mean to be heartless about it, but it is what it is, and nothing will change it. And before you get any ideas, I didn't kill them. It was a terrible accident, that's all. Life is like that sometimes, ending just when you're ready to begin it."

The tone of his voice sank deeper and deeper into his usual sharpness. He was angry. Oddly, that's what made her believe him. It also shocked Chaos enough for her to perch back into Carissa's hair. Knowing Chaos, she probably wasn't as scared as she was cold.

"So you brought Sal here, but you never told him?"

"Toffee thought it was a mistake, we fell out over it. Now he wants me to tell him, but Sal is happy enough. He doesn't need to know. Now, if you'll excuse me, I have a meal to help with." He pushed himself up to his feet, resuming the trek back to the house.

Carissa followed Fudge. She tried to argue, but he only walked faster. She debated whether she would say something to Sal when, stepping back through the sliding door, Carissa saw Holly greeting two more guests at the front entrance. While both guests were expected, it was surprising to see the two arriving together.

"Thank you," Maren said, taking her arm out of her coat and allowing Holly to hang it up. Reginald behind her was already hanging his up on the coatrack himself.

The sound of Maren's voice brought the sprite out into the open air. Carissa and Chaos looked at each other. Carissa walked up to the pair and greeted them both with a "hello." Then, she pulled Maren aside.

"Did you come here with Reg?"

"He stopped by the bakery and asked if I was all right. Isn't that sweet? Later on in the day, I bumped into him at the market, and we got to talking. He asked if I'd like to carpool here, and I thought: Why not?" Maren looked back at Reg, who was in the midst of a bow before the prince. "He's cute, don't you think?"

Carissa shook her head and smiled to herself. There was no accounting for taste, she realized the truth in the old saying.

Shortly after Maren and Reg's arrival, Holly announced it was time for dinner. Chaos found a spot right near Carissa's plate and rubbed her hands together.

"I haven't forgotten about you," Holly said.

The bean tighe set out a little plate for Chaos, already filled with a small portion of each dish, including the dessert. The sprite dug into the food, effectively ignoring the rest of the diners' conversations. That was all anyone would hear out of her for the rest of the meal.

Holly and Fudge set the plates and food on the table as everyone took their places. When it was done, Holly slid out a chair and sat with them. She turned to Fudge, who was standing at attention in a corner of the room.

"What are you doing over there?" Holly asked with a forceful tone. "Come on, the food is getting cold."

Fudge looked between her, the chair, and the Everlys. It seemed even they couldn't argue with the bean tighe. Fudge slowly stepped over and joined them at the table.

The two had outdone themselves.

The table overflowed with tempting dishes: potatoes au gratin, creamed spinach, fresh steamed broccoli, and herb parmesan rolls. The honey-glazed roast, surrounded by caramelized onions and toasted pine nuts, sat on display at the center of the table. Unlike the formal dinners at the homes of

Elixirs and Elves

the elves or even the Everly's, they filled their own plates and all ate together, complimenting the chefs sitting beside them. The prince, perhaps more than any of the others, seemed to enjoy the family feeling in the informal atmosphere.

Carissa passed him the potatoes, and he eased into a more relaxing smile, taking a small portion and passing them on to Barnaby. Though he never fully appeared to relax, he laughed at Barnaby's jokes, matched Holly's wits, and took an interest in Mr. and Mrs. Everly's suggestions for expansion of the island's resources.

Near the end of the meal, Macara said, "So, Reginald, why has Manann sent you here?"

Reginald coughed. For a second, Carissa thought he might choke on his food, but he swallowed and set down his fork and knife. His eyes hovered over the table, resting on Chaos.

"For everyone's best interest, I think it's better we discuss this between ourselves and his majesty, the king."

Reg's eyes passed to Macara but flicked back to Chaos one more time before settling back on his plate. A month ago, Cari would have thought his interest in the nature faerie was due to never having seen one before. Now, she thought it might have something to do with the note Chaos came with, the one warning about dark faeries in Moss Hill. It made her think Reg must have news about the unseelie faeries.

"Tell us something, then," Macara said, "or Moss Hill will wonder why you've come."

Carissa understood what she was doing. Moss Hill would talk about Reginald's arrival, especially since Holly had invited certain people who had learned in the course of the evening that this human was requesting an audience with the King of Sidhe and Elves. Macara gave nothing away, but Maren and Barnaby glanced at each other. Carissa lifted her fork and covered her mouth with her hand to hide a chortle. They seemed to be accusing each other with their eyes when both were well known to gossip to any and all they encountered.

Reginald looked at all the guests. Macara's words seemed to sink in. He loosened his tie and took a drink before speaking.

"The main thing is his invitation to the king, and to you, Macara, to join him in Hy Brasil."

Unfortunately, those were the wrong words to dispel gossip in Moss Hill. Everyone at the table froze. Jane seemed to grip her silverware tighter. Mr. Everly cleared his throat, and Mrs. Everly brought her napkin to her lips. Barn, Clancy, and Emony stared at Macara. Maren's bewildered look was understandable, but Carissa knew a little more than her friend, and it was enough to cause her some pause, too.

She had heard Reginald mention Hy Brasil before. Last time, he seemed boastful, but now he referred to the legendary island as if it were common knowledge. When Carissa had asked Head Elf Rolin about it, she'd received a warning not to ask. She wanted to question it now. She set down her fork and looked at Reg. The poor man seemed baffled by the reaction.

"Have I said something wrong?" he asked.

The prince tried smoothing things over with a calm tone. "Not at all. We will reschedule the trial so that you and Macara may speak with my father tomorrow."

An awkward silence followed this statement. No matter how nonchalantly the words were said, the implication of disrupting a trial by the sidhe council was huge. Holly took it upon herself to fill in the quiet with an offer of dessert. Before the table was halfway cleared, the doorbell rang.

"Wonder who that could be?" Holly murmured to herself as she made her way to the door. Since the cottage was small enough to see it from the table, every eye turned to the entryway.

A sidhe guard in full uniform stood at attention in the doorframe. Holly stepped aside and let the sidhe guard in. He walked straight to the prince with a note in hand.

Prince Zephyr stood and unfolded it. A troubling look appeared over his face.

Elixirs and Elves

"I'm sorry. There is a matter which requires my immediate attention." He looked at Macara and to Holly. "Thank you for a splendid meal. It has been a most pleasant evening."

Carissa set her napkin down and started to stand. The prince held a palm outward.

"Please, stay and enjoy the dessert. The carriage is at your disposal when you are ready to leave."

Placing his arms at his side, he bowed to Macara and abruptly turned and led the sidhe guard out of the door.

"Well," Holly said, "isn't this night just full of surprises?"

Carissa was left utterly speechless. Though the rest of the night was enjoyable enough, her thoughts kept turning to Hy Brasil. She didn't want to ask in front of the crowded room, but as the night ended and the guests all took their leave, Carissa lagged, waiting to speak with Macara.

"See you tomorrow," Maren said as Reg helped her with her coat, "bright and early at the Seelie Tree."

Holly opened the door.

"Your carriage doesn't seem to be out there," Barnaby said, peering outside.

"It's a sidhe carriage. It'll be out there when she's ready to leave," Holly said.

"Was it the one with the white horses? We saw it pass by on Main Street, didn't we, Reg?" Maren squealed.

"I told you that was a fae carriage," Reg remarked as he slipped on his gloves.

"It was beautiful," Maren said.

"Thanks," Carissa replied. "Though, I've lost my traveling companion."

"Oh, I'm sure he's sad about it too, missing out on the company of a beautiful woman," Emony said.

"And I'm sure he'll miss Carissa, too," Clancy remarked, to which Emony blushed.

"Oh, come on, Romeo," Barnaby teased as he waved his cousin out the door.

"Now, Barn," Holly said, "I think he's sweet. You could take a line or two from his book, wouldn't do you any harm."

"No harm? Have you read that book?" Barnaby retorted.

The group continued debating out on the porch. Carissa could still hear them from where she and Macara stood in the entryway. Macara, seeing that Cari wasn't budging, closed the door.

"You're wondering about Hy Brasil," Macara stated.

"I've heard it before, from Reginald himself. Though, at the time, he thought it was Moss Hill," Cari said.

"No," Macara's lips curved upward. "It's not Moss Hill."

"Then what is it?" Cari asked.

Macara paused. A cloud passed over her face. Carissa recognized the look.

"Head Elf Rolin had the same expression when I asked him about it months ago. It was followed by anger."

"Fear looks a lot like anger given the right circumstances." Macara walked into the living room. She and Carissa sat opposite one another on the sofa chairs by the fireplace.

"Will you tell me what Hy Brasil is?" Cari asked.

Macara watched the fire for a while before responding.

"It's the home of the Tuatha de Danann."

Carissa followed Macara's gaze on the flames. "Your home?"

"Not anymore. Not since we joined you in this realm." She smiled.

"Why is Rolin scared of it?" Cari asked.

Macara shifted her eyes to Cari and smiled. "That's simple. He's seen what we can do."

Macara reached a hand toward the fireplace, and the flames went out. It reappeared as a flicker in the palm of her hand. She blew it out. Carissa hadn't seen anyone do that before but knew that some of the sidhe had such power over flame. It was surprising to see, but not surprising altogether. Carissa shared a smile with Chaos, but Chaos shook her head and wagged a finger at Cari.

Elixirs and Elves

No, that's not all, is what the faerie was saying. The sprite pointed at Macara. Carissa looked where she directed and gasped.

The flame danced in Macara's eyes. She looked at the fireplace. Without any noticeable transfer, the fire danced in the hearth once again. Carissa breathed, not realizing when she had stopped. She found herself gripping her chair. Cari imagined the awe in her face was visible.

Macara's eyes now held sadness in them. She held a palm up.

"Please, do not be afraid."

"I've never seen magic like that."

"And you'll never see it again, if I, if we, can protect you from it."

"Are the Tuatha de Danann evil?" Carissa hesitated to ask but managed to get out the words.

"Are humans evil? Or the sidhe? Or the elves?"

"No. People are not that simple."

"People are never that simple. Even if you think you've found the least complicated person of all, once you start to understand them, you'll find they're more than what you expected."

"So, you're saying we shouldn't fear the Tuatha de Danann?"

"Fear the bad, love the good, and most important of all: recognize both when you see them."

"I understand." Carissa felt Chaos land on her shoulder. She turned her head to see the little sprite yawning. Cari smiled. The nature faerie often found conversations dull that didn't include her. Carissa's first thought was that she ought to get Chaos home, her next was that Chaos was very much part of this conversation after all.

"Were the Tuatha de Danann the fae that Raven Corvus warned us about?"

"Possibly." Macara stood.

Carissa took that as a cue for her to stand, too. But she didn't abandon the line of questioning.

139

"Are you going with MacLir and the king?"

"All will be decided tomorrow."

Holly entered at that moment from the front door.

"Getting cold out there," Holly said. "A nice cup of hot chocolate might be in order, I think. Oh, Carissa, would you like one, too?"

"No, I should be going." Carissa looked between Macara and Holly, adding, "Thank you for everything."

She walked past the foyer and let herself out. As Holly predicted, by the time Cari had left the porch, the carriage appeared in front of it.

A sidhe guard appeared beside the horses and opened the carriage door. Carissa briefly wondered from where in the Otherworld they had shifted or whether there was a mound beneath her feet through which they could see her.

Either way, she entered the carriage. The sidhe attendant closed the door behind her. This time, Chaos curled up next to her and drifted to sleep. Carissa stared out the window as they traveled. She allowed her mind to wander but regretted it as her imagination conjured images of the Tuatha de Danann and the unseelie, or evil faeries, who might be threatening Moss Hill.

Chapter 13

All That Glitters

Parker Greer had some nerve. He showed up outside the apothecary shop right before lunch wearing a dark business suit and a smug smile. Chaos, who'd joined Carissa at the apothecary shop to help her repair the goblet as punishment for the crime of breaking it, was in the middle of throwing a piece of the gold across the counter. Super glue, elf-light, and nature faerie magic had all failed, and the sprite was giving up. The metal skid and clunked on the counter by the register. Before Cari could reprimand Chaos for losing her temper, she saw her assistant in her bright orange sweater and jeans spring out from an aisle.

"Maren?" Cari asked.

She scooped the gold pieces into the handkerchief she'd brought them in and walked to the edge of the counter. Chaos took to the air and hovered over the shop assistant.

"I'm not here." Maren disappeared in the hallway that led to the back room.

The shop door chimed, and Cari realized the source of her friend's agitation. Maren reappeared a second later, jerking her head around the corner. Parker would not have been able to see her from the front door.

Maren made sure he couldn't hear her by whispering, "And if he's pressing charges, I'm suing him for, uh, emotional trauma, or something like that." She ducked back. Just when Cari thought the drama was over, Maren shot out again, adding, "And he ought to get another pie in the face just for coming in here today."

Finally, Maren vanished into the back storeroom—for good this time. Carissa shook her head. *Forget baking*, she thought to herself, *Maren ought to try for an acting career.* Neither she nor Parker had a case worthy of a lawsuit, in Cari's opinion, but it would make for an exciting courtroom scene. Ladies and gentlemen of the jury, the emotional trauma of my client is worth not one but two pies in the face. The levity of the joke in her mind made it easier to stomach the fishiness of the Failte Abhaile hotel heir.

A confused Chaos scratched her head while flying back to sit on a storeroom shelf and watch the trouble afoot. Parker pushed the door aside. He unbuttoned his coat and lifted his sunglasses as he walked up to the counter. His bravado matched his overdressed style: complete with an overcoat, suit jacket, tie, and the obnoxious chain of a pocket watch strapped to a matching vest. It wasn't the clothes itself that annoyed the eyes, but the swagger with which he wore it.

The businessman put one hand in his pants pocket and the other in his suit jacket. From his chest pocket, he retrieved a business card.

"Good morning, Cari," his pompous voice filled the whole space of the apothecary shop.

"If you're looking for Maren, she's not in at the moment."

"No, I'm sure she's told you her version of events, but I assure you that was a misunderstanding. I'd apologize if she were here."

Carissa hoped Maren hadn't heard that, but with his volume and her tendency to eavesdrop, there was little chance she hadn't. She expected Maren to storm out of the back room at any moment. Parker reached the counter and set down his card.

"I'd have been in here yesterday, but I had a little mishap, as you know."

"Is there something you need, Parker?" Carissa couldn't keep the edge out of her voice.

Elixirs and Elves

"Cari, I hope you'll see past any personal disagreements and hear me out." He slid his card to her side of the counter. "I think it's time for local businesses to come together and take a stand. The mayor has not done what he's promised. We're only halfway through the reconstruction and have barely done any advertising to increase tourism."

Carissa disagreed. "Business is doing well. The castle is nearly restored. Moss Hill is thriving."

"That's short term, small-minded thinking. We could be doing so much more. Businesses could be thriving."

"Have you forgotten about Vale?"

"Not at all." He put a palm on the counter and casually leaned against it. "They can keep to themselves if they want, that's no reason to limit our interaction with the world."

"The more tourists, the greater the risk of their exposure to the world." Carissa slid the card back.

"Do you know some of the tourists actually come here for the myths about this place being home to faeries? And do you know what happens if they come away with a story or two about meeting a fae? Nothing. No one out there believes them. Even the tourists themselves, once they're home, start thinking it was a trick of their mind or the townsfolk having fun with them. The fae of Vale are in no danger. We must help them understand that."

Carissa maintained her disinterested stare, but there was no sense in arguing with him.

"Is that all, Parker?"

"I was hoping you'd join the businesses in support of my candidacy. Take some time to think about it. I'll be in touch."

He glanced down at his card and noticed the broken pieces of gold peeking out of the corner of the floral embroidered cloth. Without asking permission, he unfolded one side of the handkerchief.

"What's this?" he asked.

"It's nothing," Carissa responded.

She reached for it but was too late. Parker had already grabbed two pieces with one hand. He swiped a thumb across the gold, examining it. A gift from Manann MacLir in the greedy businessman's hands made Cari nervous.

"Parker, I'd rather you not touch that."

"I'm not exactly going to break it, am I?" Bringing it closer to his face, he said, "What is this, anyway? This isn't the goblet the elfkin was drinking from when he died, is it?"

Cari slid the remaining piece on the cloth closer to her. "No, it's not. Do you make it a habit of touching other people's goblets?"

He raised his eyes in mock hurt. "What's that supposed to mean?"

Cari bit her lip. She was practically accusing him. That would be going too far. "Nothing, sorry." She slid one step over and pulled the small cutting board she used for the herbs toward her. From under the counter, she pulled out a pair of herb-cutting scissors. Carissa assumed that if she went about her work, he'd get the idea and leave. Her walk to the herb baskets on the side of the store was cut short a single step in.

Parker grasped the metal in his fist while saying, "You should be careful about making accusations."

Carissa held the pair of scissors against the counter's edge. Her other hand rested on the edge of the cutting board. "Is that a threat?" She laced her words with venom.

He clapped back as if avoiding the bite. "I didn't put any poison in any goblet, Carissa."

Parker tossed the gold so that it landed on the handkerchief. Chaos leaped across the counter to where it had fallen. She pulled at the fingers of Cari's free hand as it tapped against the tempered wood.

Carissa glanced at the nature faerie, who pointed at the gold pieces. The brief sight made it seem like a single curve of gold on the napkin. Carissa had to do a double take. Parker put his hand over the tissue.

"I don't know how the elfkin was killed, but I had no part in it, and, quite frankly, it's slander for you to suggest otherwise."

Elixirs and Elves

He lifted his hand off the gold. Chaos snatched up the pieces, counting. There were still four of them. Parker didn't seem to notice. He was too busy feigning hurt feelings.

"I know you have a low opinion of me, but considering where you're getting your information, it's no wonder your facts are wrong. Personally, I wouldn't trust the source."

Cari raised an eyebrow and put a hand on her hip. "If you're going to make injurious statements against Maren, I think it's best you leave."

"I wasn't talking about Maren. Whatever Cameron Larke has said against me, it's not true."

Carissa held her tongue. Parker strutted out the door. When the sound of the bell faded, Cari walked to the back room. She knocked on the door.

"You can come out now, Maren. He's gone."

She waited. There was no response. Carissa opened the door.

"Maren?"

There was her assistant, happily texting away on her phone. Carissa crossed her arms. Chaos floated past her onto Maren's shoulder. The little faerie made herself comfortable, sitting on Maren's shoulder and looking at the screen of her phone.

"Who are you texting?" Carissa asked.

Maren looked up and then back down. "Huh? Oh, no one. Just Reg."

Carissa and Chaos looked at each other. Maren got up, still looking at her phone, and walked past Carissa.

"You really like him, don't you?" Cari followed her assistant back to the storeroom.

"Who? Oh, he says he's almost here." Maren slipped the phone into her back pocket and finally engaged in conversation with Carissa. "He and Macara are on their way back from Vale."

"How did it go?" Cari came forward, putting both hands on the counter.

145

"Good. Reg says he did something so amazing, but he wouldn't tell me about it over the phone. He wanted to see me in person." Maren's grin reached her ears.

The bell above the door chimed. "What a day!" Reg's voice entered the store before he did.

Carissa walked over to him and Macara. Whatever they had to say, she decided it would be better to hear it without any customers. Since they customarily closed for their lunch break and it was about noon, this was a convenient time to flip the sign to CLOSED. Macara waited for her to turn it and then followed her and Reg back to the counter.

"So?" Maren asked from the counter. Her tone was expectant. "What was this marvelous thing you did?"

"Saving an ankou!" Reg tried to contain his excitement, but it burst right through his teeth. "That's an accomplishment for a day, I'll say."

Carissa's face grew long. Maren propped her elbows on the counter, placing her chin in hands. Her eyes lit up.

"An ankou? What do you mean you saved him—I mean, it?"

Macara looked at Carissa. Her slip up hadn't escaped the Tuatha de Danann's attention, but Macara was already aware of her association with the ankou. She'd helped Alden during his tribulations around All Hallows' Eve.

"The ankou was apparently wandering the mounds of the sidhe last night," Macara said.

"But how did you save him?" Maren asked, with her eyes still entranced by Reginald Smith.

Reg leaned over the counter. "It's simple, the ankou falls under the purview of Manann MacLir. By the sidhe's own laws, if a representative of the Tuatha de Danann is present, they must hand over the ankou to him."

Carissa cringed at the thought of Reg being in charge of Alden's destiny. For that matter, he seemed to be gaining hold of Maren as well.

"Is he all right?" Cari asked.

Elixirs and Elves

Reg puffed his chest as he spoke. "Yes, yes, he's fine. He's off chasing some squirmy spirit who refuses to leave for the afterlife.

"Is MacLir really the same man as the one from legend?" Maren asked.

She and Reg slid farther down the counter. Macara touched Cari's arm, signaling her over to the opposite end.

"He's fine," Macara reassured her.

"It's my fault," Cari said. "I shouldn't have told him that the sidhe may have targeted Jane. I should've known that would cause him to act rashly."

"I wouldn't worry," she said. "No harm is done."

The woman's gaze fell over the goblet pieces sitting on the napkin.

"It's broken," Carissa said. "I've managed to glue two of the pieces together, but the last won't stay on."

"May I?" Macara asked as Parker should have done.

"Yes, please," Cari replied.

Macara reached down and pulled up what Cari thought was two pieces, but were, in fact, fused into one.

Cari's eyes nearly doubled. "How did you do that?"

"I did nothing." She held the cup in one hand while reaching down into the cloth and pulled out the third piece: the base of the cup.

"But it was split in two," Cari said.

Macara smiled. She held the cup and the base together, pinching the broken area with her fingers while holding it straight in her other hand. "You really shouldn't underestimate yourself. You are possibly the most powerful Mossie alive today." Macara's hand came away. The cup stood tall, proud, and in one piece in the center of her palm.

Cari laughed. "That's brilliant! You've fixed it."

Carissa took it, cradling it with her hands and admiring its shine.

"I only spoke the truth."

Cari looked between Macara and the goblet. She set the cup down on the counter. Chaos came over and circled around it a few times.

"Whatever you did," Carissa said, "thank you."

"Is that the goblet MacLir gave you?" Reg's eyes suddenly turned toward something other than Maren.

He bent over the counter, using his index finger to push up his glasses and examine the cup.

"Yes, how do you—" Carissa began to ask how he knew that MacLir had given her such an item, but Reg dove into a lengthy summary of the cup's history.

"The Cup of Life that restored MacAirt's family from the land of the dead: it's a well-known legend. It's also called the Cup of Truth."

"Why is that?" Maren asked.

"Because," Macara replied, "it was designed to protect one from drinking a particular poison—"

"Lies." Reg just couldn't seem to help himself from interrupting. His giddy schoolgirl attitude was contagious—at least to Maren.

"That's so neat, isn't it, Cari?"

The Tuatha de Danann pulled her gloves back on. "We've made your stop, Reginald. Let's not tarry all day."

"Right, okay." Reg and Maren did not break their stares until Cari cleared throat. "All right, well, see you later, Maren, Carissa." He nodded at each of them.

"Take care," Macara said. With her, every greeting and goodbye seemed like a warning.

Carissa swerved around the corner and followed them to the door. She noted that Maren, even though she stood in one place, followed Reg with her eyes. She had a look on her face Cari had seen before, but never this quickly after meeting someone. Macara exited first. Carissa grabbed the arm of Reg's coat before he took a step outside.

"Wha-What are you doing?" Reginald protested.

Elixirs and Elves

"Serious question," Carissa said. She glanced back at Maren, who now dropped the goofy grin and walked around the counter. "Did you put a spell or something on Maren?"

Reg's lips spread wide. "Why? Did she say she's interested?"

Carissa studied Reginald's innocent-looking face. He was odd, but at least he wasn't evil. Maren could do worse. She had done worse, in fact. Twice. Cari let go of the coat.

Carissa relented, a little. Maren had been hurt so often, she hoped this time would be different for her best friend.

"Just be good to her." She drew closer, eyes narrowing. Chaos did the same. "Or you'll have one very angry elf to deal with."

The nature faerie on her shoulder probably made her look less intimidating. Reg's expression flickered between a smile and a frown as if unsure of the seriousness of the threat. With a final gulp and a tug at his collar, he nodded and left.

"What was that all about?" Maren asked, hands on her hips.

"Nothing at all," Carissa said. And as long as Reg was a gentleman, it would stay that way.

***

AT ABOUT 3:30 p.m., after Maren had left for the day and the last half hour of the workday dragged toward the end, a newspaper writer entered the shop looking for a story. Star reporter, Tilly Brier, looked left and right, then marched straight back to where Carissa was packing up the herb baskets to put into the freezer.

"Hello, Carissa," she said in a friendly tone. "Was Parker Greer here earlier, by any chance?"

Carissa let go of the basket and frowned. Turning to face her, Cari smiled without her usual warmth. Tilly seemed immune to the cold. That was true both of her reaction to Cari's attitude and of Tilly's resiliency against the pinkness of the nose and ears that always crept into Carissa's face at such low temperatures. Instead, the reporter's face was beaming with a dazzling smile and a sparkle in her eye.

Since Carissa hadn't answered, Tilly repeated the question. "I'm sorry if I'm interrupting you," her voice was kind and soft, "but I was hoping to get Parker's side of the story."

On top of the good looks, she had to be kind, too. *Dam her*. Cari found her voice. "What story?"

"The pie in the face? You know, Maren Raines and the cheating? Cameron alerted me to the story in our meeting last night."

"Meeting?" Carissa asked. Cari was really going all in on the dumbfounded look.

"Yes," Tilly's eyebrows pulled together, "I'm sorry, I thought you knew since you two are so close."

"Knew what?"

"About him helping me with an investigation into corruption in the business deal with MacLir Industries. Apparently, the project was originally proposed by Parker to MacLir Industries, and the majority of the funds for the project came from the Greer family." Tilly brought her head forward. "Between you and me, I don't think Parker's campaign will be going anywhere, especially when I reveal all the cheating he's been doing—and not just romantically. He's got some financial shadiness he might not want to come to light."

"I see," Carissa whispered. Financial cheating, that meant something, but at this point, Carissa didn't know what. The truth was she was distracted by her own jealousy. She wasn't thinking about Parker as much as she was basking in the knowledge that Tilly and Cam hadn't been on a date last night. Even a workaholic reporter wouldn't refer to a date as a "meeting."

"Well, if you see or hear anything about Parker, let me know." She handed her a business card and waved goodbye.

"Wait," Carissa said, gripping the card between her fingers and staring at the words without reading them. She

Elixirs and Elves

debated whether to ask. Curiosity finally won out. "You and Cameron...you two are just friends?"

Tilly gave her a knowing smile. "He talks about you all the time. I'd say he only has eyes for you."

Carissa could feel her lips curving along the whole width of her face as she watched the reporter exit the shop. Slowly, the smile faded. He only had eyes for Cari. So, why had Carissa been making eyes at someone else all week? She could imagine how Cam must have felt. The question was, how did she feel about Zephyr? She wished she had a simple answer.

Chapter 14

Carol of the Alarm Bells

Carissa nearly dropped her keys while locking up for the day when the shadow of a sidhe guard fell over her.

She rescued the keys mid-air and held them tightly while the honey-sweet voice of the prince drifted through the chilled air.

"I didn't mean to startle you." He bowed. "The guards are overzealous in their duties."

"Zef," she acknowledged the prince.

While she curtsied, Carissa spied the impressive carriage along with three sidhe guards in their red and black uniforms. Zephyr's clothing matched the fitted tunic-style jackets, the straight pants, and the sword at the hilt, but his uniform was crimson, and the buttons were gold. The badge where the rank and name of lower officers were usually indicated was only a symbol of the crown. The mark of royalty was a rank above all of the sidhe in Moss Hill. The prince nodded, permitting Carissa to rise, and graciously offered a hand to bring her to her feet.

Her first thought came tumbling out of her mouth before she'd even stood up. "Did you find out anything about the magic in the elixir?"

"Yes," the prince said, letting go of her hand. "It matched with a Rhys Dwfen, which is why we are here. He was taken into custody in Moss Hill a short while ago." The prince hesitated to add the last part, "I believe you know him."

Elixirs and Elves

"Fudge." Carissa acknowledged. She felt the need to quickly explain. "I don't believe it was him."

The crinkle at the prince's eyes and his raising lips expressed goodwill. "You trust your friends, I know. And I hope you're right, but I must do my duty diligently. I hope you understand that we must have a hearing tomorrow regardless of how we feel about those accused."

"Those?" Carissa picked up on the plural. "Won't Varick be acquitted now that you know the elixir wasn't poisoned?"

The prince mixed a nod with a shake of his head as if agreeing and disagreeing at the same time. "I'm sure he's innocent, but we must rule out any doubt that the killers did not conspire together." He reached a hand to Carissa's arm, assuring her, "The council will be fair."

She was not reassured. The frosty air was getting to her cheeks, and she looked to the building, longing for warmth. Zephyr brought both arms behind his back and faced the building.

"So, this is your pharmacy?"

Carissa brushed back her hair and pointed the keys toward the storefront. "You're welcome to see it inside."

The prince nodded and signaled to his guards to wait outside. Carissa pressed her lips tightly together as she opened the door and flicked on the lights. She had cleaned the counter and shelves at least three times more than usual throughout the day subconsciously, wondering when or if the prince might visit. What must the natural pharmacy have looked like to the prince? Carissa supposed the little shop, with its cute sea-breeze blue storefront, pearl walls, and azure shelves inside, could not compare with anything in Tir-Na-Nog.

"It is lovely," Zephyr said as he circled the shop.

Carissa never wandered through the shelves without purpose before. She felt like a customer browsing. The store took on a winsome character from that perspective. The garland Maren had used on the windows added a cozy feel to it. *It's a little store with a lot of charm*, Cari thought.

Then she spied the paint chipping on the baseboards. Did customers notice that? She made a mental note to talk to Maren later about it.

Zef examined the items on the shelf, remarking, "The items are similar to what I've seen among sidhe and elves."

"As I said they would be," Carissa couldn't help but say.

Zephyr grinned. "Yes, you did. I'm glad to see such similarities in a human town."

The prince finished a round about the quaint shop and meandered back to the entrance. Carissa jingled the keys in her hand, finding the right one. She smiled to herself, pleased that the prince had thought well of the store.

Prince Zephyr held the door open for her and said, "I thought we could see more of the town today. I haven't been here in ages, and I'd like to see how it's changed."

In Zef's case, ages took on new meaning. It might've meant a hundred years.

Carissa locked up while replying, "You're just in time. Actually, I was going to see my neighbor's child and his class caroling tonight at the square. We'd be a little early, but I was planning to stop by the library first anyway."

"Carolers, a marvelous human tradition!" The prince sounded genuinely joyful. "To the square," he said as they entered the carriage.

One of the sidhe guards clicked the door shut behind them. The carriage sped at an incredible rate. Carissa worried this time that more Mossies would be out and about with the celebration at the square.

"I think we're breaking the speed limit," Carissa said with a nervous half-smile.

The prince's face lengthened. "Am I?" He waved his hand and the carriage slowed.

Carissa raised her eyebrows.

"What?" the prince asked, seeing her reaction.

"Nothing. I just always thought the sidhe would be annoyed by anyone altering their magic."

Elixirs and Elves

The prince's ears twitched. "I can understand the confusion. The sidhe magic is often more complex than other species'. They don't like less trained fae to interfere because it can destabilize it."

Cari's face fell, and the prince stammered.

"I didn't mean that about being trained. I know your parents didn't teach you all the skills, but you're still—"

"It's okay," she said. "Enhanced movement is one I happen to know."

The prince looked relieved. Still, Cari had been hurt. She turned her head toward the window. Thirty years old and it was a known fact that she hadn't mastered her magic. That was slow, even for an elf with a longer lifespan.

She couldn't sulk for long. Her ears picked up the sound of a crowd talking and laughing. Singing followed shortly after, but the voices were not in sync. The singers were warming up. The sound restored her good nature.

"Look," Carissa pointed out the children singing in the square beside the tall Christmas tree. Proud parents watched their children run ahead of them into the stands set up by the tree. They checked their recorders for batteries, and some stopped or pointed their cameras to Carissa and Zephyr as they passed by. The fae carriage caught some of the students' eyes and that of the teacher directing them. Carissa recognized Timmy in the front row and waved to the Harbridges as she passed them. Timmy waved back. His mouth stretched wide across his face as he sang.

The carriage moved onward toward the library two streets down. It was far enough away from the event that there were only a few people and plenty of street side parking. It was also close enough to the Moss Hill Hospital for Carissa to recognize a person just exiting the building.

"Wait," she said, pointing across the street from the library. "Would you park there, please?"

The prince didn't hesitate or even ask but signaled the driver with palm held flat against the air. The vehicle came to a halt in front of the Moss Hill Hospital.

155

"What's wrong?" the prince asked as Carissa began opening the door.

"It's the mayor." She looked back at the prince as she hopped down from the carriage. "He's been hurt."

Mayor Belkin came out of the hospital hobbling on crutches with Cameron Larke by his side, looking at his phone. Cari rushed up to them with a questioning look and concerned eyes. Belkin responded before she had even said a word.

"Now, now," the mayor said, "don't look at me like that. I'm fine." He stopped in place, resting on the crutches and holding his hands up to reassure her.

"What happened?" Carissa asked. The prince had approached them. Carissa could see his shadow falling on the ground beside her.

"Just a silly accident." The mayor smoothed his beard with one hand as if embarrassed. "A sprained ankle, that's all."

"He fell down the stairs at City Hall," Cameron said.

His phone made a "sending" sound, and he placed it in his pocket.

"An accident," the mayor repeated.

"The third this week," Cameron firmly stated, "which I don't think are coincidences."

"What other accidents have occurred?" the prince asked before Carissa could.

The mayor responded to Cam instead of either of them. "Cameron, don't make a fuss. I think I know the difference between a little clumsiness and an attack."

"Attacks?" Carissa asked, looking between Belkin and Cam.

"Cam has a notion that someone is still targeting me, but the sidhe have said it's likely I wasn't the target at the dinner. Now he thinks every stubbed toe is an attempt on my life."

"You never stub your toes," Cam said. "You've never been a clumsy one—not before this week."

Mayor Belkin lifted his left crutch and lightly tapped Cam on the shin. "You watch who you're calling clumsy. And

Elixirs and Elves

anyway, it's called age, my boy. I'm not as spry as I used to be."

The mayor set down the crutch and straightened his shirt. A glimmer drew Carissa's eye to the tie pin at his chest. It was a clover, as Jane had mentioned. She was sure it was the one the Everlys had given him.

"I am pleased to see that you're all right," the prince said, but it occurred to Carissa that Mayor Belkin might be far from fine.

She would have said so, except that the mayor interrupted with a hurried tone. "Ugh, here comes the press." The mayor tidied his hair, and Carissa and Cam stepped back.

There was a group of them emerging from a couple directions. Carissa recognized a few of the Moss Hill press, including Tilly.

"Did you send a message to Tilly?" Carissa raised an eyebrow while standing alongside Cam, watching the news folk ambush the mayor and the prince.

"Yes, Carissa, I messaged Tilly, and she showed up a second later." Cam crossed his arms to match his sarcastic tone.

"I'm sorry," she relented. She held her hands together in the chill, trying to warm herself. She didn't know why everything she was saying to Cameron lately just wasn't coming out right. Opting to keep silent a while, Carissa listened to the mayor's and prince's assurances that the investigation on Toffee's death was under control, and that no killer was running amuck around Moss Hill.

Eventually, Cameron turned to her, dropping his arms. "It was Jane on the phone, actually. You might try calling her. She's been messaging me for the last hour since Fudge was arrested. I'm not sure if your boyfriend told you that."

"He's not my—"

Cam's cold-as-winter eyes stopped her. After a moment of silence, she admitted that Zef had told her about Fudge. The look that followed seemed like disappointment as if she should be more upset about the arrest. She was unhappy about it, but she wasn't going to blame Zephyr for doing his job.

Carissa sifted through her purse and retrieved her phone. There were two missed calls and a few texts asking for updates on Varick. She looked up at Cam again, who was now straightening his tie.

"Cam, I—"

"It's fine." He said in a gentle, weary tone. "I've convinced her to come to the singing tonight. Maybe between you and the prince, you can comfort her."

Carissa didn't like the businesslike tone he'd resorted to using with her. A feeling deep at her core told her this wasn't how it was supposed to be between them.

"Tilly told me about your investigation on Parker."

"He's corrupt, Carissa."

"I know, Tilly gave me a synopsis."

She rested a hand on his arm and removed it just as quickly as Cam looked at her. She glanced ever so slightly in the prince's direction. He was telling the Mossies about the Christmas party at Fairfield Castle, urging them all to attend. It didn't look like the interview would end anytime soon.

"I think you're right about Parker," Carissa kept her voice low enough for the reporters not to hear. "I'm not sure that he's the killer, but I think he was involved somehow."

Cam slid his hands into his pockets and smirked. "You do?"

She shook her head and smiled irksomely. He didn't have to look so pleased. But convincing one person he was right was a win for him, she supposed.

"Yes, I do," she continued. "I'm not sure about it, and I don't want to implicate the Everlys. I can't imagine how Jane must already feel, but I do know that Parker made a comment to Fudge about the tie pin at the party. When the sprites were playing around the tree and spreading faerie dust all over, Parker told Fudge he ought to put a protection spell on the pin. Jane said it was a good luck charm that Mrs. Morgan had used magic on years ago. If there was already magic on it…."

Elixirs and Elves

Cam's eyes lit up. He took his hands out of his pockets and ran them through his hair. "Fudge might've messed up the charm. But would that create an opposite effect? Bad luck instead of good?"

"I don't know." Carissa brought a hand to her chin.

Cam made another good point. "If it did mess up the magic on the pin, why wouldn't Fudge have known that could happen?"

Cari was ashamed to admit that she didn't know it could happen. She hadn't known that more complicated magic could react so severely with less skilled powers. She had so little knowledge of magic, it didn't occur to her until now that a protection spell could destabilize existing magic. Fudge left his people when he was a young man to come to Moss Hill. If he were anything like Carissa, maybe he wouldn't have known either, solely because he didn't understand all the properties of magic.

"And I assure you, everything is in line for a very happy Christmas," the mayor was saying.

Cameron said, "All right, I'll get the tie pin from the mayor. This would be easier if we had Varick, but I'll try to get one of the lower ranking sidhe or elf guards to test it for unstable magic. If we're wrong, it won't even get to the court. If we're right...."

"It'll at least prove a connection to Parker. But how will you get a guard to test it? Shouldn't I do that?" Carissa raised a skeptical eyebrow.

Cam straightened. "I'm the ambassador to Vale, Cari. I do have some connections."

Carissa nodded, impressed. "I don't doubt that you do."

He paused, looking into her eyes. His weren't the prince's ocean blues, but those cognac eyes were intoxicating. A moment passed between them, and she felt...right.

A few flashes from cameras and the interview was done. Cam and Carissa rejoined the mayor and the prince. The mayor insisted on watching the carolers and giving his yearly

159

speech of warm winter wishes, even if it was at the end of the show instead of the beginning.

They parted ways as Cari and the prince went to gather Nan from the library. Nan bowed low this time when they entered and walked to the front desk. She conversed easily with the prince as they walked out of the library and down the street, asking about how he and his parents were doing and what their plans were for the rest of their stay in Moss Hill. Carissa knew Nan was making an effort to get to know the prince, and she appreciated it. Yet, when they entered the square, Carissa found her eyes sweeping the crowd for Cameron every now and again. It wasn't fair to Prince Zephyr. He fit well with Cari's parents' expectations, the king and queen approved, and even Carissa had thought it might be the right choice. But, if Nan was right, Zef didn't belong at the heart of Cari's affections. That space, Cari was beginning to realize, might belong to Cam.

***

AT HOME THAT EVENING, Carissa was determined to confront Nan about her strange behavior with the prince the previous evening. She fully expected Nan to feign a headache or to invent some critical task that required her immediate attention. This time, however, she would not allow her grandmother to squirrel out of the conversation.

There were no nature faeries around to distract them since they were all still out with Maren and Reginald. Nan went straight to the sitting room and lit the fireplace, choosing a novel from the bookcase to pass the rest of the evening. Carissa set down her keys and purse on the end table beside the sofa and crossed her arms.

"Tea would be nice," Nan said. "Maybe some peppermint."

Nan came away from the shelf having selected a mystery novel. She ambled to the couch. Her glasses slid down the bridge of her nose as she opened the book and began reading.

Elixirs and Elves

She didn't seem to notice that her granddaughter lingered in the foyer instead of getting the suggested drink.

Carissa opened her mouth, but before she could say anything, Nan piped up.

"If you're going to start a conversation annoyed, you're most likely going to end it being angry."

She looked up at Carissa. Cari let her arms drop and walked to the sofa chair near her grandmother.

"I'm just trying to understand. I've been trying to make sense of what happened last night when Zef gave you that gift. You left me to wonder about it all day since you weren't inclined to come out of your room this morning for breakfast. That isn't like you, Nan. What's going on?"

Nan set the book on the coffee table. Turning to her granddaughter, Nan took both of Cari's hands into her own.

"You've heard the stories about the first mayor of Moss Hill, who created the treaty between the people of Vale and us."

Carissa nodded. Nan tightened her grip on her fingers and pursed her lips. It was as if she had locked in the words and was now struggling to release them into the air. Finally, her grip relaxed.

"That mayor was your grandfather."

"My grand...," Carissa felt out of breath, "but that was well over two hundred years ago!" Carissa's mind raced. The math didn't add up. The first mayor must've been in his forties, at least, at the time the contract was made, and even if he lived to a ripe old age after that, he would've been well over a hundred by the time Nan was born. The math did not add up.

Nan let go of her hand. The truth rushed out of her. "Yes, well, that would be because your grandfather was 120 years old when I was twenty. Believe me, I know how strange that sounds, but keep in mind that the lifespan of a fae is different than that of a human."

"You mean, my grandfather was an elf?"

161

Nan's eyes skirted the baseboards of the walls. She met Cari's eye for a second here and there.

"Not an elf," Nan said.

"A sidhe?"

Her grandmother tilted her head as if wriggling out of the question.

"Then what?" Carissa threw up her hands in frustration.

Nan closed her eyes and sighed, touching a hand to her temple.

"He wasn't fully fae. In many ways, he was like many of the residents of Moss Hill, with faerie blood from generations before him."

"If that were true, then the magic would have faded, and he'd have a regular lifespan like the rest of Moss Hill." Cari crossed her arms.

Emotion rippled across Nan's face. "He was a descendant of a Tuatha De Danann."

Cari's bottom lip dropped and hung there for what seemed like forever. She stood up reflexively.

"Which one?" she finally asked.

"One that was at one time loved and later feared by humans—and for very, very good reasons."

"Who?" The impatience in Cari's voice was growing.

After a full minute of sitting in silence, and Cari staring at her without budging, Nan resolved some inner battle and looked up at her granddaughter.

"Queen Maeve."

But Carissa hadn't heard of the person before. She wondered why she'd even asked. She knew very few of the Tuatha de Danann. Nan knew more, she suspected, but she was too distraught by the conversation to recount the history now.

"There's a reason we don't teach much of the legends here on Moss Hill. This was supposed to be a sanctuary for the fae and fae-touched—those humans with faerie ancestry who didn't want to be part of the problems of the world. But

Elixirs and Elves

it seems no matter what we do, we can't escape the lands outside."

Carissa wasn't sure she could take a history lesson right now anyway. She paced the room.

"Then my mother, she'll live to be as old as my dad?"

"Quite possibly. She would have some of her father's magic, I'm sure. It's why she fits in so well in the fae world. Her father taught her some about the fae magic, but she was fairly headstrong as a child. How he complained about her inability to sit through the lessons!" Nan laughed.

"So, my mother has powers?"

Nan shrugged. "Some, I think. Less than he did. But I honestly don't know that much about it. They didn't share much with me about the training. The fae of Vale were less inviting to humans in my time, and I wasn't interested in knowing about that world."

"But you married a Tuatha de Danann."

Cari felt like pointing out the contradiction. She wasn't usually one to talk back, but her words had a bite to them now. She couldn't help but feel a little angry that Nan hadn't shared this with her before. Even her mother had never said a word about it.

Nan defended herself with a fiery voice. "I married a human with fae in his family line. He was a Mossie, through and through, and did much for this town. When O'Brien took over after him, he called him the greatest mayor a town could ever have."

Cari heard the ire in Nan's voice and backed down, accepting her logic.

She continued her pacing. The lights of the Christmas tree helped calm her mind, but the back and forth was making her feel sick. Or maybe it was all the information being stuffed into her brain.

"Wait," Cari stopped, too fast. She felt a bit dizzy. "That still doesn't add up. We just celebrated your 80th birthday in April."

Nan cleared her throat. Sheepishly, she admitted. "Actually, it was my 180th birthday."

Carissa fell back into the sofa chair, too exhausted to stand anymore.

"So, you're fae too?" she asked.

"No." Nan looked up. Her eyes drifted, reminiscing. "I wasn't from the island at all. I didn't know anything about faeries, except that they were tales told to children. I'd come here to be a governess to a wealthy family. I didn't realize at the time that the O'Briens were connected with the fae."

"You raised Mr. O'Brien? Or—wait, no, don't tell me, it was his father?"

"Grandfather and great-aunt. The two were the best children on the island."

"So you were human?"

"I am human. I just have an extended lifespan."

Carissa put a hand to her head. She rubbed her temple. "You took an elixir," she said the realization aloud.

"And then your grandfather died instead of me." Nan laughed. "Fate is funny like that."

Carissa leaned forward, putting a hand on her grandmother's knee. "How did he die?"

Nan patted Carissa's hand and gave a smile to show she was all right. Carissa could see through that look a little better now.

"He was ill. You were little, but I think you might remember."

"You said it was the flu," Carissa replied.

Nan rested her elbow on the arm of the couch and brought her hand to her forehead.

"He had walking pneumonia for weeks without realizing it. He was very driven, much like you." She smiled sadly. "He felt himself slowing down, but by the time he realized it was pneumonia, he had already contracted a particularly nasty strain of the flu. It was too much for him to take."

A descendant of the Tuatha de Danann brought down by illness sounded suspect to Carissa. She wanted to debate it,

Elixirs and Elves

but her grandmother was on the verge of tears. She seemed to believe what she'd said. Carissa wouldn't push her further at the moment. She only had one last question, since her nan had never specified the fact before.

"How old was he when he died?"

"Almost exactly 225 years." Nan took a sharp breath and rose from the sofa.

Cari could see she was fighting back a flood. Her eyes were shining, though Nan tried to brush it off with a smile. Looking toward the kitchen, Nan circumvented the coffee table.

"I think that tea is in order. What do you say, Carissa?"

Carissa sat there, looking out the open curtain to the cold street. Two houses down across the street, the Harbridge's car pulled into their driveway. Life went on, it seemed. Cari's world, already mysterious as it was with fae and humans living together on this strange out-of-the-way island, had changed.

She got up and put on the kettle, musing as she did. She'd always known that the fae had secrets. Her father had his elf-magic, which he'd never thoroughly taught her to properly use. But her mother and grandmother had never been a mystery to Cari. Nan didn't care much for fae magic, which might have rubbed off on her mother, because she never used it at all. At least, she didn't use it around Carissa. It suddenly dawned on her that her father might not have taught her to use her elf-light because her magic was different than that of a typical elf. If she had any of the Tuatha de Danann magic, then her powers wouldn't work precisely in the same way as any of the elves of Vale. Maybe her mother hadn't taught her for the same reason, because her powers wouldn't work the same as her mother's either.

A troubling thought occurred to her next. What if her father had deliberately not taught her the elf-light because he distrusted her power? Did Carissa's mother also hide her magic out of fear? If this Queen Maeve really was a force that humans had come to dread, then her father might've thought it best that Cari did not learn to control her powers so she would not become anything like her ancestor. She needed to find out more about the legend.

Chapter 15

Redwood and Evergreen Lies

On the top of the tallest tree in the Vale woods, the chamber of the Sidhe Council loomed over the fae village. Carissa trudged up the multitude of steps, breathtaking both in beauty and in rigor, until she was on the final floor. Outside the council room, a crowd of sidhe and elves had already gathered for the trial.

She spied Jane in a corner of the waiting area. Cameron stood between Jane and the sidhe with the air of an older brother. Alden would've been relieved to see his old friend watching out for his sister. But the fact that he was there meant that he must've found something of value to the sidhe. Then Jane saw the mayor was there, too. He was still on crutches and speaking with Head Elf Rolin.

She almost wondered if she'd come to the right place. Humans were here in the redwood, she never thought she'd see the day. She wanted to ask Cameron what he'd found, but the council doors opened just seconds after she'd set foot on the top floor of the redwood. If it hadn't been for Chaos being up half the night with a stomach ache, Carissa might've arrived much earlier. Reg and Maren had allowed her too many sweets at the square, but that was a problem she would confront Maren about later.

Carissa had been in the council hall once before, but she noticed the astonished faces of her human friends as they entered. There was no ceiling, but the space was warm. The leaves in the distance proved that they were on a flattened branch. Instead, it was a fusion of branches between several trees. The last time Carissa was here, it had been night, and she hadn't realized that the great redwood of the sidhe people was actually multiple redwoods fused together into one through faerie magic. What made it even more impressive was that at the very top of the tree, there was no layer of snow. The weather seemed to happen around the tree but not on it.

The area appeared to be a small amphitheater. The sidhe took their places at the top row of seats. The lower rows were reserved for witnesses and spectators. The fae royalty took a spot front and center in the bottom row.

Carissa felt strange taking a place between the members of the Elven Council and the Queen of Sidhe and Elves. Prince Zephyr sat on the other side of the king. It may have been too presumptive to place Cari beside Zephyr, given that she was not engaged to the prince. They seated Reginald next to the prince instead. Being a servant of the Tuatha de Danann apparently placed him on a status high enough to sit with the royals.

Led by a sidhe guard of lower status than himself, Varick entered from a small door to the side of the room. Carissa hadn't noticed that entrance before. Varick's hands curled into fists. His wrists were bound in silver cuffs. A solitary bench, halfway encircled by guards, awaited him. He walked with his chin up, though his eyes did not raise from the floor. When he took his seat, he did so with his back straight and his head held high.

Fudge managed the same proud demeanor, except for his eyes, which shifted more than once across the crowd. That would not bode well for him. The sidhe took everything, including body language, as testimony.

Since Carissa Shae was a descendant of the Tuatha de Danann, or possibly due to her recent closeness to the royal family, Cari was called to speak first. Carissa kept herself very still as she spoke; she dare not give them a reason to suspect her words to be untruthful. They questioned her on her conversation with Varick, which she recounted—minus the

Elixirs and Elves

information about Jane. She recounted precisely as much detail as she safely could. This made for a speech.

"Carissa Shae," the eldest asked when she was done, "I must note that you have not told us the full truth."

His voice crackled like thunder. Cari felt struck. Her elf-light crackled at her palms. She squeezed them and concentrated on calming her heartbeats.

The elder continued, "You have not told us that Varick divulged the name of both the maker of the vial and the recipient for whom it was intended."

Carissa stifled a gasp. Had the prince overhead them? Would he betray her like that? Carissa would've looked at the prince but couldn't risk it when they already doubted her. With her elf-light already swirling within her chest, she didn't want to risk dishonesty.

Tiache spoke in her silence. "I have already told the council that I made the elixir. Do you deny that Varick told you this?"

This was a losing situation. If Carissa answered with a "yes," the sidhe would believe she had been lying. If she said "no," it might prove she was keeping the truth from them.

"I apologize, honored councilors, I had assumed that the council knew this and did not go into enough detail."

"Then do so now," the eldest said. "For whom was the vial made?"

Carissa could not afford to hesitate or think about it. Regrettably, she had to say what she knew. But Carissa's grandmother had taken an elixir before. The admission didn't expose Jane as a druidess. She made the admission.

"Respected elder, it was Jane Everly."

A grunt came from the stands to her left, but she couldn't see who had made the sound. It might've been approval or indignation. She couldn't tell which.

"Enough," said the eldest of the sidhe, sitting in the middle of the panel. "Your testimony has been heard. Be seated."

Astoria Wright

They hadn't asked her anything about the night of Toffee's death. Carissa had almost raised an eyebrow but caught herself. She bowed and left the center spot to take her place on the stands. Once the spotlight was off of her, Carissa couldn't help but bite the inside of her cheek and wonder about why she'd been dismissed so easily. As it turned out, several of the witnesses were easily excused.

Perhaps the sidhe realized the trial was a formality and were speeding things along? She wanted to think that. The first person to be questioned at length, surprisingly, was Sal. Poor Sal couldn't help but show some of his nervousness, though he was clearly trying not to move. He stood before them, still as a statue with his hands to his sides as if someone had tied a rope around him and propped him up on a spike.

"Recount for us the night of Toffee's death. Leave out no detail," the eldest sidhe commanded. Carissa took that as a direct insult to her.

"Your Excellencies, we were in the kitchen."

"No," the eldest held a hand up. "The whole night—from your arrival to your departure."

Sal spoke slowly and seemed to be trying to recount every detail he could remember. He recalled his early arrival with the Everlys and greeting guests with the appetizer tray. Carissa didn't see the point of making him go through such a lengthy recollection, except to cause him visible anxiety. At one point, Sal wiped his brow with the back of his hand.

As Cari predicted, there was no information she thought was relevant until Sal came to the same point where he'd initially begun.

"We were in the kitchen," he said, "me and Toffee and Fudge, and we were preparing the food. The sidhe guard, Varick, sir, he came in to speak with Fudge, and he gave him the vial, which we both saw. Toffee asked him what it was, to which Fudge said he should keep to himself."

Sal's eyes darted around the room. Carissa was sure Head Elf Rolin would have counseled Sal against such actions,

Elixirs and Elves

but he seemed oblivious to the rules of conduct. It felt like torture for Sal to have to speak for so long.

"Then," Sal said, "a guest came in asking a question about the tree lights that had gone out on account of the sprites and Fudge left to take care of it. Toffee and I stayed behind in the kitchen. Fudge came back into the kitchen a while later. He and Toffee were, I think, tending to the food, but they got into some type of argument. Fudge went off and left the vial there and Toffee, well, he…."

Sal paused, wiping his brow again.

"You will continue," the sidhe elder ordered.

Sal tugged at his collar. "Well, I don't really know, I guess he must've been curious about the vial because I saw him pouring it into a glass."

Immortality was a temptation to anyone, but from what Prince Zephyr had told her about Toffee, it wasn't a temptation for him. If he knew what it was, he would more likely have poured the glass into a cup for someone else rather than himself. How he'd come to drink the elixir himself still seemed like a mystery.

But Sal's testimony concluded, and still, there was no explanation of it. The sidhe called their next witness.

"Bring out the human called Cameron Larke," the eldest sidhe commanded.

Cameron Larke was brought to the center of the court. Cam bowed. Carissa had only been to a sidhe trial once before, and there had been no humans or spectators. This whole procedure was unusual from what she understood of the sidhe. Perhaps because she thought of the trial being odd, she noticed movement to her right. The prince gave a subtle nod. Once she witnessed that, she began noticing other things, too. Carissa had assumed Zephyr could not see the elders from his seat, but he held a mirror-like object in his hand. She'd seen it when she was being questioned. It reflected light with the same color as the elders had from their seats. He was directing the trial through the use of this device. She understood more and more with passing years why the fae rejected technology. They had a magic of their own.

The eldest began with Cameron. He did not address Cam by name. His voice carried the subtle tone of disgust.

"You alerted the sidhe to a series of accidents occurring to the mayor in the last few days. Answer in detail," the eldest implored.

Carissa was convinced the part about details was only added as a rib against herself. She ignored it and watched Cameron, impressed by his composure. Cameron kept an even tone. Even though he looked slightly downward at the ground instead of looking directly at the council, he also kept his back straight and his chin up. He had nothing to fear, having done nothing wrong, but the sidhe were always intimidating.

"I did, Your Honor. It was the Everlys' gift of a good luck charm embedded in a tie pin. Miss Morgan had blessed it for the family long before her death."

"And what bearing does this gift have on the death of Toffee?"

"Sir, the mayor's luck since receiving the pin has been opposite of what the magic had intended, which is why I brought it to the elf council, who tested the item for its magic."

"And what was the discovery?" the eldest acted as if he wanted this part of the trial to be over as soon as possible.

"It had been magically tampered with, sir."

Elder Tiache spoke in Cam's place, "Let it be known that the sidhe have discovered magic in the pin not belonging to the Tuatha De Danann. It was the magic of a Rhys Dwfen—of the Faeries of the Deep Rhys."

The announcement itself hadn't surprised Carissa. If they had let her speak, she could have told them that it was not Fudge, but Parker who'd told the elfkin to use his magic. *Maybe the next witness will clarify*, Carissa thought upon seeing that they had called on the accused himself: Fudge.

Chapter 16

The Gift of Truth

Fudge stepped to the center of the room. Unlike Sal, he was measured and calm in their presence. He bowed to them deeply.

The eldest spoke, "Tell us of the events immediately preceding Toffee's death."

Carissa wondered why they hadn't allowed Sal to do the same. The only thing she could think of was that they knew Sal was an innocent. As an unbiased witness and the one, aside from Fudge, who had been closest to Toffee all night, he could recall events with impartiality. At least, Carissa hoped that was the rationale for their logic.

"Elder ones," Fudge said in a brazen voice, "I do not dispute what Sal has told you. I admit that I used magic on the vial only to add a protective charm to it. One of the humans at the party suggested that I ought to add a protection to the charm of luck they'd purchased for the mayor. Given all that has happened in Moss Hill, I thought it a good idea. Later, it occurred to me that the same should be done for the elixir. If you examine the magic, you will see that it's a protective spell and nothing more. I do not believe it could've caused anyone's death."

"And did you persuade Toffee to drink the vial?"

"No, elder one, I did not."

"Who was the human who suggested you add this protective charm?"

Fudge did not hesitate. "Parker Greer, sir."

"Is he a druid?" the eldest asked. His tone spoke of genuine curiosity.

"To my knowledge, he is not."

"And did he tell you to use this magic on the vial?"

"No, that idea was mine alone."

Carissa had never seen someone look so defeated. The longer she looked at him, the more she noted little things, such as his sunken eyes and messy hair. He seemed like one who had not slept for days.

Tiache spoke next. "Are you aware of the ingredients of an elixir of immortality?"

"Veritable one, I am unfamiliar with it."

"You admit you used magic on a substance which you did not fully understand. Do you realize how dangerous it is to do so?"

The slightest crease appeared in Fudge's eyebrow. "No, I do not know of any danger, unless…."

Elder Tiache's voice boomed at an unexpected volume, "Unless it contained one of the sacred herbs."

The revelation was striking. Carissa knew immediately what he'd meant: the mistletoe. It was a sacred herb because of its potency with magic. But, the magical properties in the sacred herbs were challenging to master. Enhancing the magic or changing it in any way might cause an unpredictable reaction.

Tiache continued, "Both the Morrigan's charm and the elixir contained mistletoe and both were made unstable by the use of your magic. The tie pin's magic involved the use of the sacred herb to a much lesser extent, which is why it was not lethal."

"If I had known," Fudge began.

He restarted, realizing that he hadn't addressed them adequately.

"Esteemed elders, I did not know that the magical items contained mistletoe. If I had, I would not have used my magic."

Elixirs and Elves

"What kind of fae does not know mistletoe magic when he sees it?" one of the elder's voices rang out.

"Elder one, I...I," he stammered, "I know these things are well known among my people, but I am not a skilled Rhys Dwfen. It's one of the reasons I left the island. I was never good with magic."

Carissa suspected as much. Her heart sank for him. She could relate. He shouldn't have to pay for not being well trained with magic. Surely the elders knew that meant that Toffee's death might just have been a terrible accident. They couldn't punish Fudge for that, could they? In Cari's mind, this meant the trial was over, but the sidhe never seemed to think the same way as an elf.

"We have one more witness to call." The eldest excused Fudge and asked for the next witness to come forth: Jane.

"You are the daughter of Arin Everly, formerly Arin MacAirt?" the eldest asked.

"Yes, sir, I am," Jane said.

She was by far the most collected of all of them. Although she was clearly sad, her soft-spoken voice was powerful in its clarity. It seemed to hush even the rustling of leaves, and the sidhe listened more deeply to her words because of it.

"And you are a druidess in training?"

The question shocked Cari so that she had to keep her elf-light at bay. Her heart was pounding out of her chest, but Jane remained unscathed.

"Yes, sir," she said simply.

Tiache intervened. "And do you swear your allegiance to the king and queen, and to use your powers solely in protection of the people of Vale?"

This was the crux of it, Cari realized. Bringing her to this trial may have all been a pretense. Tiache brought himself forward in his chair. All the sidhe seemed interested in her answer. They had called her here solely for the reason of her declaring her allegiance.

"Wise one," Jane said, "I swear that no harm will come to Vale or Moss Hill by my hand."

"Do you swear allegiance to the king?" Anger seeped into his tone.

Jane broke protocol completely by turning to face King Finvarra. She addressed him directly.

"Your Majesty, I am loyal to the Morrigan. By order of the Tuatha de Danann, I am to swear my allegiance only to her. I seek your counsel now in front of the assembly: Do you wish me to break my vow?"

The hint of a smile appeared on the king's face. He nodded. "Your answer will pass."

The prince intervened. "Place your hands on the book of promises."

A sidhe guard walked up to her with a sizeable leathery tome in both hands. He stood beside Jane, and she turned and set both palms on the top of the book.

"Repeat your oath both to the Morrigan and to the island."

"I swear allegiance to the Morrigan sisters, Macha and Babd Catha. By this allegiance, I swear no harm will come to Moss Hill or Vale by my hand."

Carissa found it interesting that Jane twice had avoided the oath of protecting the island. She was still avoiding the responsibility of being the island's protector.

Upon taking the oath, Jane's hands glowed green. The hue spread over the book as if surrounding it. The Book of Oaths had recorded her words. She was now bound by magic not to break it.

"Wait," Prince Zephyr said before the book was taken away again.

To Carissa's surprise, the prince rose and placed his own hand on the Book of Oaths.

"I swear before the Councils of Elves and Sidhe of Vale that I, and through me, my people shall protect the lady Jane of Moss Hill from harm now and in the future. So long as she abides by her oath, I shall abide by mine."

He lifted his hands. Again, the words were inscribed. Carissa understood. This wasn't about whether he'd betrayed

Elixirs and Elves

her trust by eavesdropping or withholding information, or whether he was controlling the trial or anything that she'd imagined he'd done. This was about uniting Moss Hill and Vale. Everything Varick had worried about was out in the open, and the people were bound to protect the woman he loved. Now, even if someone conspired against Jane, she'd have an army of sidhe protecting her.

The eldest concluded, "The truth aligns with all testimony presented here today. The magistrate will deliberate with the council. You may return to your homes."

The elders rose, and bows were exchanged all around. It appeared to be over. After all of this, Carissa was reasonably convinced that they would rule Toffee's death an accident.

Chapter 17

The Magic of Christmas

Reginald Smith arrived in the apothecary shop bearing flowers. He held a ring of freshly picked fairy primrose to encircle the heart of his fair maiden. Maren seemed to be captured by offering. She held the flowers in her hands and breathed in deeply. Carissa brought a hand to her chin and watched the exchange.

"What's the occasion?" Maren asked.

Carissa stifled a sarcastic laugh. Maren was determined to make him express his affection aloud. It was so like her.

But Reg wasn't professing his love just yet. "You'll be happy to know that the sidhe have found Varick and Fudge not guilty. They have stripped Fudge of his magic temporarily for reckless use, but overall, they agreed it was an accident."

"That's wonderful news," Carissa said.

Maren either didn't hear or didn't care. Her mind was in the flowers.

"Aren't these lovely?" Maren held them up so Cari could see.

"Absolutely," Carissa approved, giving a thumbs up.

"I wasn't sure what type was your favorite," Reg removed his gloves and hat as he spoke, "but the druids consider these sacred. They're said to cure many ailments, which I'm sure you know, Carissa. But most importantly, they're said to protect one from evil."

Reg was a wealth of knowledge. He continued.

Elixirs and Elves

"Supposedly, the primrose is abundant in Tir-Na-Nog. I guess I'll be finding that out for myself soon."

"When do you leave?" Maren asked.

"Christmas morning."

Maren frowned. "Not Christmas! That's not a day to spend traveling."

"Actually, it's the perfect day," Reginald said. "There aren't many people on the water that day, and the mists aren't likely to cause much harm. No one will see us traveling the sea to the secret island."

"I suppose you won't return to Moss Hill for a long time."

Maren sounded miserable at the thought. She had always been quick to form attachments, but Carissa was surprised at how deeply this one had seemed to develop in so short a time. She patted Maren's back.

"I'm sure it won't be long. He's MacLir's right-hand man, so he'll likely visit often."

Reginald nodded. "Actually, I think that I will. This island may not be Hy Brasil, but it's possibly even more important than that."

"How so?" Carissa raised an eyebrow.

"Well," Reg pulled at the collar of his shirt as if suddenly warm, "because, well, it's the home of someone who is becoming quite special to me."

He changed shade so that Carissa had to admit the possibility that pink was a viable color for human skin. Maren's smile grew at the display. Carissa's didn't find it flattering as much as embarrassing, but she supposed it showed how deeply Reginald felt his affection. Reg straightened himself out.

"Moss Hill is important to MacLir, you know. It's the first experiment testing whether humans and fae can live together in harmony."

"Yes, but all of us Mossies are part fae somehow," Carissa pointed out.

"Are we?" Maren asked. "I don't think my family has ever had any faerie blood."

"You must have had some going far back," Reg said. "That was intentional. When the original mayor had the idea, there were mostly fae living here already. When more and more humans left these islands, and the government decided that all the residents would relocate and abandon the island, the mayor at the time, who was part fae himself, decided to appeal to the sidhe and elves here to open more of the island to the humans. They did not agree at first. As a compromise, the residents with fae blood were allowed to stay, and anyone else with fae heritage was also allowed to move here."

"The tourism," Carissa realized, "it's a next step in the experiment."

"Yes, it was. Only, if the fae had known that the unseelie had discovered the island, they may have reconsidered that plan."

Carissa looked down. If she'd been open with the sidhe about Raven Corvus's note from the very start, that's what Reg meant. Whether he knew about it or not, it hurt to hear it.

"Anyway, that's not why I came here today." He pushed up his glasses. "Maren, I was hoping you'd agree to accompany me to the Vale party on Christmas Eve. What do you say?"

"Yes," Maren replied in a high-pitched squeal, nodding eagerly.

Reg's face lit up like a kid on Christmas. It made Cari smile, too.

"And no worries about your offering to the king and queen, I've got a gift that will cover us both."

Maren didn't know what he meant. "Were we supposed to bring gifts?"

"Only those in the official dinner," Reg explained. "The whole of Moss Hill is invited to celebrate at the castle, but only the king's guests will join him inside the grand hall for the dinner."

"Speaking of which," Carissa frowned, "I still need a gift. Mum and Dad said it needs to be of special magical value."

Elixirs and Elves

She thought of the sprig of a magic dragon-blood tree from the faeries of Socotra that her parents would be giving. "I don't have anything so valuable," she added.

"Sure you do. You had a goblet here of incredible value. I saw it just the other day. Wasn't it yours?"

"That was given to me by MacLir. I can't regift it. He'll be insulted."

Reg waved a palm. "Not at all, he gave you the use of it and you saw the best use as being in the possession of your king. You're not throwing it away."

"But then the gift would be from MacLir, not from me."

Reg picked up his gloves. "The fae don't see regifting the same way as humans. It makes the magic stronger to have more people caring for it over time. The older and more well-loved a magical object is, the greater its sentimental value. And having one is a temptation to most, so giving up an object of magical power is not an empty gesture."

Carissa thought about that a moment. "So, the Everlys gave the use of the goblet to me?"

"They gave up their right to it. That is a gift to you, and it technically means you owe them or that they were showing gratitude for something you'd already done."

"They never said anything to me about the goblet," Carissa said, almost to herself. She might owe them thanks.

"Since they were the previous receivers of the gift, it should've been obvious."

A chime at the door told them that someone new had entered the shop. All three of their heads turned to see Alden marching straight from the entrance to the back counter. He didn't seem happy.

"You," he pointed at Reginald, "you sent me to Greenland in an alternate dimension! I had to figure out where I was before I could come back. I don't think I would've managed it without Chaos's help."

Carissa noticed Chaos on Alden's shoulder, wagging a disapproving finger in Reg's direction.

"I, well, I...I was sure I had the spell right, it was supposed to send you back to Moss Hill." He scratched his head. "I'm sorry. I'm new at magic."

"Don't use magic on me ever again," Alden warned.

To see his face shift between human and ankou while he was pointing an accusatory finger at someone was a terrifying sight. Reg's face drained of color, and Maren's shock was palpable. "Wha-what kind of druid are you?" Maren asked.

"Alden," Carissa used a commanding tone, "you're scaring them. Shift back."

He became human again. Maren regained enough sense to start piecing things together.

"You're not a druid at all, are you?" she asked.

Alden ignored the question and walked up to the counter, smoothing out a piece of paper.

"Before you sent me to the middle of nowhere, I managed to snag this from Tiache's chambers in the sidhe mounds."

Reginald used his index finger to push the bridge of his glasses up his nose. Then, he bent over the parchment. Maren leaned over him too, but the sidhe script was one that she couldn't have understood.

"I'm still learning all the symbols," Reg said. "I think this one says *soup* or something liked that."

"Here," Carissa reached a hand outward. "Give it to me, I can read it."

Reg handed her the parchment and Maren continued to look at it, over her shoulder this time. Chaos flew to her too, also peering at the paper as if she could read.

"It's the recipe for the elixir of immortality," Carissa said. She pointed to a long list of words. "These are ingredients. But, it's a lot more than what Varick purchased from me." She scanned the directions. "It looks like an involved process."

"What's that?" Maren pointed to a word in the ingredient list with a line crossing it out.

"Holly berry extract," Carissa said.

"Why would it be crossed out?" Reg asked.

Elixirs and Elves

"Because he left it out, to sabotage the elixir," Alden said.

Carissa dropped her hand to give him a look. "We don't know that. There could be any number of reasons for crossing out ingredients."

Maren shrugged. "We do it all the time in cooking. There are many different recipes for the same thing."

"It's more than that." Alden grabbed the paper. "There's a whole line crossed out here about how to mix in the holly berry."

"I hope not," Maren said. "Holly berries are poisonous."

"If ingested, but this part of the recipe isn't about the actual contents of the elixir." Cari set the paper in the middle of the counter so they could all have a look. Pointing to the top, she said, "This part is about the ingredients that go in the elixir, and this part," she slid her finger down the parchment, "is what is needed for the spell."

"What about this?" Reg pointed in the margins.

Carissa squinted at the tiny text. Alden said it before she could make the words out.

"It's a note about the holly: still stable without the protective element."

"That is something," Carissa admitted.

"So," Reg said, "if Tiache removed the holly from the spell, the elixir was still stable enough to put in the drink, but what does that prove?"

"Maybe that he conspired with Parker to get Fudge to use his magic on it, and without holly, it would destabilize?"

Carissa and Alden both looked sharply at Maren. Her tone was downright vindictive, but she did have a point.

"It's a bit of a leap in logic. It could mean any number of things."

"I could ask Macara," Reg offered, reaching for the paper. "She'd know for certain."

Carissa looked at Alden, who nodded. She rolled up the parchment and handed it to him.

"The ankou!" Maren suddenly burst out as if it had taken all this time for her to realize it. "That's who you are! The skeleton face—it's so obvious!" She pointed at Carissa. "You knew he was the ankou this whole time and you didn't tell me!"

"Maren, I didn't want to scare you." Carissa tried to shrug like it wasn't a big deal.

Maren pinched her arm. Carissa swore she twisted her thumb so it would burn, too. While she let out a yelp, Maren reprimanded her. "Best friends don't keep secrets like that from each other."

"I'm not going to harm you," Alden tried to pacify her.

Maren shook her head. "That's not the point—it's the lying."

All three of them shared glances with each other. Most people would find the ankou himself the big deal. Maren saw the secret itself as the problem.

"I'm sorry, Maren. I should've told you."

Maren nodded by way of accepting Cari's apology, but the cold shoulder silence said she was still feeling hurt.

"Well, I'll let you know what Macara says about this." Reg slid on his gloves and picked up his hat.

"Wait, I'll come with you," Maren said, turning the corner into the back room.

Carissa bit her lip. Maren really was upset. She had never just left the store during her shift before. If only Maren could understand that she hadn't told her in order to protect her. Maren could get caught up in the mysteries a little too easily. With her tendency to let secrets slip, knowledge like this might put her in real danger.

***

WHEN REGINALD AND Maren left the shop, Carissa noted that Chaos was strangely absent. She and Alden went to the back room looking for the sprite. When she finally called out to her, Carissa found her at the computer. Chaos, oblivious to Cari's presence, kept hopping on the keyboard as if she could type.

Elixirs and Elves

The sound of the door meant Carissa was needed back in the shop, and the store quickly filled with the morning rush of customers. She was more than a little annoyed with Maren for leaving.

This put her in a fairly sour mood by the time Varick stepped through the door. Seeing him free helped snap her out of her bitterness and she met him with a faint smile, which was as much emotion as was acceptable to a sidhe. Varick strode to the counter with his usual scowl. It was not the face of a man grateful to be free. Carissa wanted to say how happy she was that he had been found innocent by the sidhe, but given his expression, she skipped the pleasantries altogether.

"If you're upset that I said Jane was the one the elixir was for...."

"No," the sidhe grunted. He kept his voice low, considering that there were still customers in the shop. "I asked that you discover Tiache's guilt, yet you galivanted across the countryside with the prince instead. Perhaps I was too hasty to call you a friend."

Never mind the fact that, to her knowledge, he'd never called her a friend, he was also wrong about her actions in the last few days.

"I questioned Fudge and talked to Macara. I tried to keep Jane away from the trial. I even planned to speak with Tiache, but the evidence appeared to be pointing away from him."

"Toward whom?"

Carissa bit her lip. She had thought it was Parker, but considering he probably didn't know about the mistletoe, that had been a dead end.

"Well, that didn't exactly work out," she said.

"As I thought, you wasted time."

"But the sidhe ruled it an accident, didn't they?"

"I'm not satisfied with that. So long as there's a possibility that Jane is in danger, I will not rest. If you are her friend, neither will you. Come with me." He turned.

"Where?" Carissa asked.

He turned back, baring his teeth as he answered, "To the sidhe mound. I can sneak you into the potions, and we can create a truth potion."

"I wouldn't know how to make a truth potion." She gave an exasperated laugh.

Varick's eyebrows sank. "You are an apothecary, aren't you?"

"Human apothecaries don't specialize in truth potions."

He paused, staring blankly for a minute. "You have enough training, you can use our scrolls to figure it out. I will just have to ensure you have more time."

"Varick, I can't leave. I have customers." She placed her open palms out, indicating the customers wandering the shelves on either side of the store.

Varick looked left to right. "You have that other human, don't you—the assistant?"

"She's a little angry with me at the moment."

"She's your worker, isn't she? If she is not doing her job, find another."

Carissa stomped away from the counter, waving an arm for Varick to follow her to the storeroom.

Opening the door revealed Alden on the chair by the computer and Chaos by the keyboard. The faerie tried to pull Carissa in, but she stayed in the doorframe. Varick entered instead.

"What is this?" the sidhe asked.

"This is why Maren is upset," Carissa said softly. "She found out that Alden is an ankou and not a druid."

Varick raised an eyebrow. "She knew you were a druid?" he asked Alden.

Carissa let out a frustrated groan. "No, she found out he's not a druid."

Varick and Alden both paused. Chaos held her little head in her hands.

"What?" Carissa asked. She tilted her head and looked at Alden. "Are you a druid?"

Elixirs and Elves

"Did you ever wonder how I knew the spell to summon the ankou?" he asked.

"Because you were the ankou," she said as if it were apparent.

"When I became ankou, MacLir didn't come and give me directions on what to do. I became ankou and knew what my duties were the moment I realized what I was. But I only knew it because of my training."

"Your training as a druid?"

He nodded. Carissa felt a dizzying sense of betrayal. Did this whole town have secrets? Chaos seemed to sense her discomfort. The sprite flew up and patted the top of her head.

"I was being trained by the Morrigan before I died," Alden revealed. "Jane only learned of it after I passed on, but our family has a duty to protect Moss Hill. When our grandfather passed, I became the one to take on that responsibility."

"So when you died, Jane became the next druidess?"

He nodded.

Varick placed a hand on the hilt of his sword. "Which is why it's important to discover who might be targeting the druids of Moss Hill."

"You don't think that…." Carissa didn't want to finish the sentence. Was Varick really suggesting that Alden had been murdered?

"Neither of us can be sure," Alden said. "I wasn't even in Moss Hill when I became ill. But I do know that the sidhe fear any druid who doesn't swear loyalty directly to them."

"Why didn't you declare loyalty to them?" Carissa asked.

"Because Miss Morgan ordered us not to—Jane, too. Even though she didn't know what she was promising at the time, Miss Morgan made us promise not to pledge loyalty to anyone but her and her sisters."

"But why?"

"I never knew. But I suspect because there may be someone among the sidhe who does not have the best interests of Moss Hill in mind."

"So you think the vial was deliberately poisoned?" Carissa asked.

"Either that or someone knew Fudge would use his magic on it. The only accident was the target," Alden answered.

Varick said, "I believe someone was targeting Jane, but accusing an elder comes with costs if we're wrong. We need a truth potion to get an answer for certain. If we use it correctly, Tiache won't know we've used it at all—unless he lies."

"You're sure he did it?" Carissa asked.

Varick eyes flicked gold. "If I were, we wouldn't need the potion."

"All right," Carissa said, mainly to quiet him down before the customers wondered why there was yelling in the storeroom. "I think I have something better than a potion: the Cup of Truth."

"That won't work," Varick snorted. "We can all recognize the goblet."

Chaos zipped around in a frenzy at that. The sprite sped full force and grabbed Carissa by the hair.

"Ow! Chaos, what?" Cari exclaimed.

"Chaos already thought of that," Alden said.

He adjusted the computer screen so that Carissa and Varick could see. The nature faerie pointed madly at the words she'd pulled up from the Moss Hill Faerie Archives.

The Potion of Concealment, it read.

Carissa skimmed it. While Varick was still reading, she said, "It looks like it could work."

"That's not all," Alden said.

He and Chaos looked at one another. He toggled to another screen where it described the magical properties of several sacred herbs, including mistletoe. Alden highlighted a sentence at the very bottom of the screen.

"Use of magic on items sealed with mistletoe charms may cause harmful effects on the item, including death to those attempting to use the charm."

"We already know this," Carissa said.

Elixirs and Elves

"Yes," Alden agreed, "but since this is on the library server, anyone in Moss Hill could have known it, too."

Chapter 18

All the Trimmings

Fairfield Castle stirred from its two-hundred-year slumber. Its lifeblood had returned in the flow of people coursing through the courtyard and the buildings. Its heartbeat could be heard in the ringing bells, the laughter, and the flow of conversation. The recently restored halls decked with holly made for a jolly affair, and Carissa couldn't help but smile at everyone she met.

She felt like royalty in her red gown and the elaborate gold jewelry her parents had brought back for her from their last trip. The material the prince had given her, and Barnaby's skills as a tailor, had combined to create a masterpiece unlike anything she'd seen before. It had an intercontinental look to it, borrowing from multiple cultures. Barnaby said that the long scarf and flowing layers of red and gold were a style common in Tir-Na-Nog. While he hadn't been to the island in decades, everyone from the Mossies to the Sidhe complimented her on the gown. She clutched a red velvet purse strung around her wrist and mingled in the crowd.

The Mossies and citizens of Vale had all dressed in their best. The castle matched their elegance. Evergreens maintained the perimeter up on the ramparts as if they'd grown naturally on stone walls ten meters off the ground. Garland hung all around. Rectangular patches of red winter flowers checkerboarded across the stone ground. Skirting the courtyard was a long table of refreshments with a bright green tablecloth and food for human and fae guests to take. Cari

Elixirs and Elves

strung the velvet bag she was holding around her wrist. Her gift to the royals was safe. She took a hot chocolate, only for one to reappear in place of the one she chose. It was like Sal's platter—magically refilling.

Carissa closed her eyes and savored a sip of the rich, whipped cream-topped delight. Upon opening her eyes, she spied a group of children down the way snapping off pieces of a magnificent gingerbread house. A black-haired boy giggled. A brown haired girl's green eyes widened in wonder.

The most stunning sight stood at the center of the courtyard. It was a Christmas tree so large it passed the tops of the rampart walls. Carissa walked closer and touched the needles. It was real as could be. More than that, the nature faeries rustled about the branches freely without fear of it toppling over. Cari nearly dropped the hot chocolate when she saw little houses tucked into the pine. They appeared to have been carved especially for the faeries to dwell inside, and at the very base of the tree was a faerie village of sorts built into the roots. The little cottages, roads, and even a clock tower were displayed in dazzling detail.

Beyond the green branches, Carissa spied Maren out of the corner of her eye. She was happily gabbing away with Hela, who still called her Marnie. She might never learn, but it made Cari happy to see them enjoying each other's company. More than that, it was the company of a certain gentleman that Maren seemed to be enjoying most. She clung to Reg's arm. He leaned her way, ever so slightly nodding while she spoke.

Carissa would have to join them later. The prince awaited inside. A carriage and a note were all she'd heard from him tonight. *Duties requiring my full attention...*said the cold paper sitting on brown leather, where the prince should have been. If it hadn't been for Chaos, she would have been traveling alone. But traveling with Zef would have made it harder for her to tell him what she needed to say: that they would have to go their own ways after tonight.

Chaos was somewhere with the other nature faeries as Carissa made her way to the center of Fairfield alone. The doors at the center of the castle stood open, and a sparkling silver glow invited the guests inside. Beside the entrance, Cari found the embodiment of Christmas cheer. Sal, the elfkin, dressed in a refined reddish-brown suit, offered her his arm. Dependable Sal, with his toothy grin and his happy face, was a most appreciated escort. She didn't even blink before holding on to her old friend.

"I hope I've got everything right," Sal said. "I've never done a human Christmas party before."

If this were a human party, Carissa would believe it was fake snow, but the fae hosts had ways of keeping the dazzling winter dusting crisp. Nothing affected it, including the footprints of passing visitors. Carissa and Sal walked up to the top, where yet another marvel sparkled in their sights.

Sal led Carissa into the enormous entryway. The grand room, warm and toasty, smelled of orange and clove. The décor was alive with garland, poinsettias, holly berries, mistletoe, and more. There were mini evergreens livening the corners of the room. The roaring fireplace stole the attention. The exquisite human-made carvings of nature faeries and flowers above the hearth drew the eye. The fire dancing below it brought out the pictures so that they appeared to move.

"You did this all yourself?" Carissa marveled.

"I learned some of it from Toffee. Cameron helped with the design, and Hela added a few touches. 'Twas the elves who helped to put it all together."

An elfish smile crept onto Cari's lips.

"How did that feel—ordering the elves about for a change?"

A rosy blush rose on the elfkin's cheeks, and he twiddled his thumbs.

"Ordering them around? No, no, I never…. Well, I wouldn't say that's what I did…not at all."

Carissa rested a hand on his shoulder. "I think it's lovely," she reassured him.

Elixirs and Elves

"Lovely is the sight of you." Zef's voice came from Cari's right.

Zephyr, Prince of Sidhe and Elves, appeared in white garb that sparkled brightly as if made of tiny gems or captured starlight. A crown of silver dipped leaves embraced his head. If the mug in Carissa's hands had still been full of hot chocolate, it would have ended up on the floor. She caught herself before the bit that was left spilled.

"I'll take that if you're finished with it," Sal said. Did he wink at her as he took the cup from her hands? Cari winced at the thought. Given what she had to say to Zef, the levity broke her heart.

With the mug of hot chocolate gone, Carissa bowed low and made a proper greeting.

"Your Majesty," she said.

Zef's hand hovered over her shoulder.

"Cari," he said. "There's no need for that."

She stood, looking up at his smiling eyes. She hesitated to speak. Should she tell him now or after dinner? She gave a half-hearted smile, attempting to leave tough conversations for later. Her eyes turned briefly to the window right beside them.

A chorus of Christmas carols resonated from the courtyard. Carissa watched the background of snow and carolers. Slowly, the curve of her lips became genuine. Humans, sidhe, elves, and more talked, sang, and danced together. Could there be a more perfect Christmas Eve?

She could think of one. It was one where she wouldn't have to break a prince's heart. Or perhaps he wouldn't be affected. It was hard enough to sort out one's own emotions. Could one truly ever know another person's?

"You're sad." The prince's eyes saw straight through her. Maybe she was the only one who couldn't read other people so well. Prince Zephyr reached a hesitant hand to tuck back a strand of hair from her face to her elfish ear.

Carissa could feel the heat rising in her face. She couldn't say it—not yet. She tried another topic.

"You had something to attend to earlier?"

Zephyr nodded. "Yes, preparations for our departure from Moss Hill tomorrow. I was hoping that—"

He stopped, standing at attention, as did everyone else in the room. Sal announced Macara at the entrance. Carissa heard gasps in the room at the sight of the woman in a fitted, black, silk gown. With bronze leaves as the waist and a matching leaf clip in her raven-black hair, her simple attire only made her stand out even more in a room full of fancier gowns. Carissa pulled her scarf a little tighter around her. She joined the other guests in bowing to the Tuatha de Danann.

From the upper limit of Carissa's vision, she saw Macara's eye traced the room toward her. Having found her target, Macara looked at Sal, who took a moment to realize he should announce to the guests that they could rise. By the time Carissa stood, Macara was already near her.

The prince bowed again. Carissa looked at him and began to do the same.

"Enough of that," Macara said. "Though I'm honored by it and thank you for your courtesy." She said it like an automaton droning through a memorized phrase. "If you'll excuse us, Prince Zephyr, I'd like to speak to Carissa alone."

"Of course." Zephyr gave one last glimpse and walked away.

Carissa, as surprised as the other guests whose eyes covertly pointed their way, asked, "What are you doing here? I thought you never come to these."

"I don't. They're far too pompous and all the same."

Carissa wasn't sure if she was talking about the party or the guests. Her dismissive tone proved only that she was bored. Macara went on.

"I'm here to stop you from a dreadful mistake."

Which one? Carissa thought. Her eyes drifted over to Cameron, whom she'd hurt deeply in the last few days. She saw Varick by the curtains conspicuously watching Jane, who stood beside her parents, looking dreary. He thought Carissa hadn't done enough investigating while he had been in prison.

Elixirs and Elves

That may have been a mistake, too. Or was her error not seeing Parker's involvement in the crime? Watching him deep in a conversation with elves while a new date clung to his arm only made Carissa think he was guilty of something. Being a bad person, that was one thing at least.

"Carissa?" Macara brought her out of her thoughts. "Focus. I'm keeping the crowd from hearing us, but if eavesdroppers are unable to understand us for too long, they'll start to think it's not just bad luck that they couldn't catch what we said."

Carissa gave her full attention to Macara. "Sorry," she said, regretting her wandering thoughts immediately. It could not have been a small thing that brought Macara here. "What was the mistake?"

"Reginald told me whom you suspect and why, but the absence of holly in the elixir doesn't mean he was trying to poison Jane."

"Then what does it mean?"

Macara shifted her gaze and began to walk about the room. Carissa followed. Their movement along the perimeter of the great hall might prolong the illusion that those listening had just not caught the words.

"It's a change in the elixir's effectiveness. It makes Jane immortal while also leaving her vulnerable to illnesses that the sidhe are usually protected against."

"So he was trying to make her an immortal with a weakened immune system?"

"She'd keep her human immune system, which to the sidhe, would be considered weak, yes."

"So Tiache did sabotage the elixir," Carissa concluded.

"It's one way to look at it, but the sidhe might not see it that way. Jane never pledged her loyalty to them, so Tiache making the elixir in the first place would have been against the rules if he hadn't had the approval of the council. Knowing he lessened the elixir's effectiveness might please them, though Finvarra, as an elf, likely won't feel the same. The only person who can try an elder is the king, and since he hasn't called for any disciplinary action against Tiache, it's likely the council hasn't told him that Tiache acted against their will."

Carissa looked at Tiache, who was scowling by the piano as if the sound of the Mossie playing was hurting his ears. He wasn't a pleasant person, but at least he wasn't a killer. That was one theory disproved.

"Don't think about it, that's your mistake," Macara said. "Accusing an elder, even if you're right, will pit the council against you. If an accusation is made, the sidhe will have to not know it's you. The elixir wouldn't have killed Jane, Carissa, it's enough that you know they don't trust her. You don't have to act on this."

"If they didn't try to kill Jane, then was it just Fudge's magic that made the elixir toxic?"

"It would seem so," Macara said.

Carissa sighed. She wasn't sure if it was relief or disappointment.

"Maybe it was just an accident after all," she said.

"You don't seem certain about that." Macara gave her a knowing look.

Carissa began to explain her suspicions about Parker, but an array of musical notes interrupted her. It came from Sal, who was standing on the other side of the room with a mini mallet and what appeared to be a windchime.

"Dinner is served," the elfkin said.

The nature faeries had impeccable hearing. A few of them, namely Chaos, Hiya, and Cynth, made it indoors in time for Sal's announcement. Carissa noticed at least one alven floating into the room behind them. They zipped through the air. She called them back down to calm them.

"You are not joining us for dinner," Carissa said.

"Let them be." Macara chuckled. "They won't cause any harm."

Chaos landed on her shoulder at that point. She patted Carissa's neck as if to calm her down. By then, the prince reappeared beside them, and Macara stepped back to allow him to escort Carissa to the dining room. Chaos sat happily

Elixirs and Elves

on Carissa's shoulder as they moved to the next room. It was every bit as elaborate as the grand hall. Decorations of holly and mistletoe hung on the walls, and poinsettia centerpieces graced the dinner table.

Tonight, Mossies and Fae would cross the gap between neighbors and forge ahead with a deeper friendship between Moss Hill and Vale. There was no better setting for that than this dinner table. The long, wooden table stretched across the expanse of the room like a bridge. From where she stood, Carissa could see a glint of amber coating glazed across the tabletop. A row of chairs sat tucked in on either side.

A fizzy scent wafted over the baked apple aroma of the room. A glass of elderberry wine appeared at her left. Sal offered refreshments as the guests took their seats. Something about the scene made her stop in her tracks. It reminded her so much of the night of Toffee's death. A memory flashed in her mind. Only this time, she realized something she hadn't noticed before. Suddenly, everything that had happened the night of Toffee's death became clear.

"There's more on the table, anyone's welcome," Sal spoke over Cari's shoulder.

Carissa responded by taking the drink from his hand and saying, "Sal, could you come with us for a moment?"

She pulled him and Zephyr back into the previous room. Macara, who hadn't yet entered the dining hall, joined them by the fireplace. Carissa held up her wrist so her bag caught the prince's attention. "I know now is not the time for gifts, but I think this may be the best time to use this one."

Chapter 19

Truth in the Tinsel

The gears in Cari's head turned like a tinker toy fresh out of Santa's workshop. Parker, she realized, had knocked his own drink down after witnessing Toffee's death. It was a minor detail. She wouldn't have even thought of it, except that the sight of the glasses on the table brought the memory back. At the time, she had thought that was just an accident made in haste while trying to see over the dining table. Now, she realized it might have been much more than that.

Once she explained the plan to Zephyr and Sal and received approval from Macara and Chaos, they joined the others in the dining hall. Sal went back to his work. The Christmas party gathered around the table. The drinks were brought out. This time, there were a few glances exchanged between the more hesitant humans before the guests lifted their glasses for the toast. It was too reminiscent of the night of Toffee's death. The sidhe and elves didn't seem to mind.

King Finvarra held up his glass. "We have gathered to honor Toffee on this night, in dedication to his life and service to the crown. Please join me in standing in silent remembrance of our departed friend."

The sound of moving chairs against a wood floor filled the air. Then, the guests stood still, lowering their heads and closing their eyes. The faint jingle bell sound of nature faeries flying about made Carissa's ears twitch. They really couldn't sit still for a moment. But that was a good thing since at least

Elixirs and Elves

one of the sprites was moving about for a very necessary reason.

When the moment of silence was over, Finvarra lifted his glass. "To Toffee."

"To Toffee," Carissa said, along with all of the guests.

Again, the chairs shifted, and the people sat one by one. Macara brought a whole new dimension to the table since all but the king seemed to not want to begin a conversation or the meal until she did.

The king turned to the Tuatha de Danann with a half-smile and upraised eyebrows that awaited her action. Chaos smacked lettuce out of Hiya and Cynth's hands, as it was rude to eat before the oldest at the table. Some of the human guests seemed confused as to why no one was eating. Macara seemed profoundly amused and took a bit of her salad. Some of the sidhe did, too. A few soft conversations on the other end of the table earned harsh looks from the sidhe. It wasn't until Macara caught Carissa's sarcastic eyes that she finally said something.

"It's a shame the last party between Vale and Moss Hill ended as it did."

"Yes, it is," the king said.

A few of the sidhe and elves looked at each other in uncomfortable silence. It wasn't a topic anyone would care to discuss, and maybe not the way Carissa would have chosen to go about it. Macara never seemed to mind being direct.

"I'm wondering," she said, "how a poison would get into Toffee's cup."

"He put it there, ma'am. It was witnessed by another elfkin—uh, a Rhys Dwfen," an elf said.

Carissa smiled. All of the elves in Vale had taken to using Hela's term for the Rhys Dwfen. It was an honest mistake. Carissa appreciated the levity right now.

"Ah," Macara said, "so if this Rhys Dwfen told the truth, then Toffee was a thief."

Elder Tiache set down his fork. "Everyone in the trial tells the truth. We have ways of knowing if they lie." He took a sip from his goblet.

Prince Zephyr defended his servant, playing along with Macara. "Toffee was not that kind of person. He wouldn't touch something that belonged to someone else."

"He may have been confused by the vial being in the kitchen and thought it was something else," an elf suggested.

"Or someone suggested otherwise," Carissa said in as nonchalant a voice as possible.

Hela said, "There was only Sal in the kitchen, and it couldn't have been him."

"No ma'am," Sal said as he poured the drinks. "But Parker's the one who came in for a moment to get Fudge, maybe he knows something about it."

Sal smiled at Carissa. Not only was he far too obvious, but he also had gotten so caught up in the moment he hadn't remembered that it wasn't customary for a servant to speak. Some of the sidhe looked annoyed, but most of the guests at the table had turned their eyes to Parker Greer.

Parker set down his fork. He seemed to have missed the first part of the conversation. He was paying attention now.

"What is it?" he asked.

"Did you tell Toffee to drink the elixir of immortality?" Macara asked directly.

Parker barely concealed outrage. "What? No, of course not."

Chaos looked at Carissa, who gave a subtle nod. The sprite rushed toward Parker and tapped on his glass. It shimmered to reveal the Goblet of Truth. Parker's eyes widened.

"You recognize the cup?" Macara said. "Do you study magical objects?"

Parker set his jaw and stared at her. He understood the game now, Carissa could tell.

"Pick it up," Prince Zephyr challenged.

The sidhe and elves all gave their attention to Paker. He attempted to deflect with laughter. Waving his fork casually, he shook off the request like a misunderstanding.

"Your Highness, I'm not sure what this is all about…."

Elixirs and Elves

Macara performed the same type of magic as with the fireplace. The flame swirled around her fingertips and in her eyes. Since her gaze was set directly on Parker, he saw it before anyone else and jolted in surprise with enough force for his fork to fly across the table. Everyone across the table stopped eating.

Carissa grinned, and she said with satisfaction, "I think it would be wise for you to answer."

Parker looked between Cari and Macara.

"All right, all right," he said.

"Pick up the cup," Prince Zephyr repeated.

Every eye and ear focused on Parker now. His hand shook as he reached for the cup.

Parker closed his eyes and let out a long breath. "I overheard Varick giving the vial to Fudge. I know he put it in the kitchen. I told Toffee it was just a mood enhancer the Everlys had given to Fudge to hold onto. I said they had told me I could have some and asked that Toffee put some in my drink. He must've put some into his wine, too. I didn't know Fudge would use his magic on it, or you have to believe I would never have put it in my own goblet."

He paused. Parker seemed to make his next statement directly to his rival. "If you had the chance for eternal life, wouldn't it tempt you?"

Cam's eyebrows twisted. He seemed surprised that Parker was asking him. The king wasn't interested in Parker asking questions.

"How did you recognize the goblet?" the king asked.

Parker swallowed but tried to keep calm. "I've done a little reading in the library, and I saw it at Carissa's shop." He shrugged and looked at Cari.

Carissa didn't let it end there. "Did you know there was mistletoe in the mayor's tie pin?"

"Remember, the goblet will know if you are lying," Macara said.

Parker eyed the goblet in his hand. He whispered at a barely audible tone, "Yes."

201

"What did he say?" Mayor Belkin asked loudly.

"He said yes," an elf called out.

Murmurs flew out of the mouths of humans and fae, except for the sidhe, who waited for more.

Carissa didn't ask another question. She didn't have to. Parker, so intimidated by Macara's gaze, spilled out all that he knew.

"I didn't poison the elixir, all I did was make the suggestion to Fudge about the tie pin," Parker said. "It might have just caused bad luck, it wouldn't necessarily have killed him. I just wanted the mayor out of the way."

"Out of the way? Don't you know bad luck can kill a person when it's coming from magic?" the mayor burst out.

"You ruined everything," Parker spit out. "You weren't supposed to stop advertising and bringing in tourists. You went back on your pledge to help this town. The businesses were dying! I could do so much more for Moss Hill."

"The unseelie were entering the island." the mayor retorted. "They were threatening our neighbors in Vale. Do you really care more about money than lives?"

"Yes!" Parker cried out.

The admission was jarring. Gasps could be heard across the table. Hiya and Cynth flew to Carissa for comfort. Chaos patted the alvens back as tears welled in his eyes.

The vein in Parker's temple throbbed. "Without money, there is no life. There's a reason so many Mossies left for the mainland so long ago. This island is dying, and it'll keep dying as long as leaders like you don't help it reintegrate with the outside world. You know I'm right!" He looked across the table.

"I think that's enough," King Finvarra said.

He looked at Macara, whose eyes settled back to a pale blue.

"I've heard all I need to," the king said. "Place this man under arrest."

Varick himself stood up from the table and pulled Parker to his feet. He and two sidhe guards removed Parker from the

Elixirs and Elves

room. Cari saw a look pass between Varick and Jane before he left. At least the two of them seemed to have made up. Carissa didn't need the goblet to prove to her that their affections were real. Before looking away, she caught Cam's eye. He looked away too quickly for her to interpret any meaningful expression.

"Let us have a toast, then," King Finvarra said.

"Father, may I?" Prince Zephyr asked.

The king nodded. He and the queen both raised their glasses. Prince Zephyr raised his and stood.

"To the people of Moss Hill and Vale: may you have a Merry Christmas."

He looked at Carissa to make sure he had gotten that right. She smiled at him and gave an encouraging nod.

"A Merry Christmas!" came the chorus from the rest of the people at the table. Everyone raised their glasses and then lowered them to drink, but the prince wasn't done.

"And," he added, causing all hands to stop and hover in the air, "from every heart at this table to every other, we wish good health and long life to all here."

The rest of them raised their glasses. "We wish good health and long life to all here."

Everyone heard the shattering sound as it reverberated through the hall. All eyes looked in the direction of the noise. Elderberry wine soaked the table and dripped onto the floor. A very shocked-looking elder held the base of a goblet in his hand. The enchantment Prince Zephyr had placed on the cup in Tiache's hand faded, and now they could all see it for what it was. The Cup of Truth lay exposed in his grasp.

***

"WHAT DECEPTION IS THIS?" Tiache cried.

Little Chaos ran to the table where the broken shards lay and pointed, laughing to the point of tears. The more she giggled, the more the sidhe's face twisted with anger.

Prince Zephyr waved two sidhe guards over to the elder. They obeyed the command without hesitation, despite the status of the man they were poised to arrest.

"I regret, elder Tiache, that the Cup of Truth seems to have been in your possession and not that of the human."

"You would deceive an elder."

"It is no deception," the prince said. "The nature faerie seems to have played a trick on us. Sprites can be troublesome creatures."

"This is trickery!" Tiache accused.

"Yes," Macara said, "by the sprite."

This put Tiache in a jam. Since the sprites were not considered under the domain of the sidhe or elves, but as free spirits of nature, there was nothing he or anyone at the table could do to retaliate against a trick played by a sprite.

King Finvarra said sternly, "Sidhe elders tell no lies. Why would the Cup of Truth break in your hands?"

The Sidhe Council appeared to deliberate then and there as whispers broke over the silence that followed Prince Zephyr's proclamation.

Prince Zephyr said, "It is said of the Cup of Truth that three truths will repair the cup. If you hold the pieces in your hands, Elder Tiache, and explain yourself, it should repair."

Tiache bore his teeth in the wide grimace he displayed. He obeyed the order nonetheless. Cradling the pieces in his open palms with his head hung in shame, he appeared like a child despite his long years.

"Why did the cup break when we wished good health and long life to everyone at the table?" Prince Zephyr asked.

Tiache said nothing. Macara's hush voice fell over the room. In the silence of watchful eyes, it was loud enough.

"Did you create the elixir to grant long life but leave out the protection spell so that Jane could be poisoned later?"

The room was so empty of sound, Carissa could hear her own heart beating. In the hush, Tiach answered.

"Yes."

Elixirs and Elves

Two pieces snapped. It was a confession, but it still wasn't the whole truth. Prince Zephyr asked the next question. He worded it in a way that was non-accusatory. Even he didn't want to risk the anger of the Sidhe Council.

"But surely you did not intend to poison the druidess later?"

"No, I did not," he said.

He looked down at his hand. The goblet remained broken. Tiache glanced back up, his eyes frantic.

"I prepared a means," Tiache said, "but I would only have used it if she proved to be a threat to Vale."

The pieces snapped together.

The sidhe around the table looked satisfied, but Carissa had a final question that she had to ask. Macara shook her head at Carissa, but she opened her mouth anyway. The question was interrupted by Macara, who asked it instead. Coming from her, there would be no wrath from the council if Tiache was innocent.

"And did you poison her brother, Alden Everly?" Macara asked.

Tiache appeared genuinely confused. "No, my lady, I did not."

The goblet repaired. The sigh of relief at the table was audible. Even Carissa felt that she could breathe again.

King Finvarra smiled. "Elder Tiache was only protecting the interest of the people of Vale. He did not poison the elixir, and Jane Everly had verified that she is loyal to the island. We have no need to draw this out any further.

The queen added, "This is not a trial, but a dinner party. Let us put these matters to rest."

Cari caught sight of Sal in the corner of the room, who took this as a cue to rush into the kitchen.

"Quite right," the king said, unfolding his dinner napkin. This prompted all the guests to do the same.

The prince added, "I apologize if this situation has caused any offense."

"No harm is done," Elder Tiache grumbled. Surprisingly, next, he stood and bowed in the direction of Jane Everly. "I apologize, my lady, for not trusting you."

Jane's face reddened. She let out a meek reply that was barely heard across the table. It was something to the effect of "It's all right."

"All is forgiven, then," the prince said. "Let us enjoy this fine meal prepared by a very talented Rhys Dwfen."

"Here, here," the humans said at the table. The elf and sidhe, startled as they were, lifted their glasses along with the humans.

Sal, pushing a silver cart with the entrées, stopped upon hearing the compliment. His teary-eyed gratitude uncomfortably transitioned the table into several smaller discussions so that no one would have to look at the emotional display. Sal went about serving the first course. When he got around to Cari, he paused.

"You're okay, Sal?" Carissa whispered.

He teared up again. "It was mighty nice of the prince to thank me, but what did he call me? A Rhys-something. What is that?"

Carissa flittered between amusement and dismay. Fudge hadn't talked to Sal yet. She settled on a half-smile. "Don't worry, it's not an insult. I'll explain later." She put a hand on his wrist and gave a reassuring squeeze.

He continued serving. Every dish tantalized the tongue, from the turkey to the tarts. It was a shame Sal never entered any baking competition. If he did, he'd be sure to put any competitors to shame. Unfortunately, that would include Maren.

Carissa looked to the queen's right. Of course, Macara would have taken center stage if she ever came to such events, but in lieu of the Tuatha de Danann, Reginald took a place of honor. Maren, as his guest, sat beside him. She was all abuzz, talking with Hela. How they could have so much to talk about was unfathomable. At least, Carissa couldn't account for it. But they were getting along. Even the queen seemed to be

Elixirs and Elves

listening to their conversation. Cari only hoped Maren was careful with her words.

The prince was too far from her and her parents to speak with, but now and again she caught of glimpse of him looking her way. Every smile that passed between them was followed inevitably by a glance toward Cam, who was engaged in conversation with Tilly or the mayor or other residents of Moss Hill.

Situated between her parents and Rolin, Carissa had a view of both sides of the table. Her displacement from the royals, she suspected, was a result of Reg's presence. She guessed Hela's switch with her parents was a result of her being the one elf in Moss Hill who could bend unbendable rules. Cari never understood how that was so—even if she was the Rolin's daughter.

At the end of the dinner, the king invited the guests to dance in the ballroom. Carissa followed the others to a room of polished wood floors. Paintings of Moss Hill's mayors and the fae royals hung on the wall. Carissa stopped at the one in the middle of the king and queen.

"I recognize that one." Carissa smiled, looking up at the portrait and into Zephyr's eyes.

"I think you might find this one more interesting."

He held her hand, pulling her along the rim of the room. They stopped at the forefront of the depictions of the Moss Hill mayors. The lifelike mayor with vivid, hazel eyes and a realistic smile that spoke from the heart watched over the dancers as if he were enjoying the show. Carissa recognized the face from old photographs in Nan's album.

"The first mayor of Moss Hill," Zef remarked.

"I never knew him," Carissa reminisced, "but Nan said he was a lot like me."

"He was very much like you. Considerate and kind, hard-working, and loyal to his friends."

Cari squinted suspiciously. "Did you know him?"

"I met him once, many years ago."

The comment reminded her of his long lifespan. It was yet another difference between them. He tilted his head. His pointed ears twitched. Carissa broke into a smile before he could sense her sadness again, she hoped.

This seemed to put him at ease. He held a hand out. "Would you care to dance?"

"I'd be honored," she replied.

He led her to the dance floor and the evening passed as quickly as the music.

***

THE LAST TWIRL on the floor ended her carefree night. Prince Zephyr walked with her around the castle grounds. Those with young children had gone by now. The remaining guests were likeminded—lovers took strolls. It put a mood in the air that only made the end of the night more painful.

When they reached the gate, Carissa closed her eyes and let out a short breath. "Zef, I don't know how to—"

For the first time since he had arrived in Vale, Prince Zephyr interrupted Carissa. The tips of his fingers met Cari's lips. She froze, looking into his eyes.

"I know what you are going to say," he whispered. "I have no desire to hear it." He let go and spoke at a normal volume. "I knew it from the first night." He paused, his eyes searching. The defeat in his face made it plain he hadn't found what he wanted to see in her expression. "I have gotten the person wrong, but I had the emotion right: you love someone else."

Now, Carissa could admit it—to herself as well as him. "Yes," she said.

Zef smiled wistfully, then bowed, taking her hand and kissing it gently. He stood again, still holding on.

"You are a marvel. I'm glad to have met you, Carissa Shae."

"And you are much admired here in Moss Hill and Vale. I hope we will one day meet again, Your Majesty."

Elixirs and Elves

"We will, I'm sure of it." The prince bowed. "Please, do not address me so formally. We may not be destined to end up together, but I hope that we will still be friends."

"Always," Carissa said.

A chiming sound made both Zephyr and Carissa look up. They spied a little alven giving Chaos a peck on the cheek as she left the gate. Chaos blushed and floated down to her side.

Carissa and Zephyr shared a smile, and he kissed her cheek before they parted ways. She really did hope she'd see him again one day. Love was a grand idea, but Carissa was more than content to count Zef as a friend.

Chapter 20

Under the Mistletoe

Christmas day felt like an accomplishment. Considering all that had occurred in the last few days, just getting to the peaceful morning was an ordeal. Chaos, of course, had begun the day causing trouble.

Carissa found her sneaking in early in the morning through a cracked window. No doubt, she'd been out searching for Santa. Carissa's parents had filled the faeries' heads with Christmas stories just before sending them on home with Cari. It had been a sight, though: a carriage full of chatty faeries, hyper from the hot chocolate and jingling the whole way home with their version of Christmas carols, like tiny bells.

It had been as hard to get them to sleep as it had the night of Toffee's death. Only this time, it was for a happy reason. She'd finally tucked them all in at eleven o'clock. Well, all but one. Apparently, she'd missed Chaos.

The sneaky sprite feigned waking, but once Carissa made it clear she'd been caught, she changed her tune. The nature faerie flew to the window and reappeared with the ankou in human form.

"Alden?" Cari said.

"Am I invited in?" He hesitated.

"Of course you are." She waved him over to the kitchen table. The faeries were all asleep over everything in the sitting room.

Elixirs and Elves

Cari thought she might sit across from Alden at the kitchen table, but Chaos would not allow it. She zipped right to the cabinets, searching for her morning tea. Carissa took her cue and pulled out the kettle.

"So," she asked once Alden was seated, "is Toffee still on the loose?"

Alden and Chaos shared a look that Carissa didn't quite understand.

"No," Alden said. "He's passed on peacefully to the other side."

"I'm glad. It wouldn't be right to have a ghost still haunting Fudge on Christmas."

The chime of Chaos's laughter rang through the kitchen. Cari was sure she was missing something.

By the time the tea kettle rang, the faeries were up and ready to open their presents. Nan joined them in the living room. She tightened her red robe.

"You didn't tell me we had company," Nan said. She stopped mid-sentence and raised an eyebrow above the rim of her glasses frame, "You're not coming to take me, are you?"

Alden and Carissa both laughed.

"No, ma'am," he said.

"Well, then, you're welcome to stay and watch the little ones open their gifts."

Little ones, in this case, meant the nature faeries jumping around the small Christmas tree beside the bookcase. They all watched the little sprites tackle the gifts. It was a sight, with the presents being the same size as the faeries.

Once out of their boxes, the miniature clothes were inspected, approved, and hugged by the sprites. Barnaby's creations were a hit, as always. Chaos was the only sprite who kicked hers away.

"What's the matter?" Carissa asked her. "You don't like it?"

Chaos shook her head and pointed to the bigger boxes under the tree.

"I don't think clothes are enough for her," Alden commented.

"Quite right, too." Nan winked and handed Chaos one tiny box. "But that's what makes her special."

Chaos ripped through it eagerly. It was a mini book, the kind found at the front counters of bookstores. *'Twas the Night before Christmas*, it read.

This was a present Chaos was happy to hug. She opened it. The other faeries gathered around her. Chaos signed the words in a language the nature faeries could understand. Carissa knew enough now to understand that Chaos was actually reading.

The sound of the doorbell sprung Alden to his feet.

"Oh, don't get up, I'll get it." Nan lifted herself up a little slower than the Grim Reaper.

"You're expecting guests?" Alden asked, inching his way to the hall.

"I thought it might be nice to invite a few people whose holidays were especially stressful this year," Cari explained.

Alden nodded.

"I'll take my leave, then," he said. He began to fade.

"No, stay," Cari said quickly. "Everyone coming is a friend. Some already know who you are, like Maren. And Jane." She paused. "Jane and your parents would love to see you again. I think even Varick won't mind your being here today."

Alden looked wistfully up the hall to the red door. "They're not supposed to see me."

"I think MacLir would understand," Carissa replied.

The bell rang again.

"Well, I have to let them in," Nan said.

The two women awaited the ankou's answer.

He nodded.

Nan opened the door.

"Finally! I thought you'd keep us out there forever," Maren said.

Elixirs and Elves

Carissa froze in the doorway. "I thought you weren't coming."

"I'm sorry I was so angry with you, but Reg explained your position, and I think I understand—a little. Anyway, it's Christmas. That's not a time to be angry at anyone." Maren stepped through the door, inviting herself in, saying, "I've brought some of your neighbors."

Barnaby and the Harbridges were a surprise, but Carissa let them in. She knew Maren would have preferred to bring Reg.

"I hope you don't mind," Mrs. Harbridge said, holding a large pot and wearing a fancy green dress.

Her blonde hair was done up in curls.

"We didn't mean to barge in, but Barnaby said it wouldn't be a problem. Our family canceled their ferries due to the immense fog."

Carissa looked out the window. There was a haze over the town. Although she could see the homes across the street, the sky above them was filled with clouds.

The fog, of course, she realized.

Finvarra and his ships were leaving this morning. They would use fog to travel in so as not to be detected by humans.

"We've brought a ham," Mr. Harbridge said, pointing to his wife, who was heading straight to the kitchen. She hadn't seemed to notice the man standing beside Carissa. Mr. Harbridge, however, did.

He held out a hand. "Timothy Harbridge." The dark-haired, rotund man with the kind smile introduced himself.

The Grim Reaper appeared perplexed. Mr. Harbridge didn't seem to recognize him. Alden had been away from Moss Hill for a while before his death, so it was possible many Mossies wouldn't remember him. Even Cari hadn't recognized him right away when she first saw him months ago.

The Harbridge's eight-year-old, Timothy, dashed over to the sprites with barely enough time to say, "Hi, Cari!" before joining them on the carpet.

"The more, the merrier, am I right?" Barnaby said, pushing his way into the door with a load full of presents in one hand and a bean tighe holding the other.

"Holly," Carissa exclaimed, "I thought you'd be on the ship with Macara."

"I'm not fond of travel," Holly replied. "She'll be fine. She always is. Speaking of which, someone is waiting to speak with you outside."

Cari grabbed her red coat from its hook. The air bit right through her as she stepped through the door. The cold didn't seem to bother Macara. Her hooded coat made her look a bit like Mother Christmas and was likely enchanted with warmth the way Cari's dress had been. The same carriage the prince had lent Carissa twice before stood at the end of the drive.

Carissa wrapped her arms around her and walked down the driveway to where Macara stood on the other side of the yard.

"I thought you'd gone," Carissa said.

"Plenty of time," Macara replied.

Carissa looked down the road, asking, "How long will you be gone?"

Macara stepped closer. "A few months. I can't give you a definite answer."

Carissa nearly nodded, but another question traveled from her mind to her lips almost involuntarily. "Why didn't you just tell me about the goblet a few months ago, when I first told you MacLir had given it to me?"

"I think you know," Macara responded.

"You're testing me somehow. But why?" Cari asked.

Macara took her hand, held it between her own.

"I'm not testing you, I'm helping you. You need to learn to sense the magic yourself."

"But how can I when I don't know enough to even use my own magic? You're teaching Jane, but no one has told me a thing."

"Jane's magic is not the same as yours."

That gave Cari pause. A few days ago, she would've thought that Macara was referring to her elf-light

"I know," Carissa said. "Nan told me about my grandfather's heritage."

"Your heritage," Macara said.

"She also told me that Queen Maeve was dangerous."

"She was not without her good qualities."

"Are you not sharing information with me because you don't trust whether or not I'll be like her?"

Macara breathed in sharply. "No, not at all. Carissa, I'm not worried what you'll do with the magic. I had hoped you'd never have need of it. Only, I believe now that is unavoidable."

"Why?"

"Because 'there are fae coming whom you would rather not meet.'" Macara quoted the note from Raven Corvus sent to Cari months back.

"The unseelie?"

"Among others."

"And you're leaving us?"

"To gather more who would defend Moss Hill."

"You make it sound like a war is coming."

"There is a war that everyone is already fighting. The same one that began with the first thinking being: good versus evil. We all fight it every day within our communities, within our homes, within ourselves. The casualty is often love."

Carissa's lips pulled to one side. She wasn't one for wise old sayings that were often thinly veiled idle logic. They didn't tend to help in the real world. In Macara's case, though, Carissa would remember them. Her speech had a way of holding double meanings that she might later regret not keeping in mind.

"What can I do?" Cari said.

"Protect Moss Hill while I'm away."

Carissa shook her head. "I don't know how."

"Your magic is not like Jane's. Yours is instinctive. It doesn't involve spells to memorize. The magic of a Tuatha de

Danaan is whatever you want it to be in the moment. For you, even magical objects can act differently than they were forged—if you set your intention on it."

"But my magic has never worked differently than any other elf's."

"Because you haven't trained it to be. The truth is we don't know what the limits are to your powers. Your grandfather had something of the old power in him, even though he was mostly human. One thing is certain: the Tuatha de Danann can sense one another. The fact that the Morrigan was always here and even that your grandfather lived on this island kept most of the unseelie at bay. But they knew their powers and could control them. Since you don't have mastery over yours, you should stick to the elf-light alone. As long as it's only elf-magic you're using, you'll remain undetected."

"When you return, you'll train me?"

"That's not my specialty. Someone else is coming to Moss Hill soon enough who will train you very well. In fact, she sent Chaos to you ahead of her to tell you she was coming."

"Raven Corvus?" Carissa asked.

"The very same. Until she arrives and I return, you'll have to watch over Moss Hill for a while."

"But how? I'm not very good at magic, even with the elf-light," Cari protested.

"You've got a quick mind and a good heart. That's all the magic you need."

Macara patted Cari's shoulder and returned to the carriage. She watched it fade from view only to see a black car pull up. Out of the vehicle emerged her parents and Cameron Larke.

Cam placed a hand on the back of his neck and shut the door.

"Morning, Cari!" Her father pulled her in for a hug.

Elixirs and Elves

"Merry Christmas." Her mother kissed her on the cheek, then promptly took her father's hand. "Come on, Dorian, bring the presents."

Her father reached into the car and pulled out a velvet bag from the back seat. He strung it out on his shoulder and turned around, shutting the car door behind him.

With his green suit and hat, pointed ears, and a bag that looked like it had come from the North Pole, Carissa's father was the image of a Christmas elf.

"What?" he asked, seeing the silly grins on Cam and Carissa's faces.

They shared a chuckle rather than explaining. Cari's mother waved her father inside. His departure left Cam and Carissa standing alone on the pavement.

"Your parents insisted last night that I pick them up this morning. They didn't want to make the trek from Vale on foot."

Carissa rolled her eyes. Her parents could have come into Moss Hill in ten different ways. They chose Cam on purpose. They hadn't spent a lot of time with Carissa at the party the night before, but she was sure they heard about her and the prince deciding to be friends. It looked like her mother had moved on to another suitor for her.

"That's just the way my parents are—always pushing," Carissa said. "But I'm glad you came."

"So am I." He smiled.

The expression didn't reach his eyes. His cognac eyes, the ones she'd taken for granted would always look at her the way they had before, as if she was the only woman in the room, were sorrowful now. The joy had left them. She hoped she could help bring it back.

"Cameron," Carissa said.

"Caris—" Cam began, but Cari held a hand in front of his mouth.

"Just let me say this." She brought her hand back to the shawl and took a deep breath. "I understand how Varick feels, and even Jane, too. Elves live long lives."

Carissa paused and looked back at the house. She didn't want to add that she might be more fae than she'd previously thought. She was still processing that information herself.

"You and I are good friends. If we were to be together and it didn't work out, I wouldn't want to lose you as a friend. And if it did work out, I might lose you anyway. I might live longer than you." That was an understatement. She might live a century more than him, if not longer. There was no way to tell.

"The truth is, I," she hesitated, "I do want to give us a chance, a real one, if you want to as well."

She looked back at Cameron. He had his head turned away from her so that she couldn't see his face. He didn't look at her for what felt like a century.

"You're supposed to say something now," Carissa finally said.

"What about the prince?" he asked.

Carissa winced. Of course, he was brooding over the possibility that she still harbored feelings for the prince. "I don't love him, I...."

Her arms moved from holding the shawl around herself to crossing her arms. Cameron wasn't brooding at all: he was smiling.

"You what?" He looked at her, grinning. "Go on, say it."

She mirrored his smile. "I will, but, you know, it's not that easy to gain an elf maiden's affections. You'll have to, I don't know, lead me to the most magical place I've ever seen, gave me the strangest mix of gifts I've ever received, take me on a horse-drawn carriage—" She counted on her fingers the feats the prince had done for her. Her teasing smile was interrupted by Cam's laughter.

"All right, I see your point. I'll have to sweep you off your feet," he said. "Well, I might as well start with the first one."

Cameron, very much like a prince, took her hand and led her closer to the house.

Elixirs and Elves

"What, going inside the house?" Cari asked. "Oh, I see—friends and family on Christmas day. I suppose that might be the most magical place in Moss Hill."

"I can think of one more," He stopped in front of the door. Carissa laughed when she saw what was hanging in the doorframe. She wasn't sure which of her guileful guests had placed it there, but she silently thanked them. Cameron was absolutely right. They were, in fact, standing below the most powerful magical object that existed in all the world: mistletoe.

Want more great content?

Hi, I'm Astoria Wright, the author of The Faerie Apothecary Cozy Mysteries. I hope you've enjoyed the first book in this series.

Check out the rest of
The Faerie Apothecary Mysteries:

Chaos in the Countryside – A Novella Prequel
Book 1: *Herbs and Homicide*
Book 2: *Remedy and Ruins*
Book 3: *Elixirs and Elves*
Book 4: *Charms and Changelings*
Book 5: *Potions and Panic*
Book 6: *Talismans and Turmoil*
Book 7: *Tonics and Turning Points*

To keep up to date about this series and others by the author, check out the website:

www.astoriawright.com

Sign up for the mailing list for updates and freebies available only to members!

Thanks for reading!

Made in the USA
Coppell, TX
09 February 2021